THE
NEX

THE
NEX

by Tim Pratt

The Merry Blacksmith Press

2013

The Nex

"Dream Engine" originally published in *Orson Scott Card's Intergalactic Medicine Show*, August 2006

"We Go Back" originally published in *Escape Pod*, July 2011

For information, address:

The Merry Blacksmith Press
70 Lenox Ave.
West Warwick, RI 02893

merryblacksmith.com

Cover image is a detail from "The Tower of Babel"
by Pieter Brugel the Elder (1563).

Published in the USA by The Merry Blacksmith Press

ISBN—0-61575-104-0
978-0-61575-104-7

DEDICATION

For my son,
River Alexander Pratt Shaw

Table of Contents

The Nex

Chapter 1

My mom says stealing is wrong, my brother says it's only stealing if you get caught, and my dad used to say good artists borrow, but great artists steal. I don't know if I'm right or wrong or any kind of artist, but the best and worst and weirdest days of my life (so far) started with theft: first I stole something, and then I got stolen away.

The school bus dropped me off in front of my house, and I gave my brother Cal's dirty old Mustang the usual kick as I passed by. Cal saved up and bought a car as soon as he turned sixteen, but he never drops me off at my school, even though it's on his way. The car's so beat up Cal never notices the dents I contribute, but kicking it makes me feel better.

Mom's car was there too, and so was her stupid boyfriend's, so I was thinking about sneaking around the side and climbing in my bedroom window to avoid them all when I heard the sound. It was this weird hum, high-pitched, like a bunch of bees buzzing in hundred-part-harmony. I looked into Cal's back seat and didn't see anything hummy, but I did see a necklace, half covered in a jumble of schoolbooks and fast-food wrappers, a silvery bright metal chain all strung along with jewels like teardrops.

The jewels changed color, from yellow to blue, then shifted and shimmered to green, and it was the prettiest thing ever, even though I'm not a fancy-jewelry girl. I'd never seen a necklace change color that way, and I *wanted* it. I didn't even wonder how it worked. I couldn't imagine why Cal had something so nice anyway—he only cares about girls and drums lately, so anything without boobs or cymbals is wasted on him. I knelt down and felt around in the wheel well for the magnetic hide-a-key where Cal keeps his spare.

I opened the door and pulled out the necklace. It was heavier than I'd expected, and warm, like it had been sitting in the sun. I didn't want to *wear* it—I like jangly mismatched bracelets and that's about it—but looking at it made my heart thump and my skin warm up, the same way stealing gum from the gas station or hair clips from the mall does. That humming went on, and I realized the *necklace* was making the sound, and when I held it to my ear, it was like whispering—

"Randy, get outta my stuff!" Cal came through the front door, face all twisted and mad, and I tore off running across the street, over the ditch, through the empty field, and toward the woods. Cal chased me, calling me a dirty little thief—nothing I hadn't heard before—but I'm faster than him, especially since he started sneaking cigarettes. I knew once I got in under the trees I'd lose him. My Dad used to take me out there, teaching me what plants were edible and which were poisonous, picking wild mushrooms, stuff like that, and I know all the paths. Even though I could tell which berries were safe to eat, though, I'd have to go home eventually, and that would be no fun. Mom and Cal always team up against me, ever since we lost Dad.

Once I was in the woods pretty deep and couldn't hear Cal yelling anymore, I slowed down so I wouldn't trip on any roots. I stopped by a tree and looked at the necklace some more. Sure, it was pretty, but was it worth getting grounded over, maybe worse? Still, there was something about the way the gems changed colors, the way it hummed…. I started thinking about places I could stash it, making up a story about how I'd dropped the necklace and couldn't find it, sorry, Cal, and—

That's when I got stolen away.

The whole world went white and black and blue and everything turned sideways with a whoosh and I fell down flat on my back in the dirt. The sky spun crazily, and I swear all I did was blink, but just that quick the sky was dark instead of light. I couldn't see too well because of the tree branches above, but there were things in the sky that weren't stars or planets or satellites or low-flying planes, things like slowly-spinning chandeliers and big blue glowing orbs, and something whirring past that looked like a helicopter in a sketch by Da Vinci I saw once in art class, all corkscrewy and strange.

I sat up, cradling the necklace—the hum was a lot more like a whisper now, and I wondered if the necklace was picking up a radio station or something, the way tooth fillings supposedly can. I stood up, dizzy and slow, and leaned against a pine tree. I touched my hand to my nose and it came away bloody, but just a little. I have nosebleeds once in a while, ever since I was a little kid. I even used to get out of school because of them, until Mom figured out I was making my nose bleed on purpose sometimes just to get out of class.

I thought maybe I'd fallen down and hit my head, that I'd been unconscious in the woods until nightfall. It was a good theory, except my head didn't hurt, and there were those things in the sky. The other possibility was the whooshing and the colors had taken me somewhere else, but if I'd been kidnapped, the bad guys had kidnapped the whole forest, too, or at least the woods as far as I could see. I'd read books about people going magically or science-fictionally to other worlds, but chunks of their own worlds didn't usually go with them. I took out my cell phone, just to see what time it was, but the display was all weird, nothing that even looked like numbers or letters, and when I tried to dial home, I couldn't get a signal.

A woman's voice said something like "Over here," and twigs crunched and pine needles slithered under oncoming feet. I wondered if I should try to hide behind a tree, or if this was a search party looking for me or something. Lights approached from the direction of the voice, but not like a lamp, more like a bunch of fireflies, all yellowy-green and clustered together.

"It's ridiculous for them to snatch all these trees to get one little device," came another voice, this one deep and masculine like something out of a movie trailer.

"The Regent doesn't mind. He snatched up that whole scrapyard when all he needed was a few hundred pounds of copper. You been down to that place lately? Ha, of course not, but I hear it's full of refugees from the Walking Wars, all building clockwork siege engines and putting up flags and declaring sovereignty. Deluded bastards."

"They'll be absorbed," the man's voice said, sounding bored, just like my friend Jenny Kay sounds in math class. The teacher always calls on her, because Jenny always knows, but she gives the answers like they're so obvious that even *asking* her is a stupid question.

"We could rally them to our cause."

"This isn't a fight we'll win by force of arms."

"Force of arms is what I'm *good* at," the woman said, her voice clearer now. "Also force of fists, force of feet, force of fangs, and et cetera."

"I'm well acquainted with your strengths."

"You can—" The crunching stopped, and I hunched over into myself, back pressed against the tree, necklace pressed against my chest between my boobs (such as they are), not at all sure these were people I wanted to meet.

The woman stepped into sight. I could see her clearly, lit in the glow of the strange cloud of floating lights, which was about the size of a basketball, hovering and sparkling. She was taller than me, almost as tall as my brother, with short dark hair and a pointy-pretty face, wearing gray and black clothes that seemed to shift around on her body like shadows. She looked like she got a lot of exercise, and—

She saw me.

The woman let out a low whistle. "Lookit, Wisp. Another citizen press-ganged."

"None of our concern. We're not on the welcoming committee this time."

It was that male voice again, but I couldn't tell where it was coming from—was the woman throwing her voice?

Suddenly the cloud of glowing lights swooped down into my face and began wiggling like crazy. "She has it. She has the engine!" The voice boomed right in my ears.

The woman crouched in front of me, waving her hand through the glowing spots, which buzzed like bugs and reformed above her head. "Hello, little one," she said. "What have you got there?"

I grabbed the necklace tighter, and it shifted and twisted in my hands like a pissed-off kitten, which was a whole new level of weird. "Nothing. Just something I found. What is this place?" The last part was maybe a stupid question—it was the *woods*, the ones I'd used as a shortcut for years—but it was someplace else, too, obviously.

"I'll answer your questions, after you give me that." The woman held out her hand.

If it had been, I don't know, a candy bar, or a pair of earrings, or any of the other things I stole sometimes, I would have given it up—but the necklace, what they'd called the engine, was different. "It's mine," I said.

"I'm going to make this pretty clear," the woman said. "I'm stronger than you, and if you don't give it, I'll take it."

"Don't hurt her." That disembodied voice again—what, was there a *ghost* here, or someone in an invisibility cloak like in the movies? "If you spill her blood, a forensic dowser may be able to track us that way."

Blood? I didn't have any way to defend myself, not even a little pocket knife. I used to have some pepper spray on the ring with my housekeys, but Mom took it away after I sprayed some on Cal's mashed potatoes once. I tried to remember the women's self defense class I took with Mom, but I hadn't paid enough attention, all I could remember was stomping on somebody's instep or hitting a guy's crotch, and neither would help much here. Oh, and sticking something hard into something soft, like a key into an eye. That expression, "Stick something hard into something soft," had fuelled about a thousand dirty jokes from my friend Jenny Kay, but it seemed like a good idea, if I could reach my car keys. Getting a housekey in the eye would stop anybody.

"Shushit," the woman said. "Nobody's going to hurt anybody. Just give." She lashed out fast, got both hands on the necklace, and started pulling. I tried to get a better grip, crystals weirdly slippery in my hands, and then I felt a funny click as two crystals touched. I gasped when a sudden sharp pain stabbed my palms. It stung for a second, then stopped, like I'd had anesthetic gel rubbed on the stinging spots.

The woman let go and held up her hands like I was a cop pointing a gun at her, and she whistled again. All the tension and menace drained out of her. "Well, that's it. She's done whatever you do to activate the engine. She set the focus."

I looked down, and the necklace had stabbed my hands somehow, leaving pinhead-sized drops of blood on my palms. The necklace started to twist again, writhing over my hands, breaking into smaller pieces that twinkled and crawled, and after a second the necklace was gone… but I was wearing two bracelets on each wrist, brass and sapphire and diamond and silver, and rings of different-colored metal on three fingers of each hand.

"Oh, that's *wonderful*," the ghost said.

I looked up, my throat dry. "What just happened?"

The woman put her hand on my shoulder, and I flinched, but it felt like a friendly hand. "You just joined the revolution. What's your name?"

"I'm… Miranda. Randy. What revolution?"

The woman rose, crossing her arms and looking down at me with a smirky little smile. "My name… Is Howlaa Moor."

I thought *funny name* but didn't say it.

She frowned, and the male voice said, "She's not from here, she's from *Earth*, she doesn't know who you are."

"Ah. I guess that's some excuse." She gestured vaguely. "Randy, this is Wisp. He is annoying but I cannot hit him, and neither can you."

I looked around. "Up here," the voice said. "The *lights*."

I blinked. The lights were talking to me. Wisp was the lights. "How can you *talk*?"

"Sound is just vibrations in the air. I have no trouble making vibrations." The motes jiggled.

"This is too freaky."

"Just you wait." Howlaa grinned. "Come on. We have to get moving before they show up."

"They? They who?"

"The ones we're revolutioning against, of course." Howlaa gestured impatiently, and I got to my feet.

"Revolting," Wisp said.

"What are you nattering about?" Howlaa said.

"It's not revolutioning, that isn't even a word, it's *revolting*."

"*You're* revolting." Howlaa laughed, and I realized she must have a sense of humor roughly the same as Cal's. I found it stupid and comforting at the same time.

I followed after them, Howlaa walking and Wisp floating, thinking I could take off as soon as we got out of the woods and I figured out where I was, exactly. The trees got thinner, and now that I could see the sky clearly it was even stranger, with ribbons of shimmery color like the Northern Lights, and flashes in the corner of my eye that might have been multi-colored lightning. Pretty weird, but I had like a mental block when I tried to think about what that weirdness meant. These were the woods by my house. How weird could things get *there*?

Except when we got out of the woods, I didn't see the electric fence around the horse pasture, or the steeple of the Evangelical United Brethren Church, or any familiar landmarks in what should have been a super-familiar place.

What I saw was bleak nothing, ground like the lava rock from our vacation to Hawaii before Dad died, all pitted and black and hard. It all hit me then, the way the impossible had become factual, and I let out a long deep breath and tried not to let my knees give out underneath me. My body was freaking out, my heart all thud-thud-thudding, but my brain was working over the situation. Because Jenny Kay and I had *talked* about this, exactly this—about how, in stories, whenever the normal girl goes to a magical other world, she spends all her time trying to get home, and how stupid that is. We both agreed, if we ever found ourselves over the rainbow or through the looking glass, we'd take a look around before we tried to get away. We'd have the *adventure*.

The adventure was a lot scarier now that it was happening to me, but so far it was good scary like riding a roller coaster, instead of bad scary like listening at your mom's bedroom door and wondering if she's going to come out all day, and if she'll be drunk when she does.

What was so great about *home* anyway?

Dad used to say every journey starts with one step, so I kept on walking. I was glad to be wearing my big baggy jacket, and that I had on thick-soled stomping boots and black tights under my ragged patchwork skirt, because just looking at the endless desert night made me cold. "What is this place?"

"The outskirts," Wisp said. "The far provinces. Land waiting to be filled."

The only thing breaking up the landscape was that funny-looking helicopter I'd seen go past before, with corkscrewed sails instead of rotors and a platform with a couple of chairs bolted on, along with a few long levers and a set of handlebars. It didn't look like anything that could fly.

"There's only one seat with straps, so you'll have to hold on tight," Howlaa said. "The autogyro can be… a bit bumpy."

"She should be the one strapped in, *she's* indispensable now," Wisp argued.

"Why am I indispensable?"

They ignored me. Howlaa said, "Unless she can *fly* this thing, she gets the other chair, because only the pilot's seat has straps, you floating ball of—"

Something like a glowing red boulder came streaking out of the sky with a long whine, and it landed with a crash like ten thunderstorms… right on the autogyro, which exploded into flying fragments of metal and wood. Before I could even blink I found myself way back in the woods again, easily a football field's length away from Howlaa and the remains of the smoking autogyro. Had the explosion thrown me back? But I didn't *feel* like I'd been thrown, hadn't felt any sensation of movement at all, I was just *here*, out of harm's way, not that I didn't scream a couple of times anyway.

Howlaa came racing back into the woods, Wisp bobbing after her. After the noise of impact, it was quiet again, and I heard Wisp say "self-preservation circuit kicking in" before Howlaa scooped me up in her arms and started running, carrying me like I was a baby, like I didn't weigh anything.

"They found us, kid," she said. "And you're going to be the Ax's most popular girl if we're not careful with you."

"Must have been an orbital rail gun," Wisp said.

"I don't care if it was a steam colossus with a powered slingshot, the autogyro is gone, and that means we can't *fly*."

"Well, you and I can," Wisp said. "Albeit much more slowly. It's only Miranda that can't fly at all. Unfortunately. I don't suppose you can carry her…"

"Not a hope. It would ruin my aerodynamics." Howlaa wasn't even breathing hard, though I would've been gasping way too much to speak if I'd been running as hard and fast as she was. "What's the plan now, Wispy?"

"Find transportation. Resume our journey. Use Miranda's… unique abilities… to complete our mission."

"Short on details, aren't you? We're *leagues* from the city center. And now we know they'll be waiting. I should never have let you talk me into this. Things weren't so bad, working for the Regent—all the booze I could drink, permission to hit people, places, and things on a regular basis… There are worse prisons, you know."

"We knew this wouldn't be easy," Wisp said. "But our freedom is worth some effort, don't you think?"

"Yes, fine, it just seemed like a better idea before the shooting started. And now a lot depends on this kid, who is… a kid."

"At least we don't have to depend on Templeton now. He's the only human I've met who's *more* reliable when intoxicated, and even then not by much. We'll—"

They were talking about me like I wasn't there. I *hate* that—Mom did it at a conference with my principal after what happened to Dad, saying "We all want what's best for Miranda, I'm sure it's just because she's grieving, she'll try harder," blah blah blah—like I didn't have a say in my own life, and like Mom had it together herself, when I knew she'd probably had four glasses of wine before she got to the school.

I wriggled and arched my back and Howlaa stopped running and let me drop. "Fine, you can walk yourself, but keep up."

I scrambled away, the rings and bracelets on my fingers and wrists pressing cold against my skin as my heart thumped fast and wild, like the drum part in one of the lousy songs by Cal's band. Having the adventure's one thing, but I didn't even know what the adventure *was* yet. "Why should I go anywhere with you? Where am I? What's going *on*?"

Howlaa and Wisp—I won't say they exchanged glances, since Wisp has no eyes, but Howlaa looked at Wisp and then back at me and sighed. "We'll find a safe place, and then tell you everything you need to know." She rolled her eyes. "Wisp will try to tell you *everything*, period, all-inclusive, including a short history of space-time, but I'll restrain him from going on too much."

I hesitated, thinking about running, but wherever I might want to go, it was pretty clear I couldn't get there from here on my own.

"Please," Howlaa said. "Come with us? We're the ones who *didn't* throw a big rock at you from orbit. And you must be wondering about the thing you... found. That turned itself into your jewelry there. I can tell you about that, too."

I was suddenly so tired. A day at school, no more terrible than usual but still pretty terrible, then getting chased by Cal, and now all this craziness, I just wanted to cocoon under my covers in my room in total darkness, without even the blacklight turned on. "Is it far?" I heard the whine in my voice, the one Mom always snapped at me about, but couldn't help it, and didn't care to try.

"Not much farther now," Howlaa said, and scooped me up, and ran.

Chapter 2

We made it through the other side of the woods, and this time we didn't emerge into bleak lava nastiness. Howlaa set me down and I stared at what seemed like hundreds of oddly-shaped buildings. There were grain silos, like back home—we're only an hour or so from Atlanta, but it's still pretty countrified in Pomegranate Grove—plus big rounded things on tripod legs like water towers, and squat wooden buildings with cone-shaped roofs, and big metal buildings like airplane hangars, and even glass ones like greenhouses.

"Welcome to the breadbasket of the Ax," Wisp said. "Food for the citizenry. At least those the Regent chooses to feed."

"What Wisp knows about food could be written on the back of a small envelope," Howlaa said. "With room left over for what he knows about sex, dancing, and fashion. Are you hungry?"

I was—it must be about dinner time, unless I'd been unconscious for part of that time under the trees. "Yeah."

Howlaa sniffed. "Damn this primate nose. Excuse me."

"Howlaa, no—" Wisp shouted, but I didn't hear the rest of whatever he said, because I was screaming.

Howlaa's body changed, arms extending, head bulging, spine curving. It wasn't like some special effect of a person turning into a werewolf—more like one of those time-lapse videos of a plant growing or a dead animal decomposing, this fast organic expanding and collapsing. The shadowy clothes shifted and writhed and obscured some of what was happening, but it was clear Howlaa was turning into a monster, something with a long snout and pointy ears and lots of fur and bone spurs

13

jutting from its spine, not exactly wolflike, unless maybe it was a wolf that was also partly a *dinosaur*.

I took off running. Wisp came bobbing after me. "Miranda! It's not what you think! It's just—it's just *Howlaa!*"

The wolf-thing came loping up beside me, easily keeping pace, even as I veered and ran, until I tripped on a rock and went sprawling. My hair fell into my eyes and when I brushed it away and levered myself up, the monster was staring right into my face, eyes these blank orbs like they were scooped out of cherry jello with a melon-baller, black nose quivering… and then it licked my face, just like a friendly dog, and though it looked like its breath should smell like rotting meat it didn't smell like much of anything, just warm and wet. The wolf-thing—which was bigger than me—sat back on its haunches and shook, like it just had a bath, and then it writhed and twisted and shrank and it was Howlaa again, not a hair out of place. "Sorry to scare you. I just wanted a better nose to smell where the good food is."

"You're a were… something." My voice was a croak. I'd skinned my hands when I fell, and they stung, blood on my palms for the second time tonight.

"Howlaa is a were-*many*-things," Wisp said, motes dancing over Howlaa's head. "A skinshifter."

"I am a woman of many talents," Howlaa said. "Except when I'm a man or beast or something else of many talents. Come. Let's eat. I smelled apples." She sounded so cheerful and harmless, and the monster hadn't really been all that monstrous when it came right down to it, so I followed. A shapechanger! How cool to have a power like *that!*

Howlaa led us toward a low wooden building, and we stepped into a big, straw-lined room fragrant with apples. There were dozens of crates and great spilling heaps of fruit, golden, red, pink, and even white—I'd never seen white apples before. I was beginning to really *understand* that I wasn't home anymore… wasn't even on Earth anymore, judging by that strange sky, and the stranger people. Howlaa tossed me a piece of fruit and I bit into it, the juice filling my mouth, my stomach growling, impatient for me to chew and swallow. I hadn't eaten since cruddy school lunch, and I was so happy to have some food that simple physical satisfaction drove all the panic and confusion down for a while. Howlaa and I sat on crates and she held an apple in each hand, taking alternating bites and demolishing them down to the cores in just a few chews.

Wisp didn't eat, but only hovered, casting light. "You asked where you are. The place has many names—"

"The Nex," Howlaa said around a mouthful of fruit. "The Ax. The Magpie City. The Stolen State. The Cage. The Orphanarium. The Hub. The—"

"Its proper name is Nexington-on-Axis," Wisp said. "Or so the Regent who rules here says. The original name, what the long-dead Queen and Kings of Nexington-on-Axis might have called this… place… are lost to time and likely unpronounceable by the tongues, pheromone glands, or throat-sacs of even any creature Howlaa can transform into."

"But a name is just a name. What this place *is*… Wisp, you tell her."

"It is the linchpin of the multiverse. Or, more accurately, a sort of… barnacle growing on that linchpin. We exist at the center of all things, and any universes that are, might be, will be, or have been, all turn and churn and twist around us. We live in the pivot of possible worlds, with galaxies and stars and planets and realities whipping above and below and around."

"And the royal orphans, they can reach out. They can *snatch*." Howlaa's hand whipped out and grabbed another apple, quick as a snapped rubber band. "They steal whatever they want—or whatever the *Regent* wants—from any universe that passes by."

Wisp bobbled before me. "We don't know how their power works—wormholes, white holes, harnessing negative energy? But long ago the Queen and Kings built vast machines called snatch-engines in the royal palace, machines that enhanced their natural abilities, and by using those engines, the orphans can reach even farther and steal bigger things. Buildings. City blocks. Farmland. Seas. Nexington-on-Axis has no natural resources at all. Everything is imported. Even the people."

"It's a bloody kleptocracy, is what it is," Howlaa said.

"I taught her that word," Wisp said. "It means 'government by thieves.'"

I shook my head. "This is crazy. This is beyond science fiction."

Howlaa shrugged. "It is what it is, Randy. We're way out in the boonies now. The royal orphans are mostly filling up the Nex in a spiral pattern—who knows why, maybe that's what a straight line looks like to them—and they put your little chunk of Earth in the next empty slot, out by the food stores and reservoirs and slag pits and prison camps. It's only a few hours back to the city center by autogyro, but on foot…"

She shook her head. "So that's 'where,' and enough of 'who' for now, which leaves…" She pointed to my hands. "'*What*.' As in, what is that thing you found. Which we found first, only we found it in a locked room in a forbidden vault in the depths of the Regent's palace. It's called a jump-engine. Or *the* jump-engine, since there's only one. Built by the Regent's scientists, reverse-engineered from the snatch-engines."

"Literally reverse," Wisp said, "as the snatch-engines can only seize things and bring them here, while the engine you found can take things *away*. Or send them away. Or send *people* away."

"Teleportation," Howlaa said. "Poof! Here you are, there you go, no passing through the space between, instantaneous. Could be very handy."

I looked at my hands, thinking of the way I'd moved from the auto-gyro to the woods in a blink. Teleportation might even beat shapeshifting as far as cool powers go. I'd never really been anywhere, except Hawaii, so the power to go *anywhere* was pretty appealing.

"Except," Howlaa said. "You activated the engine earlier, and it tasted your blood, and hooked itself into your body. So now you've got the mind—"

"Really the whole nervous and limbic system," Wisp interjected.

"—that controls it," Howlaa finished. "Not exactly part of our plan."

I stared at the bracelets and the rings and thought, *Take me to Paris*, but nothing happened. Of course it had to be more complicated than that. "How did this thing wind up in Pomegranate Grove Georgia?"

"Because I smashed it against the wall when it looked like the Regent's men might capture us," Howlaa said. "It's got a self-preservation circuit, and when the choice was go smash or jump away, it jumped. Why did it jump to your town? Why not? It had to go somewhere."

Wisp said, "We knew the orphans would snatch the jump-engine back soon, and that it would get dropped out here on the edge of everything, so we escaped the palace, stole an aircraft, acquired a device capable of tracking the jump-engine's emanations, and… Here we are."

"If this thing can teleport you anywhere," I said, "why didn't you just use it to get away?"

"It needs a body to bond to," Howlaa said. "Wisp doesn't have a body, and mine is way too… flexible. If I put on the jump-engine while I was human, and later changed my shape into something else, the jump-engine might decide my body was under attack and teleport random parts of me to a safe distance, or something equally nasty. We were going to take the jump-engine to a man we know and get *him* to send us far, far away from here."

"Why do you want to leave?" I said. "The Nex sounds like a pretty cool place."

"We are slaves," Wisp said. "We work for the Regent, because if we do not obey him, he can make our lives misery. The jump-engine is our way out. We stole it as soon as we learned of its existence. We only want our freedom."

I tried to pull the rings off my fingers, but they were way too tight, which was funny, since they didn't *feel* tight—it was like they tightened up when I touched them. "If the Regent is so nasty, why doesn't he just grab you, or me, with the snatch-whatsits?"

"The snatch-engines don't work within the confines of Nexington-on-Axis itself—they can only grab things from outside," Howlaa said. "The Regent says trying to snatch something from within the Nex would be like trying to eat your own head. Lucky for us. Our tracking device doesn't work now, either." She consulted a little black box with a blinking green light on top. "The jump-engine's energy signature has changed, now that it's connected to you. Must be some kind of stealth routine that comes online when it's activated. So that means the Regent can't find us by tracking the jump-engine, either. He'll have to come after us the old-fashioned way. Though there are spy cameras, not to mention the gutless citizens of the Ax. Most of them would sell us out for a keg of beer or loaf of bread. We should be all right if we keep moving, though. Me and Wisp are good at getting places we're not supposed to go."

I stared at my beautiful jewelry, and the rings changed from glass to sapphire to ruby as I watched. "How does this thing work?" Maybe if they told me, I could get the engine to do something when I *wanted* it to.

"The device is made of conditional matter," Wisp said, "its physical nature shifting in and out of phase with the fluctuations of the axis of the multiverse, maintaining correspondences with certain distant but linked particles, or rather the possibility of particles, and—"

"It's science." Howlaa rolled her eyes. "It works by science."

"Right. So… what exactly am I supposed to do for you?"

Howlaa grinned. It looked like she still had too many teeth, maybe a few left over from that last transformation. "Travel with us a while. Figure out how the use the jump-engine. Save the day. The only other choice is letting the Regent catch you so he can remove the jump-engine. He'd probably start with taking off your skin and pulling out your bones." I must have made a pretty horrified expression because her face softened and she said, "We'll help you get home, when we're done. Which isn't an offer anybody else snatched up to the Cage here has ever gotten."

"I'm not so sure I want to go home," I said. "Home isn't so great. I wouldn't mind seeing more of the Nex."

"You'll have a chance to see more than you'd like," Howlaa said. "Enough talk. If your belly's full we should find a place to sleep, except Wisp, who doesn't sleep, so he gets guard duty. In the morning we'll find transportation. I know a man near here who might be able to help us."

"A friend of yours?"

Wisp laughed. It was weird, hearing laughter from the empty air, weirder even than words. "Howlaa doesn't have friends. Howlaa just has people she has declined to kill so far."

I blinked—Howlaa was clearly tough, but a killer?

Wisp said, "I'm sorry. That was a joke. Perhaps not the most reassuring thing to hear just now. Howlaa isn't an assassin, so much as an… exterminator. Pest control. She disposes of dangerous things snatched up and brought here by mistake. My apologies, Miranda. "

I nodded, wondering how much of a joke it was, really. "It's okay. And you can call me Randy."

"Never happen," Howlaa said. "Wisp doesn't do nicknames. Wisp is *precise*. Grab a couple of apples for the road and come on." Howlaa went to the door and stepped outside. There was a sound—sort of a brief "zap"—a flash of violet light, and then Howlaa fell, right outside the doorway. The last piece of apple dropped from my fingers.

"Hide," Wisp said, right in my ear, and I scrambled behind a pile of crates in a dark corner as quick as I could, peering around the side. Was Howlaa dead? I'd never seen a dead person before—Dad's coffin was empty, obviously—and this would be a bad night to start. Wisp's lights darkened, one by one, though if I squinted I could still see the specks—they were just more like gnats than fireflies, now. He floated behind the crates with me.

Bulky figures appeared in the doorway, three of them, holding things like vastly overcomplicated machine guns, with way too many knobs and antennas and glowing red and green lights, and miniature pitchforks poking out of the end of the barrels. One prodded Howlaa with his foot and said something harsh and grinding in what must have been a language. I couldn't see what they looked like, and was sort of glad.

"Nagalinda," Wisp said. "The Regent prefers their species for his personal guard because they have astonishingly high thresholds for pain."

I was afraid to say anything, in case they might hear me—Wisp was able to float a mote right into my ear and talk, so I was pretty sure they couldn't hear *him*.

"I'll take care of this, you stay here." Wisp's now-dark cloud moved toward one of the guards, but in the dim light I couldn't see what happened. One of the Nagalinda stiffened, then took a jerky, awkward step around Howlaa, almost falling over. He raised the gun, looked at it for a long moment, then reversed it, holding it backwards. The other guards talked to him—more guttural consonants and mushy vowels—and the clumsy guard smashed the butt of his gun into another guard's face, knocking him down. He fell into the apple room, just a few feet away from me. I gasped. This was something Wisp was doing, something he was making the guard do—mind control? *Body* control? Could Wisp possess people?

The guard Wisp controlled tried to attack the other one, but the Nagalinda knocked his legs out from under him and threw him on the ground outside the hut. While Wisp's guard struggled to get upright, looking a lot like a turtle on its back, the other one lifted his gun, twiddled a knob, and shot what looked like a stream of sparkling silver liquid all over his possessed partner.

I expected Wisp to come spiraling up into the air, maybe glowing, maybe not, but nothing happened—just Howlaa unmoving, and two guards down, and one big one still standing. He started to come into the room, and before I had time to get petrified with fear I ran out from behind the crate to the fallen guard and picked up his gun. It weighed a ton, and I couldn't even find a trigger, just a bunch of buttons, but I pointed it at the last guard anyway, hoping to scare him until I could figure out how to set the phaser on stun or whatever.

The guard came toward me, and up close I could see his face, which was like some kind of deep-sea nightmare fish—broad and flat, no nose, lipless mouth full of triangular teeth, oversized pearly white eyes—and I whimpered. He spoke, almost soothingly, then swatted the gun from my hands. After that he laughed. A laugh is a laugh in any language I guess.

Something hard into something soft. The Nagalinda's face was scary, but it looked pretty soft to me, and I had about a pound and a half of metal on each of my hands, so while it was laughing I cocked back my arm and just *punched.*

I felt the impact, but only barely, and as soon as I struck… The Nagalinda disappeared. Poof, gone, gun falling at my feet. I looked at my hands. Wisp had said the jump-engine could send things away. I guess it worked. I just wish I knew *how* it worked. The jump-engine only seemed to do anything when I was too scared or adrenaline-pumped to control it.

Howlaa groaned, and I went to her, glad she wasn't dead. She rubbed the side of her head while I helped her up. "Whatsit?" she said, and I babbled about how the guards had hit her, how Wisp had possessed one, how I'd faced the last guard.

By the end, Howlaa was laughing. "You punched him so hard he *disappeared*? That's a good trick. Keep doing that and you'll get a reputation around here. People might be more afraid of you than they are of me. Come on. We have to free Wisp. The guard must have sprayed some fixative on the body, something to keep Wisp from escaping, but the guns should have a setting to undo it." Howlaa picked up a gun and started flicking switches and turning knobs like she'd done it a thousand times before.

"So Wisp is *in* that guard?"

Howlaa nodded. "Up the nose, in the mouth, into the ears—through any hole, really, even the more personal ones. He can take over bodies, but he's crap when it comes to *controlling* them. He doesn't have a body of his own, so it's not like he gets to practice very often. Mostly he just falls over."

"So maybe he could take over the Regent, and…"

Howlaa shook his head. "The Regent and his best cronies have defenses against the Bodiless—brain implants, neural doodads, who knows what. All those things are too expensive to give every grunt and guard, but the Regent might send some better-equipped special forces after us when he sees what happened here.."

"These guys weren't special?"

Howlaa sprayed something orange and glistening from the gun onto the guard Wisp had possessed. "Nah. Bog standard. We've got a lot worse on the way if we don't move fast."

Wisp's motes, glowing again, came drifting up out of the guard's clothes and mouth, reassembling into a cloud. The guard moaned but didn't get up.

"Thank you for stepping in, Miranda," Wisp said. "I thought I was going to be stuck in that wet mush of a thing forever. And Howlaa, thanks—"

"Mutual appreciation over," Howlaa said. "Now we run."

Chapter 3

We slept in a giant bird's nest, a surprisingly soft place padded with leaves and made of what looked like whole uprooted trees, perched in a pile of tumbled boulders that Howlaa had to carry me up because there was no way I could have climbed, tired as I was by the time we got there.

Sleeping in a nest seems weird, but Wisp said it was the safest place for miles, because everybody was afraid of the creature that lived there. He called it a "Bandersnatch," which I remember is from that poem about the Jabberwocky, but I don't remember much about it, except that line about "claws that catch."

"So why aren't we afraid of the big bird?"

"It's not a bird, precisely… at any rate, Howlaa killed it," Wisp said. "Though she sometimes takes on its form and flies around the surrounding area, just to keep up appearances. We decided it would be good to have some safehouses that *weren't* controlled by the Regent. We've been planning our escape for a long time. Everything but the actual ability to escape. That's new."

"Why would the Regent want to steal a big monster bird from someplace anyway?"

"Oh, he didn't," Wisp said. "He wanted something else—an egg, a rock, a jewel, who knows?—and the snatch-engines accidentally picked up the bird along with the other things. Nexington-on-Axis is a closed system, though, so whatever comes here, stays. If we accidentally pick up something too dangerous to keep… That's where Howlaa comes in. She neutralizes the problem."

"I'm the Regent's janitor. I clean up nasty messes. The kind of messes that make *more* messes." Howlaa snuggled down into a heap of leaves that smelled like eucalyptus and cough drops. "At least, I used to. Now

I *am* one of the Regent's messes. Dawn comes soon. Go pee—take some leaves—and then snatch some sleep while you can."

I picked my way a little distance down the rocks, managed to pull down my tights enough without falling over, and did my business, glad it was only pee. Though it'd be kind of cool to crap on another planet, I guess. Back in the nest I tried to settle down and sleep, but I couldn't, especially once Howlaa started snoring. I stared up at the strange sky, and said, "Wisp, are you awake?"

The response was a whisper in my ear. "The Bodiless—my kind—do not sleep."

"Those things in the sky…"

"Ah. Some are private dwellings for those high in the government—that one, the swirly blue ball? It is a pleasure palace for magisters. The one that sparkles, that looks a bit like a crown or a chandelier? Is a mining platform, extracting strange particles from the places where other universes grind up against the Nex. That twinkle of red is an orbital railgun, and I hope it does not aim itself at us again."

I fingered the bracelets. "I wish I knew how to use this thing. How am I supposed to figure it out?"

Wisp's motes wobbled in the wind. "We'd planned to get help from a certain disgraced government scientist named Templeton, who was involved in the early stages of the jump-engine's development. We'll try to see him soon. Apparently the jump-engine has some… automatic functions, ways to protect you, but as for working it voluntarily, I wouldn't know where to begin. I would advise against experimenting with it. You could find yourself underwater, or in the vacuum of space…"

I stopped touching the bracelets. "Got it." If I could just click the rings together and say "There's no place like home…" I guess I wouldn't. I still didn't understand everything that was happening, but it seemed like I *would* understand, if I had a little more time, and this place was nothing if not interesting. And I liked Wisp, and Howlaa, even if Howlaa still scared me a little. People who can turn into monsters are sort of scary by nature.

I yawned. "Sleep," Wisp said. "I will keep watch." His motes floated away, and I closed my eyes, and eventually, I must have slept.

The sun came on, except it wasn't a sun, but a nuclear explosion frozen in time and trapped inside a sphere of unbreakable crystal, set in the sky millennia before by the Queen and Kings of Nexington-on-Axis and set to provide ten hours of light and then switch off for ten hours of darkness, or so Wisp told me. He started to explain how it worked while I had breakfast—apples, and I was already sick of apples, even the white ones that tasted like some weird tropical fruit—but Howlaa interrupted and said, "It's science, all right? Science is how it works."

Wisp's answer was cranky: "When you say 'science' like that you might as well be saying 'magic' or 'the gods' or—"

"*Super* science, then," Howlaa said. "Are you happy? Let's go. There's rough ground to cover here, so," she sighed, "I'd better let Miranda ride along. Stand back." Howlaa started to shift and wiggle and change again, and since I wasn't terrified this time I got to be fascinated instead. When the transformation was complete, Howlaa was a big spiderlike thing with at least a dozen spindly legs and a roundish central mass that didn't have eyes or a mouth but just a bunch of antennae, like snail antlers. The shadowy clothes she wore changed shape and became something like a seat or a saddle.

The spider—Howlaa—squatted down and Wisp said, "Well, climb on."

I clambered up, where the shadowy stuff, which felt like stiff cloth, shaped itself around me and held me in tighter than a roller coaster's straps. "Can she turn into *anything*?"

"Anything with blood in it," Wisp said, and then Howlaa started to run.

I thought she'd been quick as a person, but as a spider she was at least as fast as a car. The wind streamed by so hard I could barely keep my eyes open, but I could see well enough to make out the crazy piles of jagged rocky rubble we passed over, with Howlaa leaping chasms and scrabbling over treacherous slopes as easily as I'd walk across my kitchen floor. In what seemed like moments we were beyond the rubble of rocks and racing through the remains of a city, only the buildings were made of dirt and paper and resembled wasp's nests. "What is this place?" I yelled over the wind.

"Who knows?" Wisp said in my ear. "The Regent let the royal orphans know he wanted *something*, and they fired up the snatch-engines to get it. I'm sure they got whatever they needed, but they also got these ruins in the process. Eventually, as the city expands, I'm sure our citizens will take up residence. For now they're deserted."

We ran for a long time before Howlaa slowed down, and we passed so many things. A pile of blimps with holes in the gasbags. More trees, only some of them weren't trees but giant mushrooms. A thing like a big termite's nest that rose into the sky so high it made my eyes water trying to see the top. An ordinary parking lot like you'd see at the mall, complete with lightposts, sitting in a meadow of weird green flowers. A sword as big as an apartment building jammed into the ground, black metal hilt sticking out at an angle. And more. Nexington-on-Axis was a patchwork place, and the weather was like a mild spring afternoon no matter what weird stuff surrounded us.

Howlaa stopped running beside what could have been any old junked-up country farmhouse built on bare dirt, surrounded by heaps of scrap metal and various piles covered in gray and faded blue tarps. But this farmhouse was on the shores of a shining lake, or maybe an ocean for all I knew, that stretched off in the distance as far as I could see.

Howlaa squatted down again and I slid down, legs numb—we'd only stopped once in all those hours, to drink from a spring bubbling out of a rock—and stomped around, trying to get some feeling back. I'd been gone from home less than a day, and felt like I'd seen the world several times over. I didn't mind, but I could have used a hot shower and my own bathroom, even if I do have to share the facilities with Mom. (Cal gets his own bathroom because he's such a pig.)

Howlaa rippled and transformed. The shadowy stuff was clothes again, but this time it was a skimpy halter and even tinier shorts. She looked like a skank, like Tina McKenzie the day she got sent home from school for being dressed inappropriately.

"Those clothes..." I said.

Howlaa arranged her top, which made her boobs, which weren't very big really, look a lot bigger. I think she misunderstood what I was asking. "Being a skinshifter is hell on normal clothing. I got sick of ending up naked at the end of a fight, so the Regent had his scientists whip this up for me. It's smartcloth—changes to fit my shape."

"It, ah, definitely fits your shape now," I said.

Howlaa nodded. "That's the point."

"So, how does it work?"

Howlaa opened her mouth, but I held up my hand. "Wait, don't tell me. Science."

Howlaa smiled, and it was a lot like the way the wolf-monster smiled. "Smart girl."

Wisp floated near me while Howlaa walked up to the farmhouse door. "Howlaa is not above using sex appeal to get what she needs. She specializes in physical solutions. That doesn't always mean beating people up."

I thought about that. "Eww," I said.

"Indeed," Wisp agreed. "I don't know how you bodied types do it."

I started to say we *didn't* all do it, or anyway not yet, but then the front door slammed open and a skinny guy wearing patched overalls came out holding some kind of gun, but with a bell at the end of the barrel like an old-fashioned musket.

"My friend!" Howlaa said. "I've come to visit!"

The guy, who was maybe not as old as I thought at first despite his white hair, lowered the gun and frowned. "What brings the Regent's chief junkyard dog all the way out here? I haven't seen you since my change-of-address-at-gunpoint."

"We're on unofficial business," Howlaa said.

He lifted the gun again. "Don't get me involved in your smuggling bullshit. That's how I wound up stuck all the way out here under house arrest in the first place. If the Regent didn't need my schematics, I'd be in a gulag somewhere."

"Merrill," Howlaa said, and I wouldn't have believed she could purr before then. "We come in peace. I don't ask much. A chance to use the bathroom for me and my friend—the friend who has a bladder anyway—and maybe a bite to eat. Then we'll discuss things further. Unless you'd like me to tell Regent about the moonshine you're brewing out back? You know he disapproves of you drinking. It makes your blueprints go to shit."

Merrill swore. "Come in, then. And I imagine you'll want a drink from that still you're blackmailing me with?"

"Maybe one," Howlaa said. "Or two. Three at most."

"Please," Merrill said. "You drink like a goddamn fish."

"Speaking of fish…" Howlaa said, following Merrill inside.

"Piece of crap." Howlaa banged a big red wrench against the side of a twenty-foot-long metal sculpture of a fish propped up on cinderblocks near the shore. The fish had overlapping metal scales that tinkled in the breeze, eyes made of big dirty curved windows, and metal jaws full of serrated teeth. Howlaa flung open a toolbox and began rattling around inside. Her outfit looked like a mechanic's jumpsuit now. I sat in what shade I could find from a nearby pile of splintery boards, glad to be out of Merrill's crap-filled house, all heaped with engine parts and with greasy blueprints thumbtacked to the walls. The only upside of the visit had been the chance to use a real indoor toilet, even if it was almost as dirty as Cal's bathroom, and I'd had to sort of hover over the toilet seat to pee.

Wisp bobbed in the breeze. "It just occurred to me—you must forgive me, I have no family in the conventional sense—that your loved ones must be worried about you, Miranda. I wish we had a way to get a message to them. Normally, I'm afraid, it doesn't much matter, because new citizens have no hope of ever returning home, but your situation is unusual. I hope you don't get in too much trouble when you return."

"Oh, I'll get in trouble." I didn't want to think about it. Being grounded for the rest of seventh grade didn't sound fun. "But at first my Mom will just think I ran away. They won't worry much until tonight, probably."

Howlaa, kneeling to peer underneath the mechanical fish, didn't seem to be paying any attention. Wisp floated closer, motes of light stirring together, and said, "Oh? They won't think you've been kidnapped?"

Wisp doesn't have a face, so it's not like his expression made me uncomfortable, but I still looked down at my feet. "I've run away before. A couple of times. Once I slept under the bleachers at school by the football field, until the janitor woke me up at dawn. The other time I just hid out in a friend's basement." Jenny Kay's basement. It wasn't an awesome basement with couches and a pool table and pinball machines. It was just pipes and spiderwebs and old rakes. But Jenny snuck down after dinner and brought me a corn muffin with butter and a chicken leg wrapped in a napkin, so it was still better than shivering behind the school.

"Running away's a good impulse, but you went back afterward?" Howlaa growled. "Quitter." Guess she was paying attention after all.

"Why did you run away?" Wisp's movements were hypnotic, beautiful and random.

"I don't know. The first time things were just really tense at home, and I couldn't stand it, I needed to get out." That was right after what happened to Dad, with Mom all zombified on pills, Cal in his room blasting music all the time, the whole family falling to pieces. "The second time was mostly to avoid my Mom's boyfriend Ross—it was the first night he slept over. I can't stand him."

"This man beats you?" Howlaa banged a wrench or something, and the fish shuddered, tiny metal scales showering down flakes of rust. "Or tries to take liberties—"

"No! Nothing like that. He just… he sings all the time."

"I do not understand," Wisp said.

"He's… he's always singing songs from old musicals and doing dumb little dances and he makes my Mom heart-shaped pancakes and he tries to talk to me about stupid things. Like, he got my reading list from English class somehow, and read all the books, and tried to talk to me about them." The only good thing about Ross was that Mom pretty much stopped drinking once they got serious a few months ago. She was finally "moving on." But I didn't really *want* her to move on. When your husband gets exploded, shouldn't you stay broken for a while? I didn't want her getting over Dad. Especially not for a giant loser like Ross.

Wisp bobbled. "I fail to see what's so objectionable about singing and cooking and—"

"She means the man is annoying, Wisp." Howlaa climbed out from under the fish, which was beginning to move its fins with a series of squeaky shrieks of metal. "With the la-di-dah and the prancing and the sunny disposition that doesn't know when to shush."

"That's it." I nodded. "That's exactly it."

"I know it is," Howlaa said. "Now get in the fish. This lake isn't going to cross itself."

I blinked. "In *that*?"

Howlaa thumped the side of the big fish, and a hatch popped open, with a collapsible stairway unfolding down. "The only way to travel. At least, the only way to travel unnoticed. If we move on the surface of the lake, the Regent's spies might see us, but if we travel under the waves…"

"That thing's a submarine? I thought it was, I don't know, a bath toy for giants."

"The only giants here are the steam colossi, and they don't take baths," Wisp said. "And while they do enjoy toys, of a sort… this isn't the sort."

"It's perfectly safe," Howlaa said. "Or close enough. You might get wet, but otherwise. Merrill swears it's seaworthy. He knows if he tries to drown us I'll just swim out and drown *him*." Howlaa made a hurry-up motion but I didn't budge.

"Can't you just turn into a manatee or something? Swim that way?"

"Yes, and Wisp can just dim his lights a bit and float, but *you* can't, and we need you. Until we figure out how to work that jump-engine you're wearing, you need to travel the ordinary way."

I didn't think a big metal fish was very ordinary. "Where exactly are we going? You keep talking about a plan, plans for me, and I know what your goal is, but what are we *doing*?"

An old man with a neatly trimmed beard, wearing a long white robe, appeared between us. He didn't so much as glance at me, just smiled beatifically, looking at nothing in particular. "Howlaa. This disobedience saddens me. And Wisp, I expected better of you. Please, both of you, return to the palace. Whatever your objections to the terms of your service, I'm sure we can work out some mutually beneficial agreement. Just return the thing you stole, and all will be forgiven." The old man chuckled. "I can't fault you for stealing, after all. You *did* learn it from watching me. But you must choose your targets more wisely."

"Into the fish," Howlaa said. "No more talk, *now*."

I hurried around the man, wanting to ask who he was. He sighed. "I assume you're ignoring me? Attempting to flee? Really, Howlaa, all the resources of Nexington-on-Axis are arrayed against you. Didn't you realize we would have Merrill under remote surveillance, after the indiscretions in his past? Admittedly, he tends to destroy any equipment we place within his perimeter of influence, but he can't knock spy satellites out of the sky."

"Ignore him," Wisp said. "It's just a projection, beamed down from the satellite. They can see us with their remote cameras, but they can't hear us, and they can only see the tops of your heads, not your faces. And, I hope, not your jewelry."

I went up the rickety steps into the fish. There was another door immediately in front of me, like I was in an airlock, so I pushed that open and looked around. I'd been on boats before. This wasn't much like those boats. The inside of the fish was mostly bare metal and steel mesh and pipes running everywhere, and it smelled of algae. "Is that guy the Regent?"

"None other," Howlaa said. "Probably sending a fleet of autogyros and drone jets as we speak. The sooner we get into the lake the better. The satellites can't see underwater, and it's a big lake, and I know all the caves." Howlaa slammed the door shut, and I tried to find a place to sit that didn't look like it would give me tetanus just from touching it.

"Where's Howlaa going?"

"She has to push the sub in the water," Wisp said. The fish jerked, and lurched, and splashed, and I barely kept my seat by grabbing a metal cross-bar overhead. The hatch opened again and Howlaa climbed in, dripping water.

"How did you push this thing? It's huge!"

"Some of my forms are very strong." Howlaa went past me and sat down in a pilot's chair in the fish's head. She started to throw levers and flip switches and the fish sank, the big glass eyes filling up with lake water, clear at first, then murkier as we descended. Water began to drip in tiny dribbles from the inside of the fish's head, though it was dry where I sat. "I'll take evasive maneuvers, though I doubt there are other subs here. They were all in the Landlock Sea last time I saw a status-of-force report. It will take some time for the Regent to get combat vessels here, and we'll be gone by then, I hope."

"So about this plan—" I said.

"Shushit!" Howlaa shouted, and I shrunk back as her voice echoed in the confines of the sub.

"Howlaa needs to concentrate now," Wisp said, soothing. "Better to talk about… other things. You mentioned your mother's boyfriend. What happened to your, ah, original father?"

"Wisp is taking an interest," Howlaa said from the sweating head of the fish, and I wondered if her friendly tone was an apology for snapping at me. "Watch out."

"I am interested," Wisp said, sounding dramatically hurt. I guess when you don't have a face you learn to put a lot of expression into your voice. "You don't have to talk about it if you don't want to, but it's apt to be a long voyage, and Howlaa's not much of a conversationalist."

"My Dad was—" I almost used my Mom's phrase, and said "He was taken from us," but instead I said, "He got blown up. Two years ago."

"Bomb? Mortar fire? Soldier?" Howlaa sounded halfway interested.

"He was a chef. At a restaurant downtown. There was a gas leak one night, and he was the first one in the next morning, wanted to try out some new ideas for recipes, and… They think when he turned on the light there was a spark, or maybe he just somehow didn't smell the gas and tried to turn on the stove… Anyway, the restaurant blew up. We went to see it, after. Nothing left but a hole in the ground and some pipes sticking out."

"I am sorry for your loss," Wisp said, solemn.

"Hell of a thing," Howlaa said. "There may be explosions in our future, but we'll try to keep you out of them."

"Do you have a large family?" Wisp asked.

"A few cousins I don't see much, but otherwise, no, just me, my Mom, and my brother Cal, for whatever he's worth."

"Ah," Wisp said. "Your brother is… not nice?"

"He's just Cal." I almost missed him. "He won't drive me to school unless Mom yells at him, but he's not all bad. He lets me watch his band practice." His guitarist was really cute, even if the music sucked. "He's the only one who hates Mom's boyfriend as much as I do." I looked at the rings on my fingers and sighed. "Cal's the one who found the jump-engine. I don't know where. I guess he just picked it up because it was pretty, same as me, probably saw it on the side of the road somewhere. I noticed it glinting in the back of his car when I got home from school yesterday…" Was it only yesterday? "Anyway, I know where he keeps his spare key, so I unlocked the car and took the necklace. He came out of the house and yelled at me and started chasing me so I took off into the woods."

"Ha! She stole," Howlaa said. "See, she'll be right at home here."

I thought about saying "I steal lots of things," but that wasn't exactly something to be proud of, was it? I don't know why it started. The shoplifting, I mean. I never did it before Dad died. I'm not a kleptomaniac, it's not like I can't *stop* myself from taking stuff. I just like it. Jenny Kay started it, kind of, stealing some sunglasses from the mall and encouraging me to do the same, but I took it a lot farther than Jenny ever did. There's a loose board in the floor of my closet and I've got all kinds of stuff in there. I tell myself it's Christmas presents for everybody, but it's not like I even steal things anybody would *want*. Shoplifting just makes me feel a thrill, like I'm on an adventure, like life is exciting and dangerous instead of boring and annoying. I feel bad afterward, but the thrill is better than the guilt is bad, you know?

Something started beeping like an insistent alarm clock. "Piss and poison," Howlaa said. "We've got frogmen coming after us." She leaned forward and peered into the water, but I couldn't see anything but murk.

"Like scuba divers?" I said. "With spear guns or something?"

"No," Wisp said. "Literally frogmen. They're called Dagonites. They must have a settlement near here. And they have much worse than spearguns. Normally they aren't aggressive. The Regent must have sent them."

"They work for the Regent?"

"Everyone here works for the Regent, Miranda. The whole of Nexington-on-Axis. Most of the residents just hope he never thinks of a job for them. But when he calls, you answer. Obedience is the price they pay for food and security"

"Take the helm, Randy," Howlaa said. "I'm going for a little swim." She stood up and went to the airlock hatch.

"I—what?"

"Just sit there, and if the nose starts to dip, pull back on the lever with the red handle, just a little. If the nose starts to tilt up, push the same lever forward. It's simple. I don't want you to *go* anywhere, just keep the fish steady."

"But can't—" No. Wisp couldn't do it. Wisp didn't have a *body*.

"It's you, Randy."

I sat down in the pilot's seat and touched the lever lightly. I could see things moving in the water, now, but couldn't make out exactly what they were. "What are you going to *do*?"

Howlaa paused by the airlock. "I haven't been a Manipogo in ages. It should be fun. And Manipogos *eat* Dagonites." Then she climbed in, slammed shut the hatch, and was gone.

"Well," Wisp said. "Either Howlaa will win, or we'll throw caution to the wind and see if we can figure out how to work that jump-engine after all."

"Because dying in the vacuum of space is better than waiting to drown inside this fish?"

"You understand the situation completely."

We sat. We bobbed. We waited. I saw something like a snake the size of a couch but longer go slithering across the fish's transparent eyes, twisting sinuously as it passed.

I never knew screams sounded like that under water.

Chapter 4

The fish shifted in a sudden surge of water, either from invisible currents or because of Howlaa's slimy violence. I hauled back on the stick way too hard and the fish's head tilted up, up, up, but I took a deep breath and eased it forward gently, just a touch at a time, and it settled back to the comfortably horizontal again. I couldn't remember the last time I'd been so tense.

Wanting to take my mind off the ten million things totally beyond my control, I said, "That big sea serpent thing that went past the window—that was Howlaa?"

"In the green and scaly flesh," Wisp said.

"But it was like a hundred feet long. How can that be *Howlaa*? I'm not a scientist or anything, but isn't there some kind of law of conservation of… bigness?"

"I believe the Howlaa we see—in whatever form she takes—is not the *real* Howlaa. Not all of her. Skinshifters have never been extensively studied, and much about their nature is mysterious. They don't like to reveal much about themselves, and they have a unique gift for posing as members local populations. One theory holds that skinshifters are extradimensional creatures. The part of Howlaa we see is simply the part that… emerges into the dimensions you and I are able to perceive. The rest of her body—including additional mass—is somewhere *else*." He went on for a while, saying things like "M-theory" and "string theory" and "brane cosmology," and I just let it wash over me, not because I'm dumb, but because I didn't have the background—it was like learning fractions before you can add or subtract. Jenny Kay would've understood it all, I bet. I felt a stab of homesickness, but just for Jenny. It would've been good to have her here with me.

Wisp must've noticed the faraway look on my face, because he said, "Listen: think of a shark's fin, breaking the surface of the water, coming toward you. You can see the fin, and you can *deduce* the existence of the shark, but you can't actually *see* the shark. You see? The fin is all that protrudes into your world from the water. But instead of hiding under water, the rest of Howlaa is hidden away in higher dimensions of our universe."

"Like an iceberg," I said. "Nine-tenths of it is underwater."

"Apt enough, though when talking about Howlaa, a shark is a better metaphor than an iceberg."

The airlock squealed, and I turned in my chair, wishing for a speargun or something—but then, I always had my rings and bracelets, and if I had no other choice, those would maybe let me punch somebody hard enough to make them disappear, or at least get me to safety.

Howlaa came in, looking perfectly human if extremely wet in a shadowcloth bikini, dragging what looked like some kind of green garbage bag full of bones. But when she tossed the thing on the floor, I realized it had a face, and the greasy pierogies I ate at Merrill's rose up in my throat. I fought down the urge to puke by squeezing my hands into fists so hard the rings dug into my flesh, distracting myself with pain.

"I see you brought a souvenir," Wisp said.

Howlaa leaned over and spat several times, expelling ropy green slime with each hacking gag. She wiped her hand across her mouth and shuddered, then caught my eye. "Sorry. Bad manners. Wisp is always telling me to be less disgusting. But Dagonites have poisonous skin. Doesn't bother me when I'm a Manipogo—they're immune—but I had to expel the poison from this body unless I wanted to go gangrenous from the inside out. Hop up from my chair, Randy. We should get going before the second wave arrives."

I got up, though it meant moving closer to the corpse in front of the airlock. I'd never seen a dead person before, and this wasn't exactly a *person*, but then again, it kinda was. The dead Dagonite had a bracelet of its own, seashells and smooth beads on a string, and I wondered if the jewelry had been a gift, or if the Dagonite had made it, or—

"Us or them," Wisp said in a low voice. "Always pick 'us' in that situation. Anyone would."

"Here's something to take your mind off the moral torment." Howlaa reached into a pocket of the shadowcloth—a bikini with *pockets*?—and tossed me something like an oversized brown leather wallet. I opened it and found a creepy-looking syringe, the old-timey kind you see in horror movies set in abandoned insane asylums, all dull brass finger-holds and a needle the size of a ballpoint pen. "Jam that in Froggy's neck and suck out some of his blood."

"Excuse me?"

"You're right," Howlaa said. "It doesn't really have a neck. Just shove it generally below the head there. You'll probably hit blood."

"Why… would I be doing this?"

"Wisp, I have to *drive*," Howlaa said crankily, and turned away, pulling levers and twisting knobs and sending the submersible fish flapping through the lake at high speed. Occasional green lumps bumped off the windows and spun lazily away.

"Howlaa doesn't have a Dagonite in her… repertoire," Wisp said. "But if you draw the blood, Howlaa can drink it."

"You drink *blood*? I thought you were a werewolf, not a vampire."

Howlaa didn't answer me, didn't even appear to hear me, just turned on some wobbly black-and-white screen on the fish's cockpit that beeped and booped, like sonar or something.

"Howlaa can take on the form of any creature she consumes," Wisp said. "It's disgusting, worse even than the ordinary eating habits of the bodied, I know, but it is her way. Skinshifters can take in a genetic sample, extrapolate the entire organism from that sample, and duplicate that organism, perfect in every way."

I looked at the back of Howlaa's totally human neck. "So at some point… Howlaa drank the blood of a human?" *Like me*, I didn't say.

"Ah," Wisp said. "Well. In that particular situation, it was consensual. Part of a rather complex intrigue involving impersonation and espionage in the service of the Regent… but that was long ago."

"And that woman's been dead for eighty thousand days," Howlaa said. "Her genes only live on in me. But, yes, most of the other bodies are things I just *ate*. I didn't consume any of the Dagonites during that battle, though—just bit them dead and spat them out. They tasted awful. The blood won't be a treat, either, but I want it."

"Skinshifters are apex predators," Wisp said. "Masters of disguise. Once they manage to eat one example of a species, they can blend in with the herd… or society… and prey on others at will."

"Wolf in sheep's clothing," I said. I'd known Howlaa was kind of scary, that much was obvious, but somehow the total not-human-ness of her hadn't sunk in before. Turning into a wolf, okay, werewolves are just people with a weird medical problem and an out-of-control budget for safety razors. I could relate to a werewolf. But Howlaa only *looked* human, and she was really something else entirely. "Are you sure you two are the good guys?"

"Definitely, in comparison to the opposition," Wisp said. "But Howlaa only plays the predator in the line of duty these days. If she ever did otherwise, ever tried to prey on an innocent, I would step in, and stop it."

"How would you—Oh. The body control thing."

"It's why we were made partners," Howlaa said. "The Regent knew I wouldn't like being leashed, so he sent Wisp along to make sure I behaved myself. If I tried to run—not that there's anywhere to run on the Ax, not really—Wisp would hijack my body and walk me back to the palace for a bout of reeducation." Howlaa turned and gave me one of her grins. "It took me *decades* to get Wisp reeducated into seeing things *my* way."

"I owed a debt to society," Wisp said stiffly. "I sought only to pay it off honorably, through service. But the Regent abused my loyalty, and his sovereignty, and I agreed to help Howlaa find a way out of our situation. Out of this place. Beyond the Regent's reach, even though his reach extends into every corner of every possible universe."

"Now that you know the terrible true nature of beastly old me," Howlaa said, "suck out that frog's blood, Randy. Before it spoils and starts to stink. Blood dead more than a little while is no good to me—the cells decay."

I told myself the Dagonite was just a big frog. I'd dissected one of those in biology class, and while some of the other girls had flapped their hands and shrieked, I hadn't seen the big deal—I mean, I'd helped my Dad cut up chicken carcasses, and frogs were probably even stupider than chickens.

Of course, this frog had a bracelet. This frog had a *culture*.

But it was already dead. And if Howlaa could imitate a Dagonite next time, maybe she'd have an alternative to killing them. I jabbed in the syringe and pulled back the plunger, a swirl of blackish-red fluid filling the cylinder. "Is this enough?"

"That will do," Wisp said.

Howlaa beckoned, took the syringe, and squirted a long stream of blood into her mouth, closing her eyes for a moment as if to savor it, the way my Mom used to do with wine, before she got into the habit of guzzling the stuff. Howlaa's eyes opened, and she said, "Now chuck the dead thing out of the airlock."

"Sorry, but I draw the line at corpse disposal."

Howlaa sighed, twisted more levers, and told me to take the helm again. "Don't touch *anything*."

"If I'm not supposed to touch anything, why am I sitting there?"

"Because otherwise Wisp will get nervous." Howlaa opened the airlock and wrestled the dead Dagonite away while I sat quietly and didn't touch *anything*, even when the sonar thing began to beep and boop very insistently.

"That doesn't sound good," Wisp said.

When the airlock opened again and Howlaa returned, once more soaked, I pointed wordlessly to the black-and-white screen. Howlaa came over, leaned down, and peered at it. "Huh," he said. "Wisp, you remember those caves we found under here when we were after those cannibals?"

I wondered if Howlaa would be considered a cannibal if she ate something while she was in the same physical form as that something, but decided maybe now wasn't the best time for philosophy.

"Yes," Wisp said.

"We'd better find them, and soon."

"Why?"

"Because if I'm reading this screen correctly, there's a steam colossus standing in the water just ahead, and I'd rather not be stepped on today."

"You can't turn into a steam colossus?" I said. "And, you know, have an epic monster fight?"

"The colossi don't have blood," Wisp said. "They have… steam. They're seven-eighths machine. I can't possess them, either. Howlaa defeated one, years ago, when the colossus went rogue—she became small, infiltrated the mechanism, and destroyed the armored vat-grown brain inside. But it took most of a day to kill the creature, and we don't have that kind of time."

"There are only half a dozen colossi in all of the Nex," Howlaa complained, making the fish turn hard to the right. "What are the odds that one would be *here*?"

"Maybe it was coming to Merrill for repairs or upgrades. Whatever the reason, I'm sure the Regent has it looking for us now."

"Not much chance of it finding us, any more than I could pluck a protozoa from a puddle at my feet, but if we pass too close it might have proximity sensors online… Caves it is." Howlaa focused on the cockpit, muttering about lost time and too much distance and useless worthless jump-engines. I settled back down on my unpleasant bench, scared but also a little regretful that I wouldn't get to see a steam colossus, whatever it was—I imagined a giant mecha robot suit, the kind you see in Japanese cartoons.

"We were hoping to cover more ground underwater—the caves will be slower—but at least they're relatively protected." Wisp paused. "From the Regent, anyway. They're not particularly well-protected against the things that *live* in the caves."

"They're our brothers-in-arms, Wisp," Howlaa said, tone full of mockery. "Brave souls standing against the Regent, determined to live as free creatures on their own terms. I'm sure they'll embrace us with open arms. Or open tentacles. Or mandibles. Here we are." The fish slowed in its whooshing onrush, and I leaned over to look out the windows, where something that might have been an underwater mountain or the roots of an island became clear. There were big black holes in the rock, from the size of a person to the size of a house, and Howlaa aimed the fish toward one of the biggest. Soon we were in total blackness, without even the murky light from the frozen nuclear sun above, and the fish's interior was lit only by Wisp's glow. The fish scraped its metal belly on rocks a few times with horrible shrieks of metal, and the sweating in the head became more of a shower.

"Tighter than I remember," Howlaa said. "But then, I was traveling under my own power last time."

Finally the fish ran aground completely, and Howlaa cursed and smacked the controls. "End of the line. Everybody out." She flung open the hatch and went into the airlock without closing the door behind her, which meant we'd emerged into someplace dry, unless Howlaa had decided to drown me.

I followed Wisp out of the airlock, into your basic damp natural cavern. The metal fish was half-submerged in a pool of water and half-shredded against rock, several of its serrated teeth broken and gleaming in Wisp's light. Howlaa hopped down to the rock, and I followed more cautiously. There were tunnels branching off from this cavern, and I hoped some of them led to light and food and maybe a place to take an afternoon nap, though I wasn't too hopeful about any of those.

"Which way was it?" Howlaa said, but before Wisp answered, we all noticed the glows approaching from the tunnels before us, shifting blue-green specks and spirals in the dark.

"Underdwellers," Wisp said. "The glowing lights you see are clan tattoos drawn with bioluminescent fungus." I figured that informational moment was for my benefit.

"Recognize the clan symbol?" Howlaa asked. I couldn't read the tone of her voice. Worry? Annoyance? Pride? The things drew closer, and now there was a murmuring from the tunnels, a sort of chittering gnashing bunch of grunts and moans.

"Yes," Wisp said, and sighed. "I've seen the intelligence reports. They're clan Kil'howlaa. A vengeance clan formed by the few Underdwellers who survived your *last* visit here."

"It's nice to be remembered," Howlaa said, and transformed.

Chapter 5

Howlaa's new form was kind of like the armored Humvee version of a Komodo dragon, big and covered in spiky plates, with a long flat snout full of fangs. It reared up on two legs and showed off four arms, like a freaky Hindu god, each one tipped with claws like hunting knives that dripped some clear fluid—acid, venom, who knows.

"The Rendigo," Wisp said. "Her most fearsome battle form." The Rendigo rushed for the most crowded tunnel, screaming with a noise like a boiling teakettle being murdered. "Normally I would urge you to find a place of safety," Wisp said, "But if the full strength of clan Kil'howlaa is here, we'll need your help." Wisp went zipping toward one of the tunnels faster than I'd ever seen him move before, and one of the crouching shapes began to move clumsily and turn around and, from the sound of it, start to attack its fellow Underdwellers.

Well, crap. Time to earn my passage, I guess. I wasn't much of a fighter, not since some hair-pulling in fifth grade when I caught Sandy Tyler going through my bookbag when I came back from the bathroom, but I had the jump-engine all over my fists, and maybe they'd work their magic—excuse me, *science* magic—again.

One of the Underdwellers came out of an unattended tunnel and ran straight for me, low and loping. I reared back my arm to throw a hopefully-teleporting punch, but then I saw its face—*her* face. This wasn't some monster. The Underdweller was just a girl, blonde and snub-nosed and about my age, and apart from the spiraling glowing tattoo design on her face and the raggy clothes, she could've been a girl in my class.

While I was being confronted with the essential humanity of my enemy and all that, she punched me in the face.

I'd never been punched before. Slapped, once, right after Dad died, when Mom was pretty much having a breakdown and I said something that set her off, but never punched. I saw black stars bloom in the blackness of the cavern, and my cheekbone felt like it nearly cracked, and my nose went off like a busted fire hydrant, blood going everywhere. I stumbled and half-lifted my arms to defend myself, but then Wisp came streaming in, up little miss Underdweller's nose and into her gaping mouth, and she just stood there like a switched-off robot.

Howlaa came trotting up, human again and covered in specks of I-didn't-want-to-think-about-what, the whole rest of the fight apparently finished in the time it took me to get a nosebleed. "Here." Howlaa handed me a piece of torn cloth that looked relatively clean, and I pressed it to my nose, happy for the excuse to tilt my head back and look at the ceiling and not say much.

"Their numbers were greatly diminished," Wisp said, his male voice coming out of the Underdweller's open mouth, which was beyond weird. "Unless there are reserves hidden deeper. I wish I could read minds as well as hijack bodies."

"I do too," Howlaa said, "because I went far enough up that tunnel to see that it's *changed*. They've done some earthworks down here since we departed, and I don't know the way out anymore." Howlaa tugged on her shirt and a piece of shadowcloth came away, without so much as a ripping sound. A little more tugging and she held a length of thin black rope. She bound up the Underdweller's unresisting hands behind her back.

"Well, then." Wisp spiraled out of the girl's nose, and she shook her head, blinking blankly around, then snarling. She spat out a stream of words in—

"Is that German? Cal's taking a German class, it sounds kinda like that."

"It is," Wisp said. "I'll translate." A single glowing mote detached from Wisp's main swarm and floated to my ear, where it quietly spoke: "Dirty ugly bastards I'll kill you, I'll kill you all, when I get free—"

"I get the gist," I said.

Wisp laughed. "I'll only translate… pertinent information in the future." Wisp spoke to the Underdweller, English in my ear along with the German that came out directly. "Show us the way to the surface, and we will spare your life."

"Too generous," Howlaa growled. "Should have offered a quick death. Oh well."

"Don't be a jerk," I said. "Didn't you say the Underdwellers are against the Regent too? Shouldn't you be helping her instead of killing all her friends?"

"They wanted to kill *us*, Randy. I saved your life."

"But why do they want to kill you? Because you killed a bunch of their *other* friends back when you were working for the Regent, right?"

Howlaa looked at Wisp for some kind of back-up, but Wisp was deep in a German argument with the Underdweller, no longer bothering to translate for me, probably because I was about to dig in deep for an argument with Howlaa.

Howlaa spat, and her spit sizzled on the rock—some leftover side-effect from being the Rendigo, I figured. "Yes. Fine. True."

"You're plotting a revolution, so shouldn't they be part of it? The enemy of my enemy is my friend and all that?"

"Maybe if they didn't have a vendetta against me," Howlaa said. "Besides, it's not *really* a revolution. It's a mini-revolution. Wisp and I only want to break into the palace and wreck the snatch-engines and get rid of the royal orphans so that once we escape the Nex, the Regent can't bring us *back*. What happens to his government after that…" Howlaa shrugged. "Not our problem."

I stared at her. I thought I'd fallen in with freedom fighters, trying to change the world, but they just wanted to save their own butts. I couldn't see a reason not to say that: "You just want to save yourselves? I mean, if you wreck the engines, kill the royal orphans, and leave this place behind… won't everyone who's left behind starve? You said there are no natural resources here, not even real weather, so when the supplies run out, what happens to the people you liberated?"

The Underdweller tried to run—Howlaa hadn't tied her legs—and Howlaa had to tackle her. She whispered in the Underdweller's ear, and the girl stiffened, then nodded and struggled to her feet. She plodded slowly toward one of the body-choked tunnels.

"What did you say to her?" I asked.

"Something motivating, in the language of the Underdwellers, and less diplomatic than Wisp's words." Howlaa went after the girl. I hung back a bit, knowing I should follow, but wanting space between me and the skinshifter.

Wisp floated up to me. "Come, Miranda. We never claimed to be perfect. We only want our freedom. But… you have a point. There are other innocents here, who do not deserve to be abandoned. Once the snatch-engines are disabled, we can use the power of the jump-engine to send *everyone* back to their homes."

I thought about that. There were probably families who'd been on Nexington-on-Axis for generations, whose grandparents or great-grand-parents had been snatched originally—this place *was* their home. Where were they supposed to go? To planets they'd never seen before, to live with people who looked like them but had totally different cultures? "Even the Underdwellers? You'd help them?"

"The Underdwellers... are not good choices for allies. They might not accept our help. But if they alone were left behind on the Nex, the food stores would last them for decades. As it is, they eat each other here in the dark—they have become monstrous in their rebellion "

"Please, like you're squeamish about people who *eat* people. Or people who are monstrous." It was hard to sound snotty with a handkerchief shoved against my nostrils, but I did my best. I went into the tunnel after Howlaa, trying not to look at the bodies I stepped around. Most of them weren't human, at least—maybe it's speciesist of me, but it was way harder for me to see a dead human than a dead something else, even knowing the other creatures are people too. "If I hadn't accidentally turned on the jump-engine, you two would have just taken the necklace and left me in the woods."

"Yes. I suppose you're right. And I'm sorry. But Miranda... our lives have not allowed us much in the way of conscience. Howlaa is actually quite well-adjusted for a creature evolved over countless generations to become an infiltrating treacherous killer. She... drinks, you know. One reason she wanted a human form originally is because alcohol is plenti-ful here, at least in the city proper, and she prefers drunken oblivion to the sober contemplation of her lot in life. This is the longest I've seen her sober in a long time. Sober, and focused, and *trying*. Please don't judge us too harshly. We're doing our best."

You'll have to do better if you want my help, I thought, but didn't say it. Not yet.

We followed the Underdweller for a while. "How do we know she's not leading us to a room full of her pals? Or a lava pit?"

"We don't," Howlaa said. "But where's your love and trust and fellow-feeling now?"

I bit back a nasty answer—"Something about being with *you* has made me a lot less trusting"—then looked at the cloth Howlaa had given me. I hoped there wasn't anything down here that could smell blood. I pressed it back against my nostrils. At least the bleed was slowing down.

The tunnel was close and narrow and weirdly twisty, and it was kind of like being inside an ant farm—this didn't feel like this inside of a mine or something people had made, but it wasn't like natural caves, either, because the walls and ceiling were all smooth and rounded. Gradually the tunnel got brighter, light coming from smears of luminous fungus dotting the walls at irregular intervals. The passage opened up and out from narrow hallway to four-lane freeway width, and we passed crumbling statues of the weirdest things—a pickup truck, a park bench, a refrigerator, an old-fashioned jukebox. Those were just the sculptures of things I recognized. There were lots of others that didn't look like anything I knew at all, big wads of tubes and valves, weird things with spikes and loops and holes, all made out of this brownish rock that crumbled like dry sand when I touched it. The sculpture garden stretched as far into the gloom in all directions as I could see, some of the statues painted here and there with glowing fungus in weird patterns.

I touched one of the statues—it looked like a sci-fi movie robot crossed with a knight's suit of armor—and the arm fell off with a thump. The Underdweller girl whipped around and snarled at me, then launched herself. Howlaa swatted her down, but she bounced back up again and came for me. My nose started hurting preemptively. Howlaa grabbed her, shook her, and put her back on the path, and she kept on leading us, but not without a lot of sullen pissy looks over her shoulder at me.

"What'd I do? Did she carve that one or something?" My voice was all nasally from the crusted-up blood in my nostrils.

"The coproliths are sacred to the Underdwellers," Wisp said. "The touch of someone from above is considered profane."

Oh, crap. A taboo, like I'd read about on our trip to Hawaii, which hadn't stopped Cal from bringing a few chunks of sacred lava rock home in his suitcase. "Can you tell her I'm sorry? That I didn't mean to?"

"I can, but it wouldn't help," Wisp said.

Something sparked in my head, some vocabulary word I'd seen when studying for the PSAT. "Wait, did you say copro-something? Like, dinosaur crap?"

"I call them coproliths, which just means fossilized dung, but in this case, in your language, it's also a pun on 'monolith,' rather a clever one I think—"

"Wisp thinks he's *so* clever," Howlaa said. "I'm sure there's a word in your language for people like him, too."

It seemed to me they were skipping over the important point. "So you're saying those sculptures are made of *poo*?"

Howlaa cackled. "Better wash your hands before you eat your next apple, Randy."

"They are essentially rock, at this point," Wisp said. "The statues were created—perhaps 'produced' is a better word—by the gargantuan god-worms who first made these tunnels. The worms did not survive long after their transportation to Nexington-on-Axis. Something in the atmosphere disagreed with them. I never saw them myself, but by all accounts they were a fearsome and erudite race."

"For big worms anyway," Howlaa said. "Wish I could've eaten one. Ah, well. Before my time."

"I guess I'm missing the part where the worms poop out full-size models of washing machines?" We were passing exactly that just then, sculpted with the lid half-open.

"It's admittedly odd, even for the Nex," Wisp said. "But then, the universe *is* infinite, and any conceivable combination of particles is bound to show up in an infinite universe somewhere—even those unlikely collections of particles which constitute a race of giant worms who excrete sculptures. The worms were blind—more, as far as we know they had no senses at all like your own or even mine—but they still somehow created these models, perfect in every detail, altering their own internal physiology to allow them to excrete images of things they'd never seen. Indeed, they created things they couldn't have seen, even if they'd had eyes, items that didn't exist on their native world *or* on the Nex during their lifetimes. Things like that washing machine, that hadn't even been *invented* when the worms lived. They were obviously clairvoyant, and apparently capable of precognition as well. The Underdwellers worship the works the god-worms left behind, it's an article of faith among them that there is one great worm left, living deep underground in hibernation..."

I sort of shivered. Bugs and worms don't especially creep me out, but worms the size of the tunnel we'd passed through? Definitely creepy.

"Bah," Howlaa said. "They're all dead. We looked *everywhere*, in every hole, last time we were here, and no sign of life. I looked hard. I had incentive. I *really* wanted to eat one. Imagine if I'd slithered here in the shape of a god-worm? These Underdwellers would have named me king instead of public enemy number only."

"King in a garden of excrement. How pleasant. And that wouldn't have solved our fundamental problem."

"Shushit, Wisp," Howlaa said. "I'm *fantasizing*."

The big cavern narrowed again, and this new tunnel sloped upward hard. My calves were screaming. I'd played soccer a little before Dad died, but since the explosion, my exercise had pretty much been limited to running from Cal when I pissed him off or running from a store after stealing something. Shoplifting anything, even just a lipstick, zoomed me up with adrenaline I had to burn off by running. But my adrenaline was pretty well tapped-out in the aftermath of getting punched in the face, so I just trudged along.

The light up ahead wasn't really bluish or greenish, but more like good old sunlight, and a breeze came in, carrying the smell of... oil and exhaust, which at least made a change from the air full of particles of god-worm poo.

The Underdweller girl stopped and babbled at us for a while, and the Wisp-mote in my ear translated, sort of: "Euphemistic curse, biologically impossible demand, formal vow of blood revenge, all very standard."

"Guess I'd better kill her," Howlaa said.

I moved so fast I surprised even myself, getting between Howlaa and the girl, though that meant turning my back on little miss nosepunch. "No you better *not*. She's no threat to us."

"Not just at this moment," Howlaa said. "But this is the place where refugees and fugitives go, the broken and the mad, the ones who can't handle life on the Ax, and she'll have a new tribe in no time. She'll be the last high priest of the shit-worms, and everyone who comes will listen to her because she knows where the food is stored, where the escape routes are, where the good dry bedroom caverns can be found. She'll re-form Clan Kil'howlaa, and they *will* be a threat to us, and by us, I mean *me*."

"Touch her and I'll punch you off this planet."

"Well," Wisp corrected. "We're not certain the Nex is a planet. It could be an asteroid or construct or—"

"Whatever. I'll send you *away*, Howlaa, and then the Regent can slurp you up with a snatch-engine and put you back to work. You can't go around killing people just because they get in your way. Not while you're hanging out with me."

Howlaa stared me down for a while, then sniffed. "Fair enough. You're showing some backbone at least—you'll need that when we get to the city center. Wisp always tells me I'm too casual with the killing, that being pretty much immortal makes me cold-hearted, like *he* has any room to talk. The Bodiless will be around until the heat death of the universe at least. But fine. She can go back to her hole. Only don't come crying to me when she grows up and murders us all."

Howlaa untied the ropes binding the girl's wrists, and Wisp spoke to her, and the girl ducked her head and raced back down the tunnel.

"We'd better get on our way," Howlaa said. "Before she comes back with a knife. If I have to kill her *now* Randy will never let me hear the end of it."

"Thanks, Howlaa," I said, because I don't need to be a bitch about everything, and I *had* gotten my way. Be gracious in victory, right?

"Shushit," she said. "Even Wisp doesn't say thank you when he makes me do something I don't want to do."

"Where to now?" I said.

"Up, and out, and into the Machine Waste," Wisp said.

"If we can't find transportation there, we *deserve* to go on foot," Howlaa said.

Chapter 6

Two hours later we'd managed to find some wheels, but only individual unattached ones, scattered on the ground near smoking heaps of junk, which wasn't quite what we'd had in mind. The nuclear fireball sun was still up, but it was behind a mountain of dead vacuum cleaners, so everything was shadows, and I didn't want to think about the kind of things that might come out at night in a place like this.

"I can't believe the Rolling Steel Roadyard got infected with sentience and declared independence." Howlaa kicked a pile of tin cans that scuttled away in squeaking dismay—turned out they were some kind of little mechanized hermit crab, using cans for shells. Some of the cans were still sealed, though the labels were burned off, and Howlaa had sheared off the tops of a few with a scary knife and let me take my pick. I passed on the one that looked like eyeballs packed in gelatin and another full of noodles that smelled ranker than Cal's shoes, but there were some canned peaches in heavy syrup, which gave me a little sugar high, at least, and made a change from apples.

"The unexpected acquisition of intelligence is always a danger here," Wisp said. "Sentience is a virus in the Machine Waste, constantly configuring itself to run on new hardware."

"Bloody go-carts couldn't have waited until we were *done* with our trip to become intelligent? Or done it a month ago, so another shop would be set up by now? We need *transport*, and the only rental agency around is off learning about the joys of consciousness."

"There's another roadyard at the other end of the Waste," Wisp said.

"Ha, yes, it's just there's leagues of intermittently awakening occasionally radioactive *junk* between us and there, thanks," Howlaa said. "Nothing to be done about it. At least the Regent can't see us here."

I ate another slithery slice of peach. If I kept eating so much fruit I was going to get the runs like crazy, and that didn't sound fun out here, where there was nothing but scrap metal to wipe with. "Oh yeah? Why not?"

"Satellites that pass over the Machine Waste don't stay in the sky long," Wisp said. "This place is filled with sentient mechanical beings, all desperate to upgrade, and any of them would be delighted to have the sort of sensory array the Regent's spy satellites carry. There are cobbled-together tractor beams and gravity guns here that can knock satellites down and pull them out of the sky."

"Huh. So this place used to be an alien spaceship? What's with the tin cans and fridges and computer monitors and all this other junk then? They eat peaches in outer space?" I slurped the last juice out of my can. I was still hungry, but not hungry enough to try those black noodles. Yet.

"A ship the size of a city," Howlaa said, tossing sheets of metal and refrigerator doors aside and unearthing the torn leather back seat of a car, which she set upright. I whooped and joined her on it. After two hours of picking our way across uneven—and occasionally independently *moving*—terrain, my butt and legs were grateful for something resembling a couch. "The snatch-engines pulled the ship here from who knows where, and dropped it to the ground, where it broke like a whole basket of eggs dropped on a concrete floor. The royal orphans—though this was before they were orphans—swarmed all over the wreck, carrying off choice bits of machinery to build bigger and better snatch-engines. The rest they just left here. Bits of the wreck still remain. I wouldn't be surprised if your jump-engine didn't originate, at least in part, from that original wreck, though I'm sure the scientists made some major changes. For the past umpty-dozen years the snatch-engines have been grabbing whatever bits of metal and machinery they can find in the multiverse during any idle cycles, picking up junk and dumping it here. The Machine Waste has a little bit of everything from planet-destroying weapons to tin cans full of unidentified meat."

"Were there any aliens on the ship?"

"The *ship* was an alien," Wisp said. "A machine intelligence, though it had a biological brain—apparently the lump of neuron-packed meat so many of you bodied types carry inside you is a universally common data storage and processing medium. The brain survived the crash, unbeknownst to everyone, and many years later managed to assemble a new body."

"That was the first steam colossus," Howlaa said, leaning back in the seat with her eyes closed, as if turning over a pleasant memory. "Oh, I remember the terror the night it marched on the city center, bent on revenge—or so we thought. The Regent was in power then, but the Queen hadn't been dead more than a year, and everyone expected the Regent to break and run when that giant thing, big as a building, came striding along, weapons glittering, eyes made of stolen satellites, the earth shaking with every step."

"So what happened?"

"The Regent *talked* to it," Wisp said. "No one knows exactly what they talked about, but somehow the Regent… made an arrangement with it. The steam colossus turned and walked back into the Machine Waste, and the Regent configured the snatch-engines to send mechanical matter here. A few years later, a second steam colossus—but a much smaller one—appeared, and went to the palace, and the Regent greeted the thing as if it had been expected."

"Whoa."

Wisp never needed much encouragement to lecture, so he kept going while Howlaa began to gently snore. "The Machine Waste is technically under the Regent's control, but in practice, it's no-man's-land. The original intelligence on the ship made its own sentience into a sort of, ah, you might say computer virus? Only computer viruses aren't *airborne*. This free-floating intelligence tries to find usable mechanical bodies, and those bodies then awaken, and begin to upgrade themselves. Those little hermit crabs we disturbed are one of the smallest forms of such intelligence, barely even self-aware, but gradually a few of them will clump together, and they'll find something bigger to devour or be assimilated by, and before long they'll be fully conscious and relentlessly ambitious. The best, smartest, most adaptable of those intelligences grow and grow until they're big enough to be recognized by the original steam colossus… and it gifts them with an armored organic brain, presumably cloned from a chunk of the ship's original central biological computer, and sends the new child off to work for the Regent. It's only happened half a dozen times so far, and one of the steam colossi went rogue and Howlaa was sent to destroy it, but it wouldn't surprise me if the machine intelligences end up running Nexington-on-Axis in a few centuries."

"Nothing around here has paid much attention to us," I said. We'd seen mechanical intelligences go by—including some of the all-terrain vehicles Howlaa had originally been hoping to hire, spindly things with huge fat tires, only instead of being dune buggies for rent they were feral self-propelled sentients, now. There was nothing left of the Rolling Steel Roadyard but a Quonset hut flattened like a giant had sat on it. Which, out here, was maybe exactly what had happened.

"No. You two are organic—whatever *else* Howlaa might be—and I am Bodiless. Our kind don't interest the things living here. Of course," and he lowered his voice, "if any of the creatures realized what you have on your fingers and wrists there, they might become *very* interested in you."

Howlaa stopped snoring and spoke, without opening her eyes: "That's why I want to get us out of here as fast as possible. Even if the jump-engine disguises itself somehow, goes stealth, some things out here are *very* smart, and they'd all love to get their robo-claws on technology like that."

"THAT DOES SOUND INTERESTING."

I pressed my hands to my ears—me and Jenny Kay snuck out to go to an all-ages rock show a few months ago and wound up pressed right against the giant stack of speakers, and this voice was louder than the loudest guitar solo, such a deep rumble that I almost crapped myself, and all the sheet metal around us vibrated with a noise like thunder sound effects. I couldn't figure out where the voice was coming from, except for everywhere.

Howlaa sat straight up, eyes going wide.

"BUT WHAT IS A JUMP-ENGINE?"

Howlaa transformed into the spider-thing again, and without being told I scrambled onto her back and let the shadow-saddle grab me tight. Wisp didn't say anything as Howlaa started hauling ass across the junk-filled plain, and that silence freaked me out more than anything else— Wisp should have been explaining, or at least *theorizing*, talking the way he always did, but if he was quiet, something must be really wrong.

"ARE YOU RUNNING?" the voice boomed. "MAY AS WELL RUN FROM THE GROUND BENEATH YOUR FEET."

Just like that we started rising up. By which I mean the *ground* rose up, and we rose with it. The piles of smashed toaster ovens, cell phones, gears with pitted teeth, and coiled wires in silver and copper and gold all rose around us… and something gigantic started to stand up.

Picture a kid buried in the sand at the beach. The kid gets up, elbows and knees poking out of the sand, then all the sand cascades down as the kid levers himself to sitting, then kneeling, then standing. Now imagine you're seeing this from the viewpoint an ant, a sand flea, some tiny bug just walking across the sand that covered the kid's belly. From your point of view, that kid standing up, it's an apocalypse. It's the end of the world and the coming of a monster so big you can't comprehend it, so big you can't even get a sense of its form.

We were the bugs. (Howlaa literally.) I hung on as tight as I could, and Howlaa's legs scrambled and twisted and found purchase even when the ground went diagonal and then vertical, but we went sliding down all the same.

'TELL ME ABOUT THIS... JUMP-ENGINE."

"It's the steam colossus," Wisp said in my ear. "The *first* one. No one has seen it for years. It's... bigger than it was before."

Howlaa couldn't speak any language I could understand in that spider-form, but she made some noises like feedback squeals and Wisp sighed and said, "Yes, I *know*."

Before I could ask what Howlaa said, we were in a cage, surrounded by these black metal pillars that rose up and curled above us and—

Oh crap. The steam colossus was holding us in its *hand*. The thick black bars were its fingers. We rose up, up, up, until we hung before the thing's face. Or maybe I should say "sensory array" or something, since there was nothing you'd recognize as a face, just lenses and things like microphones and doohickeys telescoping in and out and vents puffing out billowing white clouds of steam. "I HAVE NEVER HEARD OF A JUMP-ENGINE," the colossus said. "AND I KNOW OF ALL THE TECHNOL-OGY IN THIS PLACE."

The shadow-saddle relaxed, and I slid down off Howlaa's back. She transformed back into her human form. "Randy," she said. "Miranda. Wait for us on the far side of the Machine Waste, if you can. Look for the Bleak Mountain Roadyard. We'll get there as soon as possible."

"What? How am I supposed to—"

Howlaa rushed at me, snarling, a knife in her hand, and I screamed, and raised my hands in front of my face, and—

—jumped.

Just like before, when the railgun blew up the autogyro, I crossed space without moving. I landed—but it didn't feel like landing, I was just *there*—on the roof of a dark blue Winnebago sunk halfway down in a sea of loose nuts and bolts. I could see the back of the steam colossus off in the distance, its huge legs all covered in hydraulics and pistons, the spikes made of smokestacks running down its back, all gushing white clouds. Its body, bigger than a battleship, bigger than a skyscraper on top of another skyscraper, gleamed with oil.

"OH," it said, turning—its upper body just turned, its legs not even moving, like its torso was on a lazy susan. "*THAT'S* A JUMP-ENGINE." I could see its arms now, all four of them, black metal covered with shining bumps that could have been the domes of telescopes or the closed noses of missile silos. It opened its hand, and a tiny black speck fell—Howlaa. I shouted her name, but the falling shape twisted somehow and became a *flying* shape, long and snaky with big wings, streaking off toward me.

I was sure Howlaa would land and pick me up, but she just went past above my head, close enough for me to feel the wind from her many wings, and I screamed, told her to come back, to save me, damn it.

"DON'T BE AFRAID," the steam colossus said. "YOU'LL BE PAST PAIN AND FEAR IN A MOMENT." It stepped toward me, and just its approach must have triggered whatever turns on the jump-engine's self-preservation circuit, because I teleported again. This time I wound up in the huge curved dish of a radio telescope, only there were big chunks missing from it. I was way up high, and though I'm not especially scared of heights, there are heights and there are *heights*, so I dropped down to my hands and knees and crawled as close to the edge as I dared. The steam colossus was still visible, but it was just a speck on the horizon, way past the point of reaching me, and I looked around, trying to figure out how I was supposed to get down off the world's biggest satellite dish.

"NOT FAR ENOUGH," the voice boomed, and I looked around, freaked out, because the voice was coming from the ground all around me. I crept up closer to the edge and looked down, and there were dozens of things clumping and grinding and rolling and spindling toward me, robots made of old lawnmowers and gurneys and tanks, things with mirror-balls for eyes and chainsaws for hands.

"Jump, jump, jump," I whispered, but nothing happened—would I have to wait until a chainsaw was coming at my *face* before I jumped? One of the things rose up on telescoping legs like two cherry-pickers until it was higher than the edge of the satellite dish, though it was still pretty far away. It lifted an arm of polished copper pipe and something went *thwock* past my ear. I looked around and there was a wicked dart with fins stuck *into the metal* of the radio telescope's dish, and the metal started to smoke.

They were shooting at me with acid-filled darts. And that *still* didn't trigger the flight-or-more-flight mechanism.

I had a stupid idea, but it was better than no idea, so I ran for the other side of the dish, and without even looking, I jumped off.

I looked down once I was falling. There was nothing fancy underneath me. Just a big jumble of rebar, steel spikes pointing out in all directions, ready to impale me twenty different ways. I closed my eyes.

This time I *did* land, though not as hard as I should have, and rolled a couple of times and ended up on my back. The jump-engine had decided to save my life, again, once I didn't give it any choice.

I opened my eyes. The sky was still there, the sun a ball of frozen fire just beyond the edge of my vision. I reached out my hand, dug my fingers into the ground, made a fist, and lifted my hand.

Grass. There was grass in my hand, and dirt. I sat up, and though I could see a bunch of white three-sailed windmills on a distant hill, I knew right away I was out of the Machine Waste. For one thing, there were trees. There were animals, too, sort of like cows but bigger and *way* shaggier, hairy like yaks, chewing the grass off in the distance. I was on a hill that lacked yaks or windmills, but was clearly part of the same geographical family. Beyond the hills was a dull gray sparkling plain that must have been the Waste.

It looked pretty far off, and I wondered how long it would take me to get back to the edge of the Waste to meet up with Wisp and Howlaa. I wondered if I *wanted* to. Sure, I sort of understood why they'd taken off and left me to my own devices like that—they trusted in my *device*, the jump-engine, to save me when they couldn't. But still. They could've told me the plan. And what if the stupid jump-engine hadn't worked? Would they have come back for me?

Then again, I didn't know where *else* to go. Off I trudged, over hill, past shaggy things, under windmills, until my feet ached and I was thirsty. I sat down on a nice big round rock and stared at the green hills in front of me, humps of grass hiding the horizon. The nuclear sun was getting dimmer, its last rays turning the sky pinkish, and things that weren't exactly stars became visible in the sky.

"Miranda. You're a long way from home."

I just sat there. I recognized the voice—sort of nice-grandpa-sounding, definitely old. "You're the Regent," I said. "Beamed down from another satellite. Can you hear me? You got microphones hidden here? Maybe in one of those big yaks over there?"

"I don't need microphones, Miranda." The Regent stepped around me, still wearing those robes, hands clasped behind his back. He stood, his back to me, watching the sun go down. When the last rays of light vanished, he turned, just a shadow among the shadows. I couldn't see the smile on his face, but I could hear it in his voice. "I'm here in person, Miranda, because you've landed on my country estate. Do you like it? It's very pretty. Reminds me a bit of my childhood home. Except for the windmills and the woolbeasts."

"Don't come near me."

"I won't. I won't threaten you by word or deed. I won't so much as raise my voice to you. I'd hate to trigger your little escape hatch." He shook his head. "It would be shame for you to run away before you hear *my* side of the story."

Chapter 7

"No way," I said again. "I'm not going anywhere with you. You want to talk, we can do it right here." I was pretty comfy on my rock. It was no worse than the other places I'd been hanging out lately.

The Regent sighed. "I'm an old man, Miranda, and the temperature drops fast once the sun goes out. Are you sure you won't come back to my house?"

"So some sniper can shoot me with a tranquilizer dart and you can snip off my fingers with bolt-cutters? Nope."

"Please, my dear. If I wanted you shot by a sniper, you would be well and truly sniped by now."

"I'm not your dear. And I'm not going anywhere with you." I crossed my arms, feeling stubborn and proud of myself about it.

"Very well. But I normally take my evening meal shortly after sunset. I hope you don't mind if I proceed."

Food. "Knock yourself out."

He put his hand to his ear and began to speak softly, whispering into some invisible sleeve microphone like a secret agent on TV. "Just a few moments." He sat down next to me on the rock.

"What's to stop me smacking you and teleporting you into deep space?"

"For one thing, you aren't sure it would work," he said blandly. "The one time you did that successfully you believed your life was in danger, and the jump-engine may not respond the same way to naked aggression against a harmless old man. You're afraid that if you hit me, and I *don't* disappear, the consequences would be grave."

I almost walloped him right there, just for the principle of the thing, but he had a point.

"Even if you did manage to send me away, I'd be back soon enough. I have a transponder implanted in my body. If I ever vanish from the borders of Nexington-on-Axis, the snatch-engines in the palace will bring me back quickly enough. And if you sent me somewhere else in my city or the provinces, some of my loyal subjects would see me home promptly."

"Snatch-engines might bring *something* back," I said. "But if I sent you to space, or the bottom of an ocean, you might not come back in very good shape. I don't think you take me seriously enough."

"You don't know what you're capable of," the Regent said. "*I* barely know. The jump-engine is untested technology. You can't control where you send me, but even if I did wind up in some such… inhospitable area… I have greater resources than you realize. The Nagalinda you punched wound up back in the barracks where he was stationed, by the way. A bit dazed, but otherwise fine. He gave me a full report. That's how I knew you had the engine, and that the device had incorporated you into its mechanism."

Incorporated me? That didn't sound good. I liked to think of the jump-engine as something I *had*, not something I *was*.

"I am a bit curious how you wound up separated from Howlaa and Wisp," the Regent said. "But we can discuss that over dinner. Those two are so misguided, the poor things. I hope they come to their senses soon."

A helicopter appeared in the sky, not one of the weird autogyros I'd seen before but a real black helicopter, the kind you see military guys rappelling down from in movies. It landed a little distance away on a flat spot, scaring a bunch of woolbeasts into a miniature stampede down the hill. The wind from the helicopter's rotors blew leaves off the trees, and half a dozen Nagalinda hopped out, dressed all in black. I tensed up, but didn't see any guns… and then they started unloading a long folding table and a bunch of trays and bringing them over. They set up the table near us, threw a tablecloth over it, put plates and silverware and bowls at either end, and started putting trays covered in silver domes down along the table's length. One came over with a couple of glasses and two sweating silver pitchers of ice water—I was so thirsty—and another put two bottles of wine and a couple of glasses by one of the plates. They even had a vase with a few yellow and orange flowers, and that went in the middle of the table. Finally they set down chairs in front of the place settings, then withdrew a short distance away.

"Thank you, gentlemen." The Regent rose and went to the table. "We'll serve ourselves. Kindly take the helicopter away—but on foot, please. I'd hate for the wind from its departure to ruin the lovely table you've set."

The Nagalinda trotted obediently away—and then picked up the helicopter, like pallbearers lifting a coffin, and walked off over the hill with it.

"Show off," I said, and the Regent actually laughed.

"Perhaps a little. I hope you'll forgive me. Please, have a seat." He sat down, uncorked one of the wine bottles, and poured a little red into a big rounded glass. He swirled and sniffed and sipped, then sighed. "Really, Miranda, a chair is bound to be more comfortable than that rock."

I felt like I was giving in to something, but it didn't feel like that *big* a concession, so I sat down.

"Have a glass of water." The Regent put on a pair of reading glasses, opened up a folder—the Nagalinda must have brought it—and started flipping through the pages inside.

He wasn't even paying attention to me, and I was crazy thirsty, so I started to stand up and reach for a water pitcher—then stopped and sat back down.

The Regent glanced at me, sighed, and stood up, coming to my end of the table with his own water glass. He filled it from the pitcher by my plate, took a long swallow, and set the glass before me. "See? No poison, no sedatives. Drink from my glass if you're worried I've poisoned yours. I'm not a monster, just a government official with a couple of dangerous rogue employees."

I picked up his glass and sipped. Water had never tasted so delicious. I tried not to gulp. The Regent shook his head like an indulgent uncle, picked up the water glass I wasn't using, and returned to his end of the table. After flipping through the folder for another moment, he set it aside, half-smiling. "I think the orphans do things like this on purpose. That they have their own little jokes, a sense of humor as alien as everything else about them. Or perhaps they just like… connections."

"I don't know what you're talking about. Maybe you should try having the *whole* conversation out loud, instead of just parts of it."

"Ha. Quite right. Let's begin at the beginning, then: You are Miranda Candle, age 13. Once a good student, though lately less interested in school work, judging by the number of absences. A note from your guidance counselor ascribes your behavior to the death of your father—"

"You got my file from *school*?" I couldn't believe it. Ruler of Nexington-on-Axis with spy satellites and armies of frogmen and monster-soldiers at his disposal? Sure. Capable of having a catered dinner flown in by helicopter at a moment's notice? Okay. But being able to get my file from the principal's office on another planet? That was *power*.

"Of course. I knew the locale where the snatch-engines found the jump-engine. I knew you were a girl of school age, and I knew you were named Miranda, because the Nagalinda heard Howlaa say that name. I simply configured the snatch-engines to bring me the files from the local middle school. Of course, our controls are not that precise. They took a large chunk of the principal's office in the process, including all the filing cabinets and a small fichus tree in a pot."

"You ripped out a chunk of my *school*?"

The Regent waved his hand. "No one was hurt. The snatch happened at night. Besides, you're from, ah, Georgia? Tornadoes aren't uncommon there. People will assume a whirlwind knocked down a piece of the school and carried the wreckage away, I imagine. People are good at explaining things away. This file is fine for the basic information, Miranda, but tell me, what do you *want*?"

I blinked. That wasn't something I got asked often, at least not in any sense larger than "What do you want for dinner?" or "What do you want for your birthday?"

"Think it over," the Regent said into the silence. "It's a large question, but be assured, whatever the answer is, I can help you achieve it. I would imagine you're hungry, having subsisted on whatever rations an omnivorous shapeshifter and a person with no *stomach* thought appropriate for a human girl. Have something to eat." He lifted the lid off a covered dish, and the breeze wafted a savory scent toward me, meats and juices and fennel and bay leaf and white beans—it was a cassoulet, one of the dishes Dad liked to make for special family dinners. His favorite was rustic cuisine, comfort food, and his restaurant specialized in that kind of French country cooking, ratatouille and roast chicken and beef burgundy. Since Dad died we got by on fishsticks and take-out. Mom's lousy in the kitchen and heart-shaped pancakes aside, her new boyfriend isn't much of a cook either. Just the smell of that familiar, long-lost food made my mouth water and my heart hurt.

"Go on, eat." The Regent ladled cassoulet into his bowl. "Please, Miranda. It's just a meal, not fairy food, not a gift from Hades to Persephone—Never mind. I suppose the reference is lost on you. They don't teach the classics anymore."

That just pissed me off. "I'm from a town called *Pomegranate Grove*, genius, like it says on the file there? It's one of the only places in Georgia where pomegranate trees bear fruit. We have a friggin' Pomegranate Queen in the town parade every year. So, yeah, I know the story of Persephone—the god of the dead tricked her into eating some pomegranate seeds, and she got stuck in the underworld for six months of every year. Everybody knows that story where I'm from."

"My apologies. But please, eat. Conversation is always more pleasant when the body's needs are met."

I couldn't stand it—apples and gross pierogies and tinned peaches just weren't enough—so I went to the pot and dished myself up a big helping, then opened up the other dishes too. Crusty French bread, a thick onion soup, a whole chicken roasted with herbs, eight different kinds of cheese—I loaded up my plate and bowl and carried the heap back to the end of the table and dug in. The Regent watched me eat, just nibbling his own food, having a few sips of wine. I thought about asking for a glass—I've only tasted wine once or twice, and then mostly just a tiny bit of Mom's champagne on New Year's Eve—but getting even a little bit tipsy seemed like a bad plan. "So tell me your side of things," I said around a mouthful of sausage and onion.

"Miranda, I don't know exactly what Howlaa told you about me, but I can make certain guesses. That I'm a tyrant. A despot. A cruel dictator." He sighed. "Nothing could be further from the truth. When I arrived in Nexington-on-Axis—long ago—there was no government to speak of. Oh, there was the Queen, and her myriad Kings, but they did not rule the other sentient beings who lived here, they merely… tolerated them. Or, more accurately, ignored them. The royal snatch-engines only took things the Queen and Kings and their children wanted, often for incomprehensible reasons, and whatever living creatures the engines picked up by accident were left to struggle and starve and fight and survive here however they could. And once the Kings died and the Queen began to sicken, even the meager resources of food and building materials that showered down irregularly from the sky began to slow.

"When I was snatched up, in a load of hay and farm machinery from a field near my home, I found myself deposited in a horrible shanty-town near the palace. The field of shacks was filled with what seemed, to my eyes, to be terrible monsters. They were, of course, only my fellow citizens, few of whom were interested in eating me. I've always had a knack for making friends, for organizing things, and for languages, so soon I managed to make the shantytown into something like a community. Eventually I dared to venture into the palace, where I discovered it was possible to communicate with the Queen telepathically. She'd never much *bothered* with communication, but she was sick, and worried about her scuttling chittering children. It takes a long time for their kind to mature—I don't know how long, I don't even know what the species is called, where they originally hail from, nothing—and I agreed to see that her children were cared for... in exchange for a certain degree of power. And so a bargain was struck, and when the Queen finally died, I took up residence in the palace, and assumed care for the royal orphans left behind. They are just children, you know, willful and easily distracted, quick to anger and quick to delight, and endlessly inquisitive. I'm the only one who can talk to them—their mother told them to obey me, and they are no more capable of ignoring her orders than a falling rock is capable of ignoring gravity. I rule in their place, until such time as they can rule themselves. I help the orphans make the snatch-engines more powerful, which is all they care about, and in exchange they bring me... whatever I need."

"Like soldiers and black helicopters?" I said. "Chunks of people's *schools*?"

"Like infrastructure, Miranda. You've seen our food stores—the people of Nexington-on-Axis need never go hungry, because I provide for them. I brought housing. I brought fields, and seeds to plant in them, and the snatch-engines can even bring rainstorms to water those fields. I've turned a savage place into a city without equal."

"That's not what Howlaa said. She said you have prison camps. That you spy on everyone. That you used to send Howlaa to kill anybody who got in your way."

The Regent sighed. "The situation here is complex. We have no natural resources of our own, only the snatch-engines. Everything that exists here is imported. The snatch-engines are powerful, but not *that* precise, and sometimes we bring in things that are dangerous. And, yes, Howlaa Moor was tasked with removing those threats. It's easy to bring things here, but nothing can get *out*. Mad carnivores, creatures that eat light, beings that feed on madness, animals with carcinogenic breath—they can't be allowed to live here and threaten the rest of us, can they?"

"I met Underdwellers who didn't seem like radioactive monsters."

"There are more... intellectual rebels as well. Some people just can't consent to being governed. In the past, yes, imprisonment was the only choice—it's not as if I can exile troublemakers." He nodded at me. "At least, until now. That's why I was building the jump-engine. To make Nexington-on-Axis less a cage, to make it a place where people can come and go freely, where those who dislike my rule are welcome to leave."

"Then why did Howlaa and Wisp want to steal the jump-engine? Why couldn't they just apply for a passport and leave with your permission?"

The Regent made a face. "Howlaa and Wisp *both* owe a debt to this society, for their past misdeeds, and the work they do for me is just… community service. Once their debt is repaid, they will be free to leave, certainly, but they are impatient, and wish to escape their responsibilities. Believe me, Wisp and Howlaa are not treated poorly. Howlaa enjoys drinking alcohol and sleeping on piles of fur and getting into fights, and I provide all those things in abundance."

"It doesn't matter how nice their jail cell is, if they're still prisoners."

The Regent took a sip of wine. "Idealism is a beautiful thing, Miranda, but it is the province of the young. I am old, and practical. Wisp and Howlaa are useful to me—and trust me, their past actions were dire enough to make a long period of servitude as punishment seem merciful. Surely you have some sense of what they're capable of? Come with me. Let my scientists get a look at you, and detach the jump-engine from your body. Once that's done, I'll send you home, safe." He smiled.

I think he thought he'd *convinced* me.

The Regent reminded me of every asshole adult I'd ever met, thinking he knew better than everyone else, just assuming people my age were stupid or naïve. Maybe Howlaa and Wisp weren't perfect, but at least they didn't *think* they were perfect, like this guy did. "Why do you think I want to go home?"

"Ah," the Regent said. "Interesting. I suppose, if you'd rather, you could stay here with your father. I just assumed you'd want to take him home with you instead."

I put down my fork. "What. Are you. Talking about."

He gave me one of those annoying looks of fake surprise. "Oh, didn't I mention? Your father. We snatched him two years ago. He made the dinner we're eating now. I had it airlifted from his restaurant in the city center." He spooned up another mouthful of soup. "Good, isn't it?"

Chapter 8

"My Dad is dead." I clenched my butterknife so hard it made my fingers hurt.

"Oh? Really? Perhaps I've been misinformed. How did he die?"

"A gas explosion destroyed his restaurant."

"Ahh." The Regent sat back, crossing his hands over his belly. "A gas explosion, of course. That's almost as popular as tornadoes or sinkholes as an explanation for where things go when the royal orphans snatch them. Did the authorities recover a body?"

"I… No."

The Regent spread his hands. "There you have it. Because his body is here."

"If he's really here, let me see him."

"No, dear," the Regent said gently. "Not until my scientists have pried those rings and bracelets away from you. Then you can be reunited."

"How can I believe you?"

"I am a thief, Miranda, by necessity—but not a liar."

"Not good enough. How stupid do you think I am? It doesn't make any sense, that *I* would be here, and my father, too? Out of all the possible people in the universe, in *multiple* universes? It's stupid to think we'd both get grabbed."

"It's improbable, I admit, but you must understand, the royal orphans are whimsical, in their way. When I asked them to find me a French chef, one who could make me the food I'd loved in my childhood, I was a bit surprised to see the snatch-engines reel in the finest restaurant in the small town of Pomegranate Grove, Georgia. Though your father has proven a satisfactory chef. Those same orphans were instrumental in creating the jump-engine. It appears they programmed its self-preservation circuit with the same sense of whimsy, as it jumped to your town for safety. That's why I said I believe the orphans make little jokes. They enjoy coincidences and synchronicities. Like your presence here. Besides, isn't the taste of this food evidence enough that your father's hands created it?"

I snorted. I was pretty sure some of the meat in the cassoulet came from animals not even native to my planet, so, no, not exactly. "Nope. Show me my father. Now."

"No, no, a thousand times no."

"You think I'm making *requests* here? Take me to him—"

"Do not raise your voice to me. I am the unquestioned ruler of the city-state at the center of space and time. I made myself Regent of a kingdom more powerful than any on the Earth where I was born. I began a refugee in mud and rose to be the single most significant individual in the whole of the multiverse. You *will* obey me, Miranda. I have made you a fine offer. Take it, or a less savory option will be thrust upon you." He'd dropped the whole kindly-grandfather pretense, which was a relief—I hadn't been fooled, not really, but seeing his true colors made it easier to resist him.

But what if he was telling the truth? If my Dad really was here?

Well, in that case the Regent was the kind of bastard who'd steal a man from his wife and kids forever just to get a good *meal*. Whatever bad things Wisp and Howlaa had done, it couldn't be worse than that. Either the Regent was lying to trick me or he was an evil jerk. "Howlaa and Wisp said taking the jump-engine from my body might kill me. You're saying otherwise?"

"My scientists are quite talented, Miranda. I'm sure it won't come to that."

Right. Not reassuring. What would he care if I did die in the process? And even if I didn't, what incentive would he have to let me see my father afterward? How could I trust the word of—of a kleptocrat?

No. If my Dad was alive, and here, I'd find him, but not this way. I hadn't known the Regent long, but I didn't like him. Maybe thinking we could overthrow him was idealism, and maybe idealism *was* the province of the young, but so what? I *am* young.

"Okay," I said. "I'll go with you."

"Marvelous, Miranda. You are wise beyond your years." He rose and walked toward me, and I stood up from my chair. "I'll summon a helicopter." He put his hand on my shoulder.

I twisted and punched him in the stomach as hard as I could, and he disappeared.

Sirens and alarms started whooping from one direction, and I ran as fast the other way as I could.

I was pursued. Helicopters whirred behind me. Nagalinda *did* come rappelling down from above this time, firing their strange guns, but I must have been terrified or adrenaline-jacked enough to trigger the jump-engine's protective circuits because my entire flight was a blur of teleportations—half a dozen hops from hills to slanting slate rooftops to giant skulls half-sunk in water to fields full of open pits and purple gas. I left the pursuit behind, but jumping so often, so quickly, took something out of me—my fingers ached, and the rings pulsed and twisted and throbbed. I landed, at last, in a dirt lot filled with big pipes, building materials for some construction project, and I crawled inside one of the pipes with aching legs and a full stomach and a whirring mind and a hollowed-out heart. At least I wasn't hungry, and the night wasn't too cold, and inside the pipe I might be invisible from above, and maybe I *had* sent the Regent so far away it would take him a long time to come back.

I was so exhausted I managed to fall asleep without thinking too much about what I was going to do come morning.

Something poked me in the ribs, and I rolled over, bumping my head on the roof of the pipe. The poke came again—it was a broom handle—and I grabbed it and yanked the stick out of the poker's hands. Somebody gasped, and then a figure squatted down before the opening of the pipe. He had a wedge-shaped scaly head like a lizard, but he wore a jumpsuit—I thought of that *Alice in Wonderland* Disney cartoon, of the lizard Bill wearing a chimneysweep's outfit. Only Bill didn't show quite so many teeth when he opened his mouth, and this lizard-man made hissing noises at me.

"Sorry, I don't speak… Lizardo." He backed off, out of sight, and I climbed out of the pipe. Lizard-guy snatched the broom out of my hands and started brandishing it and spitting more hissy words, forked tongue flickering, eyes bulgy and scary. He advanced on me, this weird spiky web of frilled skin rising up from his neck and spreading out like a ruff on a picture of Shakespeare, still hissing, so I cocked back my arm to punch him into… wherever.

"Miranda, no!" I recognized *that* voice, and lowered my fist.

Wisp floated over and babbled at the lizard in a sputtery way. The lizard shrugged and walked off, pushing the broom. "He wasn't attacking you," Wisp said. "He just said, '*You're* not a raccoon.' I don't think he expected to find refugees in his construction site. Perhaps you shouldn't try to solve all your problems by punching people into outer space?"

I laughed. "Good to see you, too, sparkles."

The motes of light bobbed in what was maybe a sort of nod. "Are you all right? We were worried, of course, when you didn't make it to the rendezvous. Howlaa's been beside herself."

"How did you *find* me?" I thought about the Regent's cassoulet and had a horrible idea. "Did the Regent fill me up with tiny edible tracking devices or something?"

"You saw the Regent? He captured you?" The motes seemed agitated.

"He tried to buy me. Bribed, threatened, wined, and dined. Well, not wined. He kept the wine for himself."

"How did you escape?"

"How do you think? I sucker-punched him and then ran like crazy, teleporting with every other step." I looked around. "So how did you find me? And where's Howlaa?"

"Searching for you elsewhere in the construction area. She'll be along. We waited at the Roadyard, but when you didn't arrive, Howlaa transformed into a chase-hound—one of her best tracking forms. She had a handkerchief you'd used, enough to get your scent, though tracking someone who can *teleport* is difficult. There were many gaps in the trail. It took us all night, starting back near the steam colossus, striking out almost randomly whenever the trail gave out until we could pick up your scent again. We ended up here."

"You guys must be exhausted."

"Howlaa is well-supplied with adrenaline, and its xenobiochemical analogues, while I do not sleep. Do not worry about us."

"Wisp, you lazy—Randy!" Another lizard-person came over, but this one was wearing a jumpsuit of shadowcloth, so I knew it was Howlaa, apparently trying to blend in with the locals. Her eyes were a beautiful deep green, and her neck-ruff was fully extended. "I thought I smelled you. No offense. We were afraid you'd been stomped by a steam colossus or captured by the Regent." She hugged me, and she smelled funny and lizardy, but then, I probably didn't smell much better myself. I should've gotten a shower out of the Regent before taking off, though I bet if I'd gone into his house I'd never have gotten out again, jump-engine or not.

"Come with us to our transport," Howlaa said. "And tell us everything."

We walked past more heaps of pipes and boards, through a gate in a tall wooden fence and out of the construction site, onto what could have been an ordinary street, except for the gleaming golden manhole covers and the fact that the buildings—also golden—were rounded and curved, without a straight-line to be seen. "What is this place?"

"Just a neighborhood snatched from some planet," Howlaa said. "These days it's mostly populated by Scapeores." She pointed backwards. "Like the one shoving a broom back there. Or like *me*, just now. Their kind mostly sleep late—they're cold-blooded and get around more easily once the sun's been on for a while—but the low-caste ones sleep with heat lamps on timers and rise early to do scutwork."

"Huh. If they're cold-blooded, why was he wearing clothes? Clothes only keep you warm by holding in your body heat, right? They're no good if you're cold blooded—just like bundling up in blankets won't keep you warm if you've got hypothermia, there's gotta be some warmth in you for the fabric to trap in the first place."

"You're right, Wisp, she *is* smart."

I was Jenny Kay's partner in science class, I thought. *I couldn't help but learn stuff.*

"The clothes are ornamental, decorative, and functional," Wisp said. "They denote caste. The highest members of Scapeore society wear only a few jewels and nothing else."

"There's only about two hundred Scapeore in all of the Ax," Howlaa said. "I give their precious caste system one more generation before it falls apart, and some high-caste lady-lizard gets her eggs fertilized by a dung-jockey, same as happened with the Beetleboys and -girls after they'd been here a while. Maybe I should wear this body and try to seduce a lizard-prince. It'd be fun to mess with them. Things out here in the provinces are still pretty conservative. Closer to the city center you'll see things get more lively."

"So we're still a long way from where we're going?"

"We're not far from the Machine Waste," Wisp said. "Your trail went well away at points but doubled-back a bit." He made a noise like clearing his throat, which was funny, since he didn't have a throat. "Howlaa, she… met the Regent. In the flesh."

Howlaa immediately turned, swept my legs out from under me with a kick, and knocked me to the ground. I landed on my back and all the air got bashed out of my lungs.

"Howlaa!" Wisp shouted, but she jumped on top of me, straddling my body and pinning my arms down by the wrists before I could even think to fight.

"Howlaa, Miranda is *with us*," Wisp said. "Release her."

Howlaa stared into my eyes, her scaly face dead blank, not that I could read lizard-people expressions anyway. "She's with us so far as she's *able*," Howlaa said. She grunted, and her body began to change, though it wasn't a complete transformation—a human hand burst from her side, emerging from a hole in her shadow-suit. The hand kept extending, an arm coming with it, and the fingers fumbled in one of the shadow-suits many there-and-gone pockets. The hand came out holding the tracking device they'd used to find the jump-engine the night they found me instead.

"A chimera-form, Howlaa? I thought your kind found such things unseemly."

"Shushit, Wisp, sometimes I need an extra hand, and *you* can't lend one." The light blinked red, and Howlaa cursed. "Lie still, Miranda. Wisp, she's infected."

"Oh, dear," Wisp said. "It never even occurred to me—"

"Because you don't have a *body*," Howlaa said. "You forget how vulnerable they are."

"Infected?" I said. "What do you mean infected?" I struggled, but there wasn't much point.

"Wisp will fix you," Howlaa said, and the last thing I remember is tiny motes of Wisp's body streaming toward me, into my mouth, into my nose, and then everything went dark.

I woke up shivering. I was sweating, wrapped in some crinkling material like tin foil that made me feel like a baked potato. I was on my back in a vehicle bumping along at high speed, and it was dark. Howlaa's face appeared above me, human again, tipping a cup to my lips. "Here, drink," she said, and I swallowed, cool water. I tried to sit up and gulp more but I was too weak to move. "It will be over soon," Howlaa said, and then it was all dark again, and I was having dreams about ants and blood and war.

"Randy. Wake up. You need to eat something."

I blinked, squinting in the artificial light, and Howlaa helped me sit up. I was in the back of a truck, parked in a windowless warehouse with nothing but a few oil drums in the empty space. Howlaa pressed a warm cup into my hands. I sniffed it suspiciously, then began slurping it down—it was chicken broth, or something near enough, and I was *starving*.

"Your fever broke in the night," Howlaa said. "You should feel better soon."

I lowered the cup, beginning to remember. "What did you do to me?"

"Wisp healed you," Howlaa said. "And saved our lives."

"What—"

"The Regent poisoned you, Randy."

Wisp floated over. "You were full of nanites, tiny machines with transponders beaming your location back to the Regent in real-time."

"That's the best case scenario for what the nanites were doing," Howlaa said. "That's why we wrapped you in the foil blanket, I don't know if you remember. Metal to block the transmissions, assuming you were transmitting. Maybe they were mind-control nanites turning you into a sleeper-agent assassin instead. One punch and you could send us into cells deep in the palace." Howlaa hopped down from the truck and went to one of the metal drums, tipping it a little as if checking to see if it was full. "Wisp went inside your body and tuned your immune system, taught your body's natural defenses to recognize the little machines as invaders. You spent two days in a fever fighting the infection."

I swallowed. "The Regent... he has that kind of technology? He can do that?"

"Not to me," Howlaa said. "It's easy for me to expel foreign stuff from my body, the same way I puke up hormones or poisons I need to get rid of. And Wisp is immune, what with having no body. But you... Did you eat any food he gave you? Drink anything?"

Fairy food. Cursed pomegranate seeds. I nodded. "I'm so stupid. I had no idea."

"Not your fault," Wisp said. "You're not from here, you couldn't have known, any more than someone from the 18th century on your planet would know to be afraid of... atomic bombs. Bazookas. Biohazards."

"But if the Regent could track me, why did he let me sleep in that pipe all night? Why not send in some guys to sneak up on me and hit me with a tranquilizer first?"

"Well, you *did* punch him all the way into orbit," Howlaa said with a grin. "I've still got some sources on the inside, and they tell me the Regent appeared in one of the magisters' orbital pleasure-palaces, landed right in the middle of an—"

"An inappropriate activity," Wisp said sharply.

Howlaa laughed. "Yeah. One of *those*. Took him a while to get back to the surface. The snatch-engines don't work on orbital objects—they're still technically part of the Ax—so he had to take a conventional craft. I imagine the Regent's lieutenants were busy dealing with his ruffled feathers for most of the night. And why hurry? He knew he could find you whenever he wanted."

"He was probably waiting to see where you would go, too," Wisp said. "Hoping you would find Howlaa and I, allowing him to capture all *three* of us."

"Nagalinda from the palace guard started coming out of the woodwork after Wisp went up your nose, too," Howlaa said. "They were watching your location, but Wisp is hard to see from a distance, and I just looked like a Scapeore. One of them must have figured out we were the dangerous fugitives, though. Took a fair bit of running to get away from them, but I bartered for the fastest ride in the Roadyard, and once I made it to our transport and got you shielded it was easy enough to lose them."

I climbed down from the truck, a little unsteady, but I felt better with hot food in my belly, even if it was liquid food. I circled the vehicle, and saw it wasn't a truck, but something much weirder. It had wheels—a lot of them—along with tank-treads and folded metal spindly spider-leg things and pontoon floats. "This is wild."

"It's a most-terrain vehicle," Howlaa said.

"Not all-terrain?"

"It can't cross lava," Wisp said. "And it might have trouble in the non-Euclidean neighborhoods. Oh, and it can't fly properly, it can only do brief powered glides. But in most terrain, it's the fastest thing around. Built from one of Merrill's schematics."

"Drunk cranky Merrill? He designed this?"

"Genius is not the sole province of the good or the socially well-adjusted," Wisp said.

"Hear hear," Howlaa said, and belched. "I had to negotiate hard to get my hands on this machine."

"What did you even have to trade?"

"I offered to let the proprietor go on living in exchange for giving me outright ownership of this vehicle," Howlaa said. She paused. "But he talked me into accepting a short-term rental and a promise to return the machine in working order within ten days. Those Roadyard folk haggle hard."

I laughed. "So now that you've got these wheels—and legs, and things—we can make good time? Get to the city proper?"

Howlaa laughed. "I never stopped traveling while you were getting well, Randy. We ran full-out for two days. We're *in* the city proper. Specifically in a very boring building in the warehouse district. We'll see about getting you a disguise, and then we'll try to track down our associate Templeton and see what he can tell us about the jump-engine. If that goes well… we'll move on with our plan."

"I have an addition to the plan," I said. "Not that I've *heard* the plan, and I look forward to it, but there's something else I need to do."

Howlaa frowned. "What's that?"

"I need to find my Dad."

Chapter 9

"He was probably lying," Howlaa said, after I'd explained.

"But not definitely lying," Wisp said. "It's *possible*."

"Not *probable*," Howlaa countered.

"This is Nexington-on-Axis," Wisp said. "Home to sentient machines, hallucinogenic swamp gas, orbital love palaces, skinshifters, the Bodiless, and many other improbable things. With everything Miranda is doing for us, we have to try and help her, if there's any chance her father is here."

Howlaa rolled her eyes. "Of course we'll *try*, I'm not saying that, I just don't want her to be disappointed when it turns out the Regent was lying."

"My Dad is dead," I said. "I was at his funeral, even if his body wasn't. I don't expect miracles. But if I don't try to find out, to make *sure*, I'll always wonder. And I couldn't stand that."

"Fair enough," Howlaa said. "We'll beat the bushes, and we'll beat the informants, and we'll see what we can discover about the Regent's favorite chef."

Wisp said, "But we can't go out at all until we get you disguised—"

"Is there any chance I can get a *shower*? I was gross two days ago, and that was before I got steamed in foil with my own sweat."

"Ah. A shower? Not… as such. This used to be a live-work space, but the tenant was a large sapient reptilian, and his cleaning chamber is mostly composed of articulated scale-buffing arms—"

"Did it involve running water? At all?"

"No… though there was a stall for rinsing off slime-mollusks before shipping them to market, and it may still be functional."

"At this point I'd settle for a sprinkler and a handful of sand to scrub myself with, Wisp."

Howlaa tossed me a blanket to use as a towel, and handed me a cloth-wrapped bundle. "Change into those, not your nasty dirty clothes. Part of the disguise. And make it quick. The government isn't going to overthrow itself."

Wisp floated through the warehouse and I followed, around a ceiling-high stack of dusty black crates the size of ice cream trucks. They smelled like shellfish just starting to go bad.

The shower—or the closest local equivalent—was the size of a horse stall with a drain covered by an iron grate in the middle of the floor. Sparkling bits of opalescent shell fragment were scattered in the corners, and there were smears of thick green slime on the concrete walls. Worse than showering at summer camp. The only control was a knob about the size of a ship's wheel, and there were nozzles everywhere, poking out from all sides. "Uh... is there hot water, do you think?"

"Doubtful. It's unlikely the slime mollusks complained about the cold."

I glanced at the swarm of glowing lights. "A little privacy?"

"Miranda, I don't have a *body*, much less a body capable of feeling anything resembling lust for a barely post-pubescent female. And I've seen Howlaa nude in any number of—"

"Not the point!" I shouted. What did Howlaa always say? "Shushit! Go away! Shoo!" I flapped my hands at him, then looked at the jewelry on my wrists and fingers. "Is it okay to get this stuff wet?"

"The jump-engine can survive most imaginable extremes of pressure and temperature. I believe it is safe to assume it is also waterproof."

"Good to know. Now float on." I watched the swarm of lights drift away, though if he'd left a mote or two behind to spy on me, how would I know about it?

I sighed and started to undress, wincing at the way my clothes stuck to me, and trying not to notice the whiff of my armpits. I stepped into the shower and twisted the knob the tiniest of tiny bits.

The water shot forth in narrow streams from all directions, and it was so cold bits of my body went numb instantly. I howled and hopped in the spray, and almost ran for dry air, but I could *feel* the dirt running down off my body, so I gritted my teeth and tried to think warm thoughts, wishing for soap and shampoo.

I couldn't stand it for more than a few minutes, but at least there wasn't any crud caked on me anymore, so I twisted the knob off and stepped out, dripping. My teeth chattered as I wrapped the blanket around me and dried off.

The new clothes were crazy. Basically it was a black unitard body-stocking thing, *not* my usual thing. Weirder, there were these dangly diaphanous purplish wings of cloth and wire attached to the shoulder blades, and a skirt sewn around the waist, only it was less a skirt and more a random spray of leaf-shaped green fabric streamers. There was a pair of glasses, too, with bulgy lenses all faceted like discoballs, but when I put them on it was just like looking through glass, only everything sort of sparkled, like the world had been doused with glitter. I pulled on the elbow-length gloves, which looked lumpy where the rings and bracelets bulged out, but at least hid the jump-engine from casual view.

I pushed the glasses up on my forehead—the sparkles were a bit much—and went back to the car/truck/whatever. "Guys, why am I dressed like an eight-year-old with a fairy princess obsession?"

"Just marking you as a member of a thriving subculture," Wisp said. "The Minions of Mab, they call themselves—mostly human females, fairly young, who owe fealty and give adoration to our city's one and only refugee from the land of mist and mirrors."

"Help me out here. That didn't clear anything up for me."

"Mist-and-mirror people are sort of like skinchangers," Howlaa said, "only they're too lazy to change their skin, so they just change the way people perceive them. They're telepathic, and our resident refugee picked up some sort of Faerie Queen imagery from a passing human girl, appeared to that girl in the form of an ethereal woman with wings and eyes like ice, and bam, she had the start of a cult. She claims to be Queen Mab of Faerie, snatched from the fields beyond the fields—stolen like a changeling, she says—but it's all so much bullshit. She's just another alien looking to make an easy living, and her minions keep her well-fed and comfortable. Her little darlings scurry around the city in droves, so you'll fit right in, and no one will look twice at you."

I tugged at the skintight fabric. "This sucks. I quit gymnastics when I was nine and I didn't ever plan to put on one of these again."

"Better to look silly and be free than to look good and be captured," Howlaa said. "Speaking of…" She took a pair of scissors from the cab of the truck and snipped them at me. "You'll need a shorter haircut to go with that. A purple one."

I backed away. I'm not really vain about my hair—especially after this many days without washing—but pixie purple didn't sound too flattering.

"The Regent has seen you, Miranda," Wisp said. "It's best if you aren't instantly recognizable here, in the heart of his power."

"Damn it." I sat down. Howlaa snipped away professionally, and I tried not to sigh too dramatically at seeing my wavy dark hair fall to the floor in chunks. "Are you taking it all off?"

"Of course not," Howlaa said. "I don't have a razor, and I don't want to blunt my knife's edge on your head-stubble. Be still."

"Is there a mirror in this place, so I can see what you're doing to me?"

"Plenty of big glass windows once we get outside, Randy. You'll get a look." He took out a tube of temporary hair dye—it was even a brand name I recognized—and that was a relief, at least. Though with the lack of showers around here who knew when I'd be able to wash out the dye? Howlaa draped the blanket around me like I was at a hair salon and started working.

With so little hair left on my scalp it didn't take long for Howlaa to get all the dye gel combed in. I wanted to reach up and touch my head, which felt about as fuzzy as a peach at best, but Howlaa slapped my hand away. "No purple fingers," she growled. We waited fifteen minutes—I could tell it was killing Howlaa, just *waiting*, because she paced around and did push-ups and made fun of Wisp—and then Howlaa rinsed out my hair with the contents of a couple of bulb-shaped water bottles, purplish water sluicing down on the blanket. "All right, let's see the whole effect," she said.

I stood up, put on the weird glasses, and gave a little twirl, purple-haired and winged and feeling dumb, but, at least, not feeling much like myself.

"I don't know," Howlaa said. "The cheekbones are the same, the nose, the build, the gait won't change, the space between the eyes is identical, the—"

"Pish," Wisp said. I didn't know exactly what "pish" means but it sounded like something British people would say to be condescending. "Ignore her, Miranda. Howlaa can change her body so radically that she doesn't appreciate how effective more minor changes can be. Most sentients don't look past the immediate surface, and your immediate surface is quite different now."

"If you say so," Howlaa said. "Time for me to make some changes too."

I'd seen her transform several times already, but it wasn't any less weird or fascinating this time—though I stepped back and widened my eyes when she finished. "One of *those*?"

"Yesh," she said, sounding like a normal human voice that got run through a food processor or something. "One of *theesh*." Howlaa had transformed into a Nagalinda, flat face, holes for a nose, mouth full of nasty teeth, eyes dead and big and watery, skin eel-smooth.

"No one bothers Nagalinda," Wisp said. "They have an aggressive culture. More importantly, they can speak in human tongues, albeit heavily accented, so I won't be stuck translating between you constantly."

Howlaa's shadow-suit shifted and spread out, becoming a shirt and pants... and then changing from fuzzy blackness to shiny blackness, switching texture to become some kind of dark leather. "Whoa! I didn't know your outfit could do that!"

"The clozhe make the man," Howlaa said. "Shadowcloth hash chameleon propertiesh. Perfect for an imposhter. I jusht usually don't bother with the fiddly bitsh."

"Aren't we kind of an odd couple?"

"No one will think so. Your purple hair marks you as a high personage among the Minions of Mab, and those often have deadly bodyguards. Howlaa looks the part of just such a hired hand."

Howlaa's lipless mouth opened wider, showing off an extra row of teeth, and I figured it for a grin. She—he? it?—beckoned and I followed toward a tall wide door.

"Are you ready for your first glimpse of the heart of Nexington-on-Axis, Miranda?" Wisp said. "For the wonders and terrors beyond this door?"

I rolled my eyes. "I'm sure I'll manage."

The first thing that hit me was the brightness—the nuclear sun seemed to shine brighter here, and my disco-ball glasses tinted automatically into sunglasses in the glare. Once my eyes adjusted I realized the light wasn't just from the sun, but was partly reflection from the twisted mirrored skyscrapers that rose on either side of the warehouse. My eye could barely follow their curves, and they more like oversized blown-glass art than buildings. I tried to imagine the kind of creatures that might live there, and could only think of huge boneless things.

And this was only a side street. Howlaa led us out, onto the main drag, and it took every ounce of my cool not to gape and gawp like a hick on his first trip to the big city.

It's funny, but the first thing I thought was, *This is like Vegas*, where we went once on vacation. They have the Eiffel tower and a pyramid and a Disney-looking fairy-tale castle and the Statue of Liberty and I don't even remember what all else, jumbled up all near each other. The Nex was like an alien's dream of the Vegas strip.

At a glance I saw:

A mountain made of glass or maybe ice, thirty stories high, and imprisoned at the center a frozen monster with red wings and a body covered in mouths and eyes, and the eyes were blinking. *But the weirdest thing was all the apartments just chiseled into the mountain, with people (not humans, mostly) going about their business, all their walls transparent, all their actions on display, completely oblivious to anyone who might be watching them cook or pee or sleep or argue, and apparently unbothered by the thing at the heart of the mountain staring at them, too;*

A lighthouse tilting at a scary angle in a patch of bubbling mud;

A geyser of foaming water shooting straight up into the air from the center of a lake, bigger than Old Faithful, with a huge cubical building bobbing on top of the spray, constantly on the edge of falling off, but never quite tumbling, and when I squinted I could see an elevator descending down through the center of the waterspout and vanishing into the lake;

The corpse of something the size of a whale, with flippers and big jaws but also little useless legs, the body shellacked or lacquered or something, with people going in and out of the gaping mouth, like they lived there;

Building-sized beehives filled with bustling figures in beekeeper outfits;

Cliff dwellings like the native Americans had in the desert, only these were standing shoulder-to-shoulder with a couple of totally Old-West-looking buildings, one even with a sign that said "Saloon";

And more, and more, and more. That was just what I saw on the couple of blocks around me. And that's omitting the people.

Out in the provinces I'd seen weird stuff, sure, from lizard people to frogmen to Nagalinda to intelligent machines, but there hadn't been all that *many* of anything, and I'd gotten the idea the Nex was sparsely populated... but I'd been in the equivalent of the badlands, the big empty spaces in Wyoming or something, and now I was in the middle of the *city*, with the city folk.

I did see a few girls dressed like me in unitards or leotards and stupid wings, with orange hair and green hair, and the one who passed by on my side of the street gave me a curtsy so deep I thought she was falling down. And there were a couple of Nagalinda, and more lizard people, and even a clattering machine-being or two, but—but—

Okay. Imagine you go to some really hopping part of a big city on a Saturday night—think of all the different kinds of people you might see. Old people going to the theater. Married guys out with their wives. Families hustling their kids home. Homeless people panhandling. Punks standing around smoking. Guys on skateboards. All those different types, you know? Now subdivide all those types by things like hair color and eye color and shoe size and every other arbitrary category you can think of, so that blue-eyed-old men with gray hair and loafers are a completely separate category from their green-eyed counterparts. Pretty big pool of different kinds of people, right?

Now imagine all of those different kinds of people are different *species*, some of them so totally non-human that you're not even sure if they're living things or weird sculptures until they start moving. We passed by conglomerations of rocks wearing shoes. Translucent slugs reading maps. A little dust devil spinning around some leaves and litter that I almost walked through until Howlaa grabbed me because, no, turns out that's an Aeolian, a distant relative of Wisp's race that shares the lack of a body but lacks the powers of possession and useful glowing. I swear we saw everything you can imagine and a lot of things you can't, everything but a hyper-intelligent shade of the color blue and a sentient kitchen sink. Things like lizard-people and guys with the faces of deep-sea fish started to look awfully normal by comparison. I guess you really can adjust to anything.

"Here." Howlaa pointed to the saloon, which was both a relief—because I didn't want to go near the glass mountain, for instance—and kind of a bummer, because it did look really normal in a kitschy way, like something you'd see in a ghost town theme park, with cheap beer for the parents and sarsaparillas for the kids. There were hitching posts out front and there were things tied to the posts, but they weren't horses, as even a non-horse-crazy girl like me could tell from the spines and the number of legs.

Inside matched the outside, with wooden tables and a piano with a drunk guy sleeping with his face on the keys and a bartender with a totally out-of-control mustache. Both human. There were no customers I could see. Wisp's translating mote was still in my ear, and it whispered: "Tell him you're here to see Templeton."

"Barkeep. I'm looking for Templeton."

The bartender raised one of his eyebrows, which was almost as bushy as his mustache. "You don't look like a geargirl. One of those airy-fairy types. I thought your kind pretended to be allergic to anything mechanical. What do you want to see Templeton for?"

Howlaa growled. It even made the hairs on the back of *my* neck stand up, and I knew I wasn't in any danger from her.

The bartender raised his hands. "Say no more. Templeton doesn't pay me enough to ask follow-up questions." He picked up a black plastic phone from behind the counter and spoke briefly, then hung it up. "He's not in."

Another growl from Howlaa, followed by a cracking of numerous knuckles.

The bartender sighed. "And the room he's not in is number 112, right up those stairs."

Howlaa flipped something round and shining onto the bar, and the bartender made it disappear quickly. We headed up the stairs, and I whispered, "Was that money? I thought you guys all just stole from each other."

Howlaa laughed, a harsh noise from a Nagalinda. "We barter. I gave him a token for the Incarnadine district. Home of legendary robo-prostit—"

"Howlaa!" Wisp said, and Howlaa gave a nasty cackle. Like I couldn't figure out what he was going to say.

"That's gross," I said.

"The robots aren't shentient, so they don't mind the work," Howlaa said. "Could be worshe."

"I'm not sure this is appropriate conversation," Wisp said.

"Thish ish a brothel, Wishp," Howlaa said. "We passhed appropriate a long time ago."

Wisp sighed. "I didn't choose the meeting place."

"So this guy Templeton is a pimp or something?"

"Jusht a schientisht," Howlaa said. "With a tashte for shlumming."

"Do try to avoid the letter 'S' while in this form, Howlaa. The lisp is distracting. You could have said Templeton has a 'predilection for low company,' for instance, and avoided both 'taste' and 'slumming.'"

"Shushit," Howlaa said, and at least that sounded the same as usual. The door to room 112 was wooden, but had a crazy lock with blinking lights and interlocking teeth. Howlaa knocked on the door, and when nobody answered, leaned close and whispered to the lock. The lights flashed and it clicked open. "Ha. That'sh the problem with artificially intelligent locksh. If you know how, you can threaten them into opening." She pushed open the door and stepped inside. "Templeton! We're here to talk about you-know-what."

I followed, and the door swung shut behind me. I'd expected some kind of four-poster-bed in red velvet, but this was more like the back room of an electronics store after an earthquake, wires and gears and electronics piled on shelves and all over the bed. The curtains were drawn over the windows, and it was dark, but I could tell there was a guy sitting in a chair in the corner. He leaned forward into the range of Wisp's glowing lights, and I couldn't help it—even after all I'd seen here, I gasped.

"I thought you said this guy was human," I said.

Templeton made a noise. I can't say if it was a laugh or a snort of contempt or what. When he spoke it sounded like the monotonous disconnected tone of the default voice on a laptop: "Human? I still have pancreas, a spleen, and most of my skin. What DNA I still possess is human." A pause. "Why, are you racist against cyborgs or something?"

Chapter 10

"No? I didn't know cyborgs were a race."

"We're persecuted," Templeton said. He glanced at Howlaa. His eyes bulged out, telescoping like spyglasses. "Howlaa, could you shed that nasty skin? A Nagalinda tore off my original arms. I don't like them much." He lifted his hydraulic limbs, all silvery and skeletal, and clenched hands with eight fingers and two thumbs each—he could count to twenty on his *fingers*. "Not that my new arms aren't great, but these hands are no good for—"

"Miranda is young," Wisp said. "Please contain your lewdness."

Templeton couldn't smile—his mouth was more of a grille—but he made a noise I think was a snigger. "Nobody's lewd like a teenager is lewd. I remember when I was that age. But, sure, propriety, I can roll with that."

Howlaa rippled and changed, taking on her human form again, shadow-suit withdrawing to something like a tank top and baggy shorts, all fuzzy black again. "Templeton, we're here to—"

"Please, I was *saying* something, trying to educate this little Mabling. I know you minions of the Faerie Queen hate tech, and hate cyborgs, but listen, we're all around you, even the human-looking ones. Everybody who wears corrective eyeglasses or contact lenses is a cyborg. Everyone who has an insulin pump or a pacemaker is mechanically augmented. Just because my enhancements are a little more obvious is no reason to treat me like a freakshow or a monster, I'm no different from someone with a titanium screw in their hip or a plastic knee—it's a difference of degree, not of kind. Understand? But I've been persecuted, stripped of my dignity, shorn of my—"

"You weren't fired for being mostly robot," Howlaa interrupted. "You were fired for testing new technology on yourself without permission."

Templeton sniffed. "Semantics."

"I don't have contact lenses," I said. "Or a plastic knee. But, ah, I do have…" I glanced at Howlaa, who nodded minutely. "I do have *these*." I stripped off my gloves, revealing my rings and my bracelets.

Templeton stared at my jewels for a long moment. He didn't lean in close to examine them, but for all I know his mechanical eyes were zooming in. "Shee-it," he said at last. "The jump-engine has already bonded to this girl? That kind of screws my plan."

"You were going to activate the engine yourself and steal it, leaving Wisp and me here to deal with the shitstorm fallout of your departure?" Howlaa said.

Templeton nodded. "Well, yeah."

"We figured. That's why Wisp was going to hijack your body to prevent such a treacherous act. You've still got one nostril and working sinuses and an organic brain, so Wisp can run you like a remote control racecar."

"Would've been a hell of a standoff," Templeton said, "Especially since my weapons system is on an autonomous AI circuit, and can protect me even if my self-control is compromised."

"It would've come to fisticuffs?" Howlaa said, sounding a little sad. "That would've been entertaining."

I pulled my hands back. "You knew this guy was going to betray you, but you were going to come talk to him anyway?"

"As we've already noted, genius is not the sole province of the honorable and the likable," Wisp said. "Knowing he would betray us is better than wondering if he *might*, at any rate. We knew exactly how to proceed. Then you came along, and…"

"How does a second-level Mabling wind up picking up a sparkling bit of tech anyway?" Templeton said. "Aren't you supposed to pretend to break out in hives if you so much as touch a digital watch?"

I rolled my eyes. "I'm just in fairy-cultist drag, Borg-o. Traveling incognito. I'm… new around here. The jump-engine thing was an accident."

Templeton grunted and abruptly rose. "Nuclear meltdowns are accidents. This is a catastrophe. Once it's activated, there's no turning the jump-engine off, folks. Which means the whole revolution-of-three is now in the hands of our unplanned fourth—what's your name?"

"Miranda Candle. Randy."

"Great. Our fate is in the hands of Randy-Candy here, who I'm guessing isn't a teenage cat burglar or super spy, but just another unlucky sap who got sucked up by the snatch-engines?"

"Miranda is quite resourceful," Wisp said. "And you are hardly the ideal of the stealth commando. Some of your augmentations could have been helpful in the event of armed confrontation, but you are... untrained."

"Better than some girl—" he said.

"What, are you racist against girls?"

Templeton stopped, then made that snigger again. "Touché, Randy. I guess you'll have to do, since the alternative for me is sitting in this room and waiting for rust or cascading electrical failures to take me out. Have you figured out how to do anything with the engine yet?"

"I can hit people, and make them disappear. And when people try to hit me, I teleport."

"Ah," Templeton said. "It's set in full manual mode, then, with only the self-preservation and non-lethal self-defense functions operating automatically. Everything else you'd have to activate by hand, and you don't have the instruction booklet."

"But you do?"

"Sweetie, I *wrote* the manual. I was the Regent's best usability expert and interface designer before my tragic accident."

"Tragic trial, conviction, and punishment," Howlaa said. "To be fair."

"Mmm. Semantics again. Hold out your hands, Randy. If I may?"

Another glance at Howlaa, another small nod. I guess this guy was our only hope. I held out my hands, palms down, and his robo-fingers touched me. "No snatching the rings off," Howlaa said.

"I'd have to snatch her whole *hands* off, and if I tried, I'd trigger the self-defense circuit and get teleported who knows where, so no thanks. Here, okay, if you twist this ring like this, and slide this ring down as far as you can, and pass this bracelet over this *other* bracelet—poof, you've got line-of-sight teleportation turned on, just turn the thumb ring and you'll teleport yourself to the farthest point in your vision." As he turned the rings, they changed color and texture, from silver to gold to platinum to copper, from smooth metal to braided wire to lumpy primitive-style twists. "It's all color and metal coded, it's not that complex, really, there's a learning curve, but once you master it, the pattern's no harder than mastering a really tough video game or high-end graphic design software. See, twist these and these, and you get coordinate-specific teleportation, just state the particular cartographic system you're using, name the coordinates, twist this thumb ring, and poof—you go right to your stated coordinates. Adjust the rings this way and you get short-burst evasive tele-porting, useful for running like hell from guys with guns. This way, and you can walk through walls—short-hop teleports, with the jump-engine's density-sensors determining where the next empty space is for you to in-habit. This lets you teleport to any place you've been before. And this—"

"I'll never remember all this." I shook my head, already forgetting which ring did what, only remembering the last step, twisting the thumb ring, and without remembering the preceding steps pulling the final trig-ger could be dangerous.

"Well, and why the hell would you?" Templeton said. "The full man-ual mode is for control freaks who don't trust the machine to do any-thing on its own, Linux types, you know what I mean? Fear not, there's a much simpler way." He twisted both my thumb rings simultaneously, and I winced, expecting to find myself on top of a mountain or inside a tree or something, but instead the rings sort of melted, and slithered, and walked across my fingers, and the bracelets evaporated or shriveled up or shrank to nothing and then...

... I was left with just one ring, a gold band inscribed with funny but familiar-looking lettering, on the ring finger of my left hand.

"There you go," Templeton said. "Full automatic mode, with the added bonus that guys won't hit on you because they'll assume you're married." He paused. "I guess you're kinda young for that though, unless you're from serious redneck country."

"What's this writing say?" I looked at the ring, amazed at how little it weighed after days of carrying around half a jewelry store on my hands. "What language is this?"

I wouldn't have thought a guy with a piece of lab equipment for a face could look sheepish, but he managed. "It's Tengwar."

"I don't speak that," Wisp said, sounding doubtful.

Templeton said "Ash nazg durbatulûk, ash nazg gimbatul, ash nazg thrakatulûk, agh burzum-ishi krimpatul."

"What does *that* mean?" I said.

"Jeez, Randy, you're disappointing me here," Templeton said. "You're from some kind of Earth, your English sounds basically like mine, and I haven't been here *that* long—they don't have Tolkien where you're from? *The Lord of the Rings*? 'One ring to bring them all'? My little joke. Seemed appropriate."

"You mean the magic ring they threw into a volcano in all those mov-ies they made in New Zealand?"

"They made *movies* from those books?" Templeton said.

"This whole conversation is confusing and I suspect irrelevant," Wisp said. "What do you mean by 'full automatic' mode?"

Templeton shrugged, with a whine of motors as his shoulders rose and fell. "Randy *is* the jump-engine now. It's part of her, she's part of it. Where she wants to go, she can go. Poof. Wishing makes it so."

"You mean… I could go home? Like, now?"

"You could," Templeton said, "but if you do, without saving our asses first, I'll personally build a new jump-engine from my own guts and use it to chase you down and throw *you* into a volcano."

"I'd come back," I said. "I just want to leave my Mom a note so she doesn't worry." More so I wouldn't get grounded quite as badly when I did return.

"Miranda," Wisp said. "Please… don't. What if something happened and you couldn't come back? If you were struck by lightning, hit by a bus?"

"Eaten by a tiger?" Howlaa said. "That happens on Earth, doesn't it? We'd be screwed. And you'd never get to find out about your Dad."

I sighed. "Fine. Okay. We'll do it your way. But… can I *send* things to earth? Like a snatch-engine in reverse?"

"Sure," Templeton said, and he even dug up a pen and a scrap of paper for me.

I wrote a pretty cryptic note: "Mom, am okay, will be home soon, sorry I couldn't call, not running away forever, promise." It wouldn't keep me out of trouble, but sending a note might keep her from *killing* me when I got home. I looked at the note, then wrote "Love" at the bottom in a loopy scrawl even I could barely read. "Okay. How do I, ah, jump-mail it?"

"You seem to like punching," Templeton said. "Just think of where you want it to go, and give it a smack."

So I did. I punched the letter and it disappeared. Templeton said it should appear on my kitchen table instantaneously. Better than e-mail. But maybe not as good as texting.

"All right," Templeton said. "Your girl has some of the most powerful technology on the Nex in her hands. What's the next step?"

"I can just poof my way into the palace and wreck up the snatch-engines, right?" I said. "Punch 'em into outer space?"

"Small problem: you've never been there. You don't know where you're going, so you can't just teleport there. I could give you coordinates and let you jump to a specific location, but the palace is… tricky. You might end up jumping blindly inside a furnace or a deathworm torture pit or something if we do that. So you'll have to get close to the engines, step through a few walls, work your way in gradually. Of course, after you've gotten a good look at the heart of the palace, you can come and go back there at will. Though we all hope more than one trip won't be necessary."

Howlaa burped. "First we have lunch. Then Miranda practices until she can teleport in her sleep. Then we help her with some personal business. Then we defeat the Regent."

"Shit. What personal business are you talking about?"

"It's personal," I said. "Are you coming with us?"

Templeton lifted one of his legs, which had some patches of actual skin and muscle left, and pointed to a blinking black anklet. "See that? It's tamperproof, and infallible, and it keeps me here."

"Ohhh. Like, house arrest? You leave and the cops come?"

"No, like self-destruct. I leave and I implode. Just as lethal as exploding, only with less property damage. The Regent doesn't want me running around loose, though he doesn't seem to care who visits me."

"You *are* probably under surveillance," Howlaa said. She turned, shivered, and began transforming back into a Nagalinda.

Templeton nodded. "Sure. Nothing mechanical, nothing in here—I can keep my own room clean, at least. But I'm sure the barkeep is an informant. Why wouldn't he be?"

"Explains his curiosity," Wisp said. "Curiosity isn't usually a survival trait in a landlord around here. But all he saw was a high-level Minion of Mab and her bodyguard come in. We just need a… plausible explanation for that."

"Good luck." Templeton began sorting a pile of wires heaped on his bed. "Might as well come up with a plausible reason for oil to hang out with water."

"I can think of shomething," Howlaa said. She knocked Templeton down and began beating his head and chest. Fragments of plastic and metal sprang free.

"Damn it!" Templeton shouted. "A little warning next time, let me turn off my sensory inputs, or at least flip the switch that lets me interpret pain as pleasure." He made a low moan. "Ah, there, yes, just like that. Bash away, big boy."

"Eww," I said.

Howlaa stepped back. "This ish unpleashantly non-consenshual."

"I'm just coping in my own way." Templeton sat up with a whine of overstressed motors. "It's going to take me hours to return this damage."

"That's what you get for seeding a Mabling recruitment potluck with nanites," Wisp said. "You know they're allergic to machines. Next time, our mistress the Faerie Queen might do more than send us to beat you up."

"Oh, is *that* what I did." Templeton unscrewed one of his eyes, removed it, and examined the cracked lens. "I am a bastard. Listen, you assholes—you come *back* for me when you've finished your mission. I didn't help you for free."

"We keep our promishesh," Howlaa said. She led the way out, and Wisp went dark and floated inconspicuously with us.

"You're lucky that's *all* we did!" I shouted back into Templeton's room, and tried to look like a smug brainwashed fairy fancier as we went down the stairs.

"You all need a post-brawl drink?" the bartender said.

"It wasn't a brawl," I said. "Just a friendly message."

"I thought the noise of crunching components and breaking glass sounded pretty friendly," the bartender said.

Back on the thronged street, I said, "Okay, so what are we doing now?"

"I was serioush," Howlaa said. "Lunch. We've been living on shcraps for too long. Now we're in the city. Now we can get shomething *good*."

"The restaurant district it is," Wisp whispered in my ear.

My belly growled—it had been growling pretty regularly, but now it *really* growled, apparently alerted to the possibility of real solid food. I hadn't had anything substantial since the Regent's dinner party. "What are we going to eat?"

"The best food in the universes can be found here," Wisp said. "Come along."

I had to do my playing-it-cool thing again as we navigated the broad avenue. Howlaa led the way to a moving walkway that snaked up through the air, apparently unsupported, like a silver ribbon in the wind. We stepped onto the walkway along with a cross-section of the bizarre residents of the Nex, from dolphins with legs and bubbling fluid-filled helmets to tiny wizened men on robotic stilts to a girl about my age in a ballet dancer's tutu smoking a long black cigarette. All these people had names, cultures, histories, lives—they'd all been stolen away to this place, or descended from others stolen long ago, and made their lives here. I remember how stunned I'd felt in school when one of my teachers told me there were almost 300 countries on Earth, and 7,000 living languages—how could there possibly be so many? How could I ever hope to visit all those places, and speak to everyone I found there? And Nexington-on-Axis made Earth seem like a little hick town, smaller even than Pomegranate Grove.

As we rose into the air—high enough that I clenched the rail as hard as I could—I got my first look at the Nex from above, and the city spread out as far as I could see in all directions. Out where we were, the streets were more-or-less straight, a pretty comprehensible grid, but closer to the center things got narrow, jumbled, and cramped, like an old historical district surrounded by modern outskirts. And at the very center rose a building that stood high above everything else, a curved thing of domes and minarets and swooping arches, all made of stone that changed color in the sun and seemed, in places, to flow like water. I half-turned and craned my head to keep looking at the thing.

The ballet dancer glanced at me. "Yeah, it's got some new towers today. Kind of pretty. Hope they keep them."

"What?"

The girl rolled her eyes. "Stupid Mabling," she muttered, tossing her cigarette over the side and walking away.

Apparently I was not disguised as the member of a universally popular clique.

"The palace," Wisp said in my ear. "The building at the center of the city. It is a living thing, in its way, changing shape, growing new towers, new arches, rising up, changing daily."

"Awesome," I said.

"Makes it difficult to break in," Wisp said. "There are no blueprints, no floor plans—that's why you can't jump to specific coordinates inside safely. But with the jump-engine, we should be able to navigate, room by room. Once you've practiced a bit and feel comfortable with your abilities, you can take us inside with you. The snatch-engines are vast, but smashing them is within Howlaa's powers, and you can scatter the fragments throughout the universe. Then we'll be free to go wherever we like, without fear of being recaptured."

"Eat now, plan later," Howlaa said, and tugged me toward a branching side-path on the walkway. We went down a drop so steep I had to close my eyes and breathe slowly to keep from puking, then leveled out close to the ground again and stepped off the walkway. I stumbled a little coming off it—*Way to look like a tourist, Miranda*, though I guess the Nex doesn't have tourists, just immigrants, pretty much by definition—and Howlaa caught my arm and steadied me. "The reshtaurant dishtrict," she said.

The buildings were as weird and varied as they were elsewhere: a mammoth tree with rope ladders and platforms loaded with diners, all pulling fruit from branches; a dead Ferris wheel with a guy serving cotton candy and fried dough from one of the cars; a slowly-revolving glass globe filled with fluttering bugs, with bug-people inside snatching live food from the air; and more. "Is there any human food here?"

"Some," Wisp said. "But mostly fusion restaurants. Nagalinda-Peruvian is quite good. And Dagonite-Mediterranean is marvelous seafood, with delicacies shipped in from the Landlock Sea."

"Could I maybe ease into the multicultural thing?"

"There are some purer examples of human cuisine," Wisp said. "Mostly clustered a few streets down. Though they do make use of local ingredients, which won't always match your previous experience." We passed street vendors serving everything from hot dogs to twitching things impaled on sticks, and the air was a mosh pit of smells, savory banging up against sweet knocking over sour shoving rotten aside. Every once in a while I'd get a noseful of something mouth-wateringly delicious, and then some millipede thing would go by eating from a plastic bowl that smelled like an open sewer and my guts would churn.

I was relieved when we turned a corner onto a street lined with pretty-much conventional-looking buildings. Funny how a street with an adobe Mexican restaurant and a wooden steakhouse next to a Japanese teahouse with paper walls looked familiar and normal here, when such a combo back home would've been weird and jarring.

"What are you in the mood for?" Wisp asked. "Thai? Mexican? French? Guatemalan? Hmong?"

"Wishp talksh a lot about food for shomeone who doeshn't *eat*," Howlaa said. "Like a virgin going on and on about shex." She paused. "Not that, ah, there'sh anything wrong with virginsh, I mean, if you're…"

I stopped, staring, and lifted my arm to point.

"What is it?" Wisp said.

"That," I said, my mouth suddenly dry, my legs trembling. "That building."

"Yesh? Rushtic French Cuishine? We can eat there if you want."

"No. It… That was my *Dad's* restaurant. The one that blew up."

Chapter 11

"Suddenly the Regent's claim seems much more plausible," Wisp said.

I barely heard him. I just stared at Etienne's, the restaurant looking exactly as I remembered it—the name written in elaborate script on the awning, the big front windows revealing a bright and airy dining room that became dark and cozy when night fell. Tables covered in cloth and set with crystal glasses, the length of the bar in the back of the room, the swinging doors that led to Dad's domain, the kitchen, where he'd shown me how to crack eggs one-handed and promised to teach me fancy knife-work once I got old enough that Mom wouldn't freak. The only difference was the quality of the diners inside—instead of the more well-off citizens of Pomegranate Grove (and the occasional scattering of ordinary people out for a special occasion), the tables were populated by the usual motley that surrounded us on the street, all sipping wine and eating food that… food that my *father* had made? *Really*?

I started toward the restaurant, and Howlaa laid a hand on my shoulder. I shrugged her off, and then it was both hands, one on each shoulder, and her leaning down to whisper in my ear: "The Regent ish sure to have people watching thish place, Randy. We should get away."

"My Dad might be in there."

"All the more reason to tread carefully," Wisp said. "So your reunion can be a happy one."

"I am *not* going to risk my life without at least trying to see if my Dad is alive first, guys. What do you think will happen? They'll catch me? I can freaking *teleport*."

"Not if they have snipers armed with tranquilizers, and knock you out before you can," Wisp said.

"I'm willing to risk it," I said. "I don't know if Bodiless or skinchangers *have* parents, but I do, and if my Dad is still breathing, I need to know."

Howlaa's grip tightened, at first, and I thought I was going to have a fight on my hands, but then she let go. "Jusht be careful," she murmured. Howlaa and Wisp faded back, though I could still feel a little Wisp-mote hovering in my ear. I walked into the restaurant, trying to figure out how to get to the kitchen unnoticed—if Dad was here, he'd be in the back. He hated front of the house. Said he was comfortable cooking, but didn't like to see how people reacted to his food. His version of stage fright.

Before I got two steps in, the hostess glided up to me. She was human, tall, thin like a shishkabob skewer, with long blonde hair and a weird ruby-red monocle over one eye, with a lens that twisted and spun. "Miranda Candle?" Her voice was all warmth and welcome, and I stopped.

"Um," I said.

She tapped her monocle. "I see you've... joined a new subculture since the photograph I saw was taken, but facial feature ratios don't lie. We've been expecting you. Come with me to the private dining room?"

I glanced to the right, automatically, toward the room reserved for private parties. Cal had his thirteenth birthday party in there. "I don't remember making a reservation," I said. "How did you know I was coming?"

Her one human eye twinkled. "A certain gentleman of your acquaintance made the arrangements. He's eager to see you again."

Dad? I followed her, and she opened the door. The private room was dim, the hanging lights turned off, just a candle burning in the center of the table. I stepped inside, and the hostess shut the door behind me. I heard the click of a lock engaging and my heart sank. A lock wouldn't keep me here, if push came to shove, but it told me I wasn't meeting my Dad.

The Regent leaned into the circle of the candle's light. "Hello, Miranda. So nice to see you again. The disguise is a nice effort, and bravo for getting rid of the tracking devices, but my greatest strength has always been understanding the *psychology* of my rivals. I knew you'd come here, once I told you about your father. The hook was set."

"I want to see my Dad." I crossed my arms.

"Oh, my," he said softly. "Your jewelry has changed. Tell me, was it simple trial and error to change the settings, or did Howlaa smuggle out a draft of the user's manual? Or... no. You found someone to give you advice, didn't you? I knew Howlaa must have contact with someone who knew about the jump-engine project. She's no good at detective work, really—just extermination. Was it Templeton? I should have dismantled him, but I have a pathetic tendency to hold onto *everything*, just in case I need it in the future. A certain… hoarding mentality… comes along with proximity to the royal orphans, I think."

"If you're done monologuing, I'd really love to see my Dad now. Or would you rather get punched into outer space again? I've got a little more control now." I cracked my knuckles, thinking it was a pretty good dramatic gesture, and now that my fingers were mostly clear of rings, I could do it without pinching myself. "You might not wind up in an orbital pleasure palace. You might just end up in *orbit*."

"A counter-offer. You can come with me to a very pleasantly-appointed lab, where you'll be treated kindly while my scientists disconnect the jump-engine from your limbic system—that's the deep old *reptile* part of your brain, the fight-or-flight part, the place where the engine is most deeply entrenched."

I looked at my ring. "This is in my *brain*?"

"Parts of it, yes. You're just a cog in the engine now, Miranda. Let me disconnect it before things spin even more out of your control. Let me give you your life back."

"Fu—"

"Please!" The Regent held up his hands. "Hear my entire proposal. I remove the engine. I reunite you with your father. I use the engine to send *both* of you back home, and never trouble either of you again. How does that sound?"

Familiar. "I don't trust you."

"I'll swear before as many witnesses as you like. I'll have my magisters draw up ironclad contracts. I'll cross my heart and hope to die. I have nothing to gain from betraying you. All I want is the engine. I can give you something you want in return. Ask anyone—I am a reasonable man. I am not vindictive." He chuckled. "I prefer to outlive my enemies in lieu of exacting revenge."

I sat down. I wasn't a zillion-year-old tyrant, but I knew when I had bargaining power. "What about Wisp and Howlaa?"

His mouth tightened. "They will be returned to their regular duties, pending reeducation."

"Brainwashing, you mean?"

"Their brains are remarkably resistant to washing, which is part of why they're valuable to me, but they will be given the opportunity to reconsider their recent poor choices and dedicate themselves to my service anew. They've been captured already, you know. My people are everywhere, and we saw Howlaa in her bodyguard disguise. My forces moved on them as soon as you came into the restaurant."

Crappo. "Okay. You want to make a deal? Fine. I get my Dad back, and you have to set Wisp and Howlaa free, let them out of their contract, sign an emancipation proclamation, whatever. Send them wherever they want to go."

"Ah!" The Regent said. "I *see*. You're under the misapprehension that this is a negotiation. It is not. You will accept my offer. Period."

"Punching you. Into *space*. That's my offer. Of course this is a negotiation."

"Your father is here, Miranda. In the kitchen, with two of his sou chefs. One of them is simply a humble cook. The other is one of my agents. He will put a knife into your father's kidneys as soon as he gets the order from me through his little earpiece. Really, Miranda. Your father's a good cook, but he's not so good I won't use him as a hostage."

I took a deep breath, then let it out. "Let me see him. Let me see that he's here, and that he's all right, and I'll do what you want."

The Regent cocked his head.

"You *said* you're a reasonable man. So be reasonable."

"Fair enough. Come." He rose and headed for the door, and I resisted the temptation to punch him into the center of the frozen sun—if Templeton was right, I could control destinations now, but who knew what would happen to Dad if the Regent disappeared? He gestured for me to open the door, and stepped out after me. I was amazed—the whole restaurant was empty, all the diners hustled out during the time I'd been in the dining room. Unless maybe they'd *all* been undercover spies for the Regent, just pretending to have lunch. I was beginning to get some idea of how powerful this guy really was. "Just through here." The Regent nodded to the kitchen.

The front of the restaurant exploded, windows shattering and glass flying. We were far enough in the back that none of the really big shards reached us, but a few little fragments bounced off me, and it was still enough to trigger my flight mechanism; I ended up teleported behind the bar. I stood up in time to see Howlaa in her Rendigo form come barreling into the restaurant, claws dripping venom, stalking toward the Regent, who regarded her coolly.

"I suppose this means I've lost a number of my best-trained troops?" he said. "I warned them not to underestimate your capabilities. The next wave will be more cautious, at least."

Howlaa growled and lashed out...

And her claws passed harmlessly through the Regent, who rippled like a flag in the breeze.

"A hologram," Wisp said, suddenly hovering beside me, and I realized that I couldn't have punched the Regent into the sun even if I'd wanted to—he was just a projection again. The guy was smart, you had to give him that.

Howlaa snarled, and I looked at the kitchen door longingly. Was my Dad back there? Was he okay?

"Miranda, we have to go," Wisp said.

"If you leave with them, I will have your father killed," the Regent said.

It was almost enough to make me bow my head... but instead I looked into his simulated eyes. "If you hurt him, if you *touch* him, I'll never let you have this jump-engine." I slammed my fist down on a table, and sent it—away, far, as far as I could reach, which I thought was very far. I stalked forward, bringing my fist down on the bar, and it winked out of existence, the pitchers and glasses that had been resting on it crashing to the floor and shattering. "I'll send everything in your city away. *Everything.* You like hoarding things? I'll empty your whole *world.* You can run your snatch-engines full-speed to try to get that stuff back, but I'll drop this shit into black holes, into the middle of stars. Your palace is next."

The Regent shook his head and smiled like I was a two year old throwing a tantrum. "Miranda, please, just a moment ago we were being so reasonable—"

Howlaa leapt into the air, twisting, and I jumped back. "What the—"

"He caught a sniper's tranquilizer dart, Miranda," Wisp said. "Meant for you. But there will be more. We have to go."

"Can I—how do I teleport with you guys? How do I take you with me?"

"We don't know," Wisp said. "Templeton said it should... respond to your thoughts?"

I turned to the Regent. "Remember. If *anything* happens to my father—"

"Yes, yes. This posturing is silly, Miranda. I have your father. You have my jump-engine. We'll end up trading eventually. Why waste all this time?"

I reached out to touch Howlaa's slick, scaly side. "Wisp, can you... go up Howlaa's nose or in her mouth or something? I can't touch you, so I'm not sure..."

"Of course." Wisp's motes ran into Howlaa's gaping, panting, tooth-filled mouth.

"Until next time, then," the Regent said.

I didn't teleport far. Just into the kitchen, where Howlaa took up *way* too much room and knocked over a couple of garbage cans.

My Dad wasn't there. The kitchen was empty, though it was just like I remembered it, the bank of stoves and ovens, the prep tables, the big industrial sinks, the smells of herbs and cooking meat. A pot was bubbling over on one of the burners, stew turning to burned mess, and without thinking I walked over and twisted the burner off.

"Perhaps we should go a bit *farther*?" Wisp said.

I looked around, hoping for some sign that Dad was still here—a picture of the family, a lumpy mug I'd made for him at summer camp, *something*—but it was just a working kitchen, no personal stuff. I sighed. "Okay. Where? Earth?"

"No! If we leave the Nex, the snatch-engines will be able to bring us back."

"Okay, then. Somewhere more local."

I jumped us back to the warehouse, beside the truck.

We were at the center of a ring of a hundred Nagalinda, all aiming their complex guns at us. The Regent was there, or another simulation, sitting on the back of the truck. "Ah, Miranda. I know everywhere you've been, dear. My trackers have worked out your whole backtrail. And you can only teleport to places on the Nex you've already been—otherwise, you're jumping blind, and even in your petulance I don't think you're stupid enough to try that. *All* your little haunts and way stations are surrounded. Really, now. This is the end. This is—"

Howlaa snatched me up with one of her huge arms and barreled through the line of Nagalinda. Her shadowcloth slithered up over me, changing into a hard armored shell, and I heard darts pinging off the material, and the Regent shouting "I need her alive!" and Wisp saying "Oh dear oh dear oh dear."

Howlaa darted into some kind of deep, narrow storage room and dropped me on my ass, rapidly changing into human form and shoving the heavy steel door closed. I stood up and said "What do we do now?" and tasted blood on my lips. Crap. In all the commotion, my stupid nose had started bleeding again.

Howlaa handed me a handkerchief, and I pressed it to my flowing nostrils.

"They'll be able to peel this room open soon enough," Howlaa said. "But if the Regent is telling the truth about scouting our backtrail, I'm not sure where we should go. If we flee the Nex, we get snatched, and a blind jump…" She shook her head. "Too dangerous."

"We came so close," Wisp said as the pounding on the other side of the door began, along with muffled shouting. "Perhaps it's better if Miranda saves herself, makes an arrangement…"

"We're not done yet." Howlaa snatched the handkerchief from my hands.

"Hey, I'm still bleeding here!"

Howlaa put the bloody handkerchief in her mouth and *slurped*. I winced and said "Oh my god, gross," and then realized what she was doing, if not exactly *why*. A moment later she spat out the handkerchief and began to change…

Into me. I was looking at a perfect image of me, only *naked*, and she was exactly the same, right down to the mole over my bellybutton. The shadow-cloth slithered and wiggled and changed into my stupid Mabling costume, and one little bit of it crawled to her finger and became a copy of my ring. "Regent!" she shouted. "I've sent Howlaa and Wisp away, someplace you won't find them, someplace *they* can survive. I'm coming out!" She turned to me and hissed, "*Go*. They can't have every inch of our backtrail covered. Go someplace obscure, in the provinces, and lay low for a bit—they won't look for you if they think you're already in custody. This won't buy us much time. Soon enough the Regent will realize I'm not you."

It was so weird, like if my mirror started ordering me around. "But… what am I supposed to *do*?"

Howlaa shrugged. "Destroy the snatch-engines. Get rid of the orphans. Topple the government. Depose the Regent. Reunite with your father. Oh, and *save me*. Wisp will help."

"I—thanks, Howlaa. Be careful."

"Shushit. Being careful is for others."

"If you'd open your mouth, Miranda?" Wisp said.

"Uh," I said, and Wisp took the opportunity to zip into my mouth, which was kind of like having a mouthful of gnats, only more bubbly. I closed my eyes, thought *obscure*, and jumped.

Chapter 12

I sat curled up in the same pipe in that construction site for what felt like hours, waiting to be discovered or captured or shot with a tranquilizer dart. That last wouldn't have been so bad maybe, since I would have actually been able to sleep. At least Wisp wasn't bugging me—he seemed content to just hover there indefinitely.

After a while, when it was dark, I whispered, "I messed up pretty bad, huh?"

Wisp didn't light up, but my eyes were adjusted well enough to see the swirl of motes before me. "The Regent is gifted at anticipating the actions of others," he said at last. "You only wanted to see your father. It's understandable."

"I ruined all your plans."

"Howlaa always says 'plan' is a four-letter-word for something that goes wrong. We simply have to… adapt to our new circumstances."

"So what do we do now?"

"I am primarily an observer, Miranda. I am capable of doing my part for the cause of our freedom, certainly, but when it comes to creating stratagems, tactics, making plans… these are not my strengths. I always depended on Howlaa for such things."

Which meant… what? It was up to me? Not reassuring. "How long do you think we have before they realize Howlaa's not really me?"

"Difficult to say. Howlaa is genetically identical to you, and she is an adept imposter, so she will stand up to considerable scrutiny. Once the Regent begins to study the false jump-engine, however, the deception will become apparent. For now, I think it is safe to say that no one is looking for you. Yet."

"Which means if we're going to do something, we should do it soon."
I crawled out of the pipe. The construction site was lit only by the street-lamps outside the fence. I walked around for a while, poking under tarps, until I found a long wooden box with a lid, padlocked shut. I rattled the big lock, then squeezed it in my fist.

The lock flickered, and went from hanging on the box's clasp to lying in the dirt at my feet. Very cool. The jump-engine could vastly simplify my shoplifting process, though after a few days of genuine adventure, the adrenaline rush of stealing bracelets was starting to seem kind of childish. I flipped open the box's lid and peered inside. Wisp floated close and said, "Miranda, do you have any experience with demolitions?"
"Is that, what, dynamite?" The box was full of neatly stacked cylinders, but they weren't cartoon red with fuses sticking out of one end, just a dusty dull orange.

"Yes. They're dangerous if you aren't experienced." He paused. "They're dangerous *anyway*."

I shook my head. "Sorry, Wisp. I don't know what they teach in seventh grade around here, but we don't have classes in blowing shit up in Pomegranate Grove."

"A pity. A teleporter with access to bombs... you could be a one-woman uprising."

I found another box, made the padlock disappear, and considered the jumble of dirty tools inside. There was a big sledgehammer that seemed perfect, but I could barely even lift it—I don't think it was made for human hands, even big burly construction worker hands. I picked up a wrecking bar with a curved end, about three feet long, and it felt good in my hands, something I could swing. "There we go," I said.

"Why do you want a weapon, exactly?" Wisp said. "Anything you could smash with that you could just as easily reach out and send away. Any door you wanted to pry open you could simply pass through."

"I don't know. Maybe I don't trust the whole magical ring thing. If the Regent finds a way to turn off the jump-engine, at least with this I'll still be able to *hit* stuff."

"Contingency plans are never a bad thing," Wisp said. "What now?"

My rumbling stomach answered that before my brain could think about it. "We never did get anything to eat. All aboard, Wisp. We're jumping."

A flicker, and we were back in the kitchen at Etienne's, dark, empty, quiet. The pot on the stove was cold and crusted, and everything was still a mess from the interrupted lunch service, which meant my Dad must be in custody somewhere—he never left the kitchen messy like this. I hunted around and found some cheese and fruit and bread, enough to make a half-assed repast, and dug in while Wisp floated around the room.

Once my belly was full, thinking was easier. If I could get to the center of the palace and send the snatch-engines into a black hole or something, the Regent would lose his biggest source of power… but he'd still be a pissed-off ruler with an army and a bunch of high-tech stuff at his beck and call. He'd *never* let my Dad free, or Howlaa, for that matter, and even though there was no prison on Nexington-on-Axis that could keep me out—or keep them in, once I found them—the Nex was a big place, and I didn't know where to start looking for either of them.

The snatch-engines were still key. They were the thing the Regent valued most. Just getting rid of them wasn't enough anymore, because there was more at stake than Howlaa and Wisp's freedom. Maybe I could hold the engines hostage. Put them somewhere out of the Regent's reach, but not out of mine. He'd have to agree to an exchange of prisoners then, and I could negotiate for Wisp and Howlaa's freedom, too.

I picked up the wrecking bar. "Let's go to the palace, Wisp. It's time to snatch the snatch-engines."

First I teleported to the moving walkway, much to the surprise of all the people and things riding it—apparently Nexington-on-Axis never sleeps. A steam-powered piston-driven cyborg like Templeton—only even less human-looking—growled at me, and a bunch of LEDs on his face lit up. A twisted little imp with a pearl necklace riding on the shoulders of a bored-looking human boy said "Where did *you* come from?"

"Blessings of Mab be upon you," I said, conscious of my bedraggled wings and the fact that I'd lost my faceted glasses somewhere. So much for my disguise. I looked down at the palace, glittering and shifting in the distance, towers elongating and shrinking and corkscrewing with slow grace. At night, from above, the lights of Nexington-on-Axis were like galaxies colliding.

Line of sight, I thought, and jumped to the roof of the palace. I knelt down and put my hand on the smooth surface of the roof. The stone, or whatever, was cool and slightly rough and weirdly organic, like touching the skin of a snake. I pressed down, and it yielded slightly, milky rainbows of color spiraling out from the pressure of my fingers. I walked up to the base of one of the towers, bigger around than a giant sequoia, and it didn't look like a built thing at all, but like a growing thing, a tree branch sprouting off from the main trunk. "Where did the Regent snatch *this* place from?"

"The palace predates the days of the Regent," Wisp said in my ear. "It was the first structure on Nexington-on-Axis, as far as we know, home to the Kings and Queen and their children. Perhaps it is native to this place. The engines have never found anything like it again, though the Regent has searched."

"Huh. So do we have any idea where the snatch-engines are located?"

"Just 'the heart of the palace.' But the palace extends for many blocks in all directions, and extends downward as well. There are whole wings that have never been seen by sentient eyes, sections that are utterly inaccessible, without doors, windows, or ventilation shafts. The Regent's government occupies only a tiny portion of the palace. The rest... governs itself."

"So we're going exploring, then. Will we know the snatch-engines if we see them?"

"I suspect they will be difficult to miss," Wisp said.

I walked to one of the towers and put my hands on its surface. "Here we go." I closed my eyes and stepped forward.

When my eyes opened, it was dark, and Wisp's motes lit up rapidly, his form spreading out to make a net of light. I stood on a smooth stony platform inside the curvature of the tower, with what I thought was a spiral staircase winding up into the darkness above and down into the darkness below. When I stepped closer, though, I saw there were no steps, and the curve was just a single glass rail, like a giant corkscrew. "What, am I supposed to slide down that?" I asked.

"I don't think this tower is designed for human habitation," Wisp said.

"Wonder what this lever does?" It was a crystalline rod about three feet long, set into the center of the platform, with a sparkling diamondlike knob on top. I tugged, and the lever didn't budge—it wasn't as delicate as it looked. "See?" I said. "My crowbar is already useful." I jammed the bar between the base of the lever and the wall and pulled, and the lever creaked and inched forward. "Can't use teleportation for leverage."

"I hope pulling that lever doesn't trigger something unpleasant. Like the disappearance of this tower."

"If the walls start closing in, I'll just step through them, and you've got nothing to worry about anyway, right?"

"I can't pass through impermeable solids, Miranda. My kind are difficult to contain, it's true, but an airtight container closing around us fast enough can do it. I don't know whether I'd be able to escape this tower or not."

"Better be ready to climb up my nose and in my ears and under my clothes in a hurry then, just in case."

I grunted and strained at the bar, and the lever gave way completely, slamming down against the platform with a sound like a spoon ringing against a glass.

"Subtlety, thy name is Miranda," Wisp said.

"Shhh." I listened. There was noise up above, a sound almost like whistling, like when you blow over the mouth of a bottle. "What is that?"

"Onrushing death?"

Something like a car on a roller coaster came spiraling down the rail, but it was low and sleek and rose-quartz colored. The car pivoted around and around as it descended, so even though the track spun in tight corkscrews, the front of the car always faced the same way. "I thought this palace was alive. This looks like something that was built."

"Perhaps the palace is both an organism and the *habitation* for an organism. Perhaps there is a central life form, somewhere, and the palace is merely its shell, built up around it like a nautilus. Who can say? But this is hardly the oddest thing you'll find in the palace."

The car stopped in front of the platform. It was a no-frills thing, without pads or seatbelts, and the only control was a small lever. I climbed in. "I guess we head down." I pushed the lever toward my feet.

The ride was smoother than I expected, and with the pivoting-around I didn't even feel dizzy, though the blank expanse of wall lit by Wisp wasn't all that interesting. "Think there'll be guards waiting for us at the bottom?"

"Possibly," Wisp said. "If this railway is monitored. But the palace is unimaginably vast. It has gradually consumed the buildings around it, growing around them the way a tree will grow around a nail driven into a branch—or the way an oyster will surround a piece of grit to make a pearl—utterly enclosing and incorporating them. Even at its most active, the palace can seem empty. The business of government takes place only in a few stable chambers near the front doors. It's considered suicidally foolhardy to venture much deeper, since corridors and staircases have a way of folding in on themselves, disappearing, and reconfiguring. Some say the Regent's apartments and audience chamber and courtrooms and offices are actually dead parts of the palace, necrotic tissue in the organism, since they are the only rooms that never change. You and I are in one of the living sections. I don't know what we'll find, but it's unlikely we'll *be* found."

"I just can't get over how weird this place is."

"The universe is vast and strange. Have you heard the theory that, in an infinite universe, anything that possibly can exist *must* exist?"

I nodded. "My friend Jenny Kay told me something like that once—she said that everyone on Earth has perfect doubles way out there in the universe, some impossibly far distance away. And not just perfect doubles, but also slightly imperfect doubles, people almost exactly the same except for maybe a mole, a pimple, a missing tooth. I didn't really get it." I realized I'd just given Wisp permission to lecture, but it was better than staring at a blank wall, at least.

"The theory holds that since all objects—you, me, restaurants, planets, everything—are composed of specific combinations of particles, all of those combinations would repeat an infinite number of times, assuming the universe itself is infinite. So there are countless versions of you, including infinite *identical* versions and infinite slightly-different versions. There are versions of you identical in every way, except you have the thoughts and memories of Mozart or Einstein or Howlaa—"

I interrupted. "Wait, I get that physical stuff is just made of atoms or whatever, and that if you have enough space those atoms will fall into the same patterns over and over, but you're saying *thoughts* can get copied too?"

"Thoughts, dreams, they're all just combinations of atoms, as you say, in the structure of your brain."

"So there could be zillions and zillions of Mirandas and Wisps riding down this tower? And in some places it's my friend Jenny Kay instead of me, or it's Napoleon instead of you, or it's a gorilla with a pistol and his partner the cyborg parrot? Anything I can *imagine*?"

"Not exactly," Wisp said. "You may be able to imagine things that are not possible given the existing laws of physics. Though there's also a theory that there are other universes, equally as infinite as your own, which have different laws of physics. Occasionally the snatch-engines pick up things that simply evaporate, collapse, or disappear, as if they are fundamentally inimical to this universe. We also grab humans from Earths that don't have the same history or civilization that yours does—Earths that are dominated by the denizens of the land of mist and mirrors, Earths over-run by spidery aliens, Earths where zero-point energy was discovered in the 19th century and the world became a Utopia—at least for the citizens of the Unending Holy Roman Empire."

"Whoa. There are whole parallel dimensions?"

"Not parallel dimensions—that's a *different* theory—just planets in your own universe that are unimaginably far away from your Earth, in solar systems that happen to exactly resemble your own, populated by human who are remarkably similar. Not that we've ever snatched two versions of the same person, as far as I know. The vastness of the universe makes such things unlikely—it would be like catching two identical snowflakes on two different continents the first time you stuck out your tongue in a blizzard. Only much more unlikely."

"Is there a chance the father I have here... isn't *my* father? That he's some other Miranda's Dad?"

"It's not impossible, but it's unlikely. The royal orphans tend to snatch things from the same general areas again and again, if they can—it's easier than reconfiguring the engines into whole new combinations every time they need something. So statistics are in your favor."

Sometimes, like anybody, I lay in bed and look at the ceiling and think about infinity, and I always fall asleep before I get very far. I wasn't sleepy now, but I still wasn't getting very far. It all sounded interesting, but in normal day-to-day life infinity didn't much matter. But here, in this place, with universes whirling past in the sky, it seemed like something I should get a handle on. "So there are also countless copies of Nexington-on-Axis?"

"Now *that* is a matter of some debate," Wisp said. I could tell he was warming up—he was a born lecturer, assuming he was ever born. Get him and Jenny Kay in a room together and nobody else would be able to get a word in anywhere. "Some contend that the Nex is a singular place, standing outside all possible universes—that this is the Omphalos, the Axis Mundi, the singular hub around which infinity spins. Certainly the Regent believes that, and truthfully, so do I. We are not *inside* any of the universes, but in the space between them."

Trying to imagine bubbles of infinity inhabiting a greater infinity was too much for me, but I did take one thing away from Wisp's words: "If there's only one Nex, that means I'm the only Miranda—the only *anybody*—riding this rail right now. The only Miranda in the palace. The only Miranda trying to save the day."

"That's true."

I sighed. "Which means if I screw up, there's no chance it's being done right in some *other* part of the universe."

"I… Ah. Yes. I think that's likely."

"Guess I better not screw up, then."

The car lurched to a halt. Wisp drifted up and out, lighting a corridor leading away from the base of the tower. I climbed out of the car, head still spinning with infinities, and followed him. "I wish there were some lights down here. No offense, but you're more firefly than flashlight, Wisp."

The walls began to glow with a pearly pale light until the curving corridor was totally lit up.

"Wait. Can the palace *hear* me?"

"Improbable as that seems," Wisp said, "it appears it can."

Chapter 13

I walked down the corridor. There was no point teleport-ing—I could only safely jump in line-of-sight here, and the curve of the tunnel meant I couldn't see more than a few yards ahead or behind. We hadn't passed a single branching passage or doorway. "So, palace. If you can hear me, give me a sign." Nothing happened. "Do you mind that I'm here? Blink once for yes, twice for no." The walls remained steady. "Hmm. Do you think we're going in circles, Wisp? Maybe the corridor just changed behind us and formed a loop like a doughnut, like a snake eating its own tail?"

"A troubling thought," Wisp said. "You can always teleport if this hallway goes on much longer."

"Yeah, but then we're just starting over somewhere else. Hey, pal-ace—how about opening up a shining path to the heart of you, where the snatch-engines live?"

The lights in the walls pulsed slightly. "What does that mean?"

"Squid communicate by flashing colors at one another in a spectrum their predators can't even see," Wisp said. "Ants leave pheromone trails for their compatriots to follow. And the palace is far more alien from you than an ant or a squid. What hope can you have of communicating with it? Who knows what it means?"

I stopped walking. "It understood when I asked for light. So I'm hopeful. Palace? See this crowbar? I want to find the snatch-engines, and I want to bash the crap out of them. If you like having a bunch of weirdo creatures running an industrial theft-factory in your body, you don't have to help me. But if you *want* to see the parasites kicked out of your guts, give me a hand."

The walls shimmered and parted like a slice of bread being torn apart, creating a ragged tear that revealed another passageway.

"Remarkable," Wisp said. "How did you know it would help you?"

"I didn't. I just figured, if I was a sentient palace, I wouldn't want a government bureaucracy set up in some dead part of my body, or a bunch of royal orphans and heavy machinery living in my *heart*. It's a body-having thing. You wouldn't understand."

"It's always possible the palace is leading us to an electric eel pit, you know."

"We'll jump that deathtrap when we come to it, Wisp."

This corridor angled down, and lit up in pulsing sections, so I could never see very far before me. Eventually the walls got farther apart until we stood at one end of a long broad bridge, without so much as a guardrail protecting us from a deep drop, suspended in a huge space. There were structures in the emptiness all around, things that might have been glass or stone, rising and bending and twisting like the girders of a half-built skyscraper come to life, all silent. Sparks of light ran up and down the girders, flickering. A flowing river of glowing jewel-colored liquid rushed underneath us. The silence and bigness made me feel like I was in church, though my family hardly ever went, except for a couple of months after Dad died—or disappeared.

When I stepped on the bridge it sank in a little under my feet like a mattress, and I went across fast, afraid that if I stopped I wouldn't be able to start again. If I got scared and had to go down on hands and knees, I knew I wouldn't like the feel of the bridge on the palms of my hands, all fleshy and soft. The passage at the other end of the bridge looked a lot more normal, with floors that seemed to be stone and a few arched doorways. I paused and peeked through every open door, wondering if I'd know a snatch-engine or a royal orphan if I saw one, but there was nothing obviously alive—just rooms full of strange pools and fountains bubbling colored liquid, or sculptures of trees with glass fruit, or bottomless pits, or rooms where the corners didn't come together in a sensible way and the light seemed to churn and foam against itself and my eyes crossed just trying to see inside.

Eventually, though, we reached something new.

This door was twice as tall as me, made of dull gray metal and studded with fist-sized rivets, with a round handle as big as a wagon wheel in the middle. The door wasn't something the palace had grown—the palace was trying to *reject* it, wall-flesh growing over the edges, all red and green and sick-looking where the palace's flesh touched the metal door. I put my palm against the poisoned part of the wall, and it was feverishly hot. "This must be a door the Regent *really* wanted to stay in place."

"Can you open it?" Wisp said.

I tugged the wheel, which didn't move, then slipped the crowbar between the spokes and pulled down on it with all my weight, but it still didn't budge. "How does an old bastard like the Regent get this open?"

"He probably has the Nagalinda open it for him. Assuming this is even the Regent's door. The palace, and the Queen and Kings of Nexington-on-Axis, were here long before the Regent became ascendant."

"Huh. I hate to jump in there blind. Can you squeeze under the door and let me know what we're dealing with?"

Wisp's motes fluttered around the edges of the door, then came back together. "I'm afraid not. If there ever were cracks, the palace's flesh has grown over and sealed them.

"Okay then. Let's hope it's not a room full of poison gas or lava or something." I put my hand on the door, made an effort to keep my eyes open this time, and stepped forward. The ring on my hand warmed up—was something trying to keep me out, some high-tech force field?—but I passed through, even getting a glimpse of door's insides, tumblers and locking mechanisms frozen shut with rust.

Beyond the door was the heart of the palace. Or the things that had been built in that heart.

The noise was crazy loud, hammering and clanging and sizzling and roaring. The stink was electricity and burning charcoal and hot metal. Wisp had to slip a mote right inside my ear for me to hear him, and even then, it was faint. "I've only seen the engines from above, briefly, from an observation deck, but this... I think we're at the bottom of the engine room, Miranda."

I looked up. And up. And up.

The snatch-engines were these huge towering coils of copper and silver and gold and brass and iron, glass globes the size of houses filled with lightning, sparking jacob's ladders and coils, wires and cables in spiderweb designs, pipes venting steams, pistons as big as my body pounding up and down. Bellows expanding and contracting. Pipes dripping hissing fluids. Gears the size of Ferris wheels turning against each other.

I knew I was only seeing a tiny portion of the engines, because they stretched up toward a ceiling I couldn't even see, and sprawled out in all directions, bigger around than a building, bigger than a city block. Catwalks crisscrossed the shaft above me, and I could see *things* moving up there, skittering and crawling and swinging, doing who knows what to the snatch-engines—servicing them, improving them, snuggling them.

Wisp said, "They've grown, since I was here last, though the engines were vast even then. No one understands how they work, except the royal orphans, and who knows which embellishments are necessary and which are merely ornamental? I know it's daunting, Miranda, but this is what we came to do—to destroy these things."

There was no way my plan to hold the snatch-engines hostage in exchange for Howlaa and my Dad would work. I'd imagined the engines as objects I could just stick somewhere inconspicuous—I'd imagined sending the engines to the old quarry deep in the woods south of Pomegranate Grove, where hardly anyone ever went, where they'd be unnoticed until I needed to bring them back. But these engines were huge, impossible to hide—if I sent them to Earth you could probably see them from *space.*

As for falling back on plan A, I didn't think I could destroy them, either. I looked at the crowbar in my hand and had to laugh. I couldn't smash these engines any more than I could dismantle a car with a spoon, anymore than I could smash a mountain with a mallet. As for using my teleportation powers to send the engines away, I could *try...*

I reached out and touched the nearest component, a metal strut holding up a gently spinning brass globe. I pushed, tried to send the whole snatch-engine *away*, into a desert I'd seen once from the window of an airplane.

The metal strut went, but the brass sphere came crashing down and rolled away, and nothing else so much as budged.

The engines were too *big.* Maybe because there were limits to the jump-engine's powers, or because I couldn't conceive of the snatch-engines as individual things—they looked so much like mismatched piles of parts, I couldn't even tell where one engine ended and another began. I could try to get rid of the thing piece by piece, but it would take forever. I'd have to teleport chunks of it, and once I sent away everything I could lay hands on, the stuff up higher would just collapse on me. It wouldn't be enough to take pieces out of the thing, to damage it—the royal orphans would just repair it. I had to make the whole *thing* go away, fast enough that the orphans couldn't just snatch the missing pieces back, *and* get rid of the orphans themselves so they couldn't build another engine from scraps of technology in the Machine Waste. I let the crowbar fall to the floor. I'd never felt more overwhelmed.

But I had to try. I was here, and if I gave up, what was left for me? Going to live in the tunnels with Clan Kil'howlaa? Hanging out with Templeton? Joining the Minions of Mab in hopes of scoring a free vegetarian meal? I went to the brass globe on the floor and sent it to the desert too.

I looked around for the next piece of the machine and reached out for a bolt the size of my head.

Then I sensed… something.

Ever notice a swarm of bees coming at you from the side? Or caught sight of a flock of birds changing direction from the corner of your eye? Something like that happened. I got a sense of motion, looked up, and a swarm of *things* massed on the catwalks above, and then came scurrying and leaping and gliding down toward me. I hadn't been able to see them clearly before, and now that I could… their bodies were almost too bizarre to be horrible.

"The royal orphans," Wisp said in my ear. "They've seen us."

"They're—what—Wisp, what *are* they?"

"The orphans make changes to themselves much as they do to the engines. When they see something they like on another creature, a tentacle or teeth or claws or wings… they steal it and graft it onto their own bodies."

I don't know what I'd expected. Snot-nosed kids, or slug-people, or lizard people, or frog people, or cyborg midgets, or something like anything I'd seen before. But the orphans were as weirdly patchwork and cobbled-together as the snatch-engines themselves. Their bodies were feathered or scaled or horned, multi-legged, with bodies like those of bugs or manta rays or snakes. Most weren't much bigger than a good-sized dog, though one or two were cow-sized. A lot of them didn't have eyes, though others had too many eyes, or antennae, or snail-stalks, or—

Imagine everything that creeps or crawls or runs or swims or flies on the Earth, all put in a box and shaken up and mixed together, then dumped out again, bits of one stuck to bits of another, and you might have some idea of the variety in the royal orphans. And they were coming at *me*. Because I'd smashed up their pride and joy. The same way Cal came after me when he saw me messing with his car… except Cal was my brother, and I knew he'd never really hurt me.

"We can fight them, Miranda. They aren't very strong—they're horribly inbred—and they aren't designed for fighting. And remember: you have the jump-engine."

He made a good point—faced with a wall of monsters I'd sort of forgotten I had options. I looked past them and jumped to one of the catwalks, up as high as I could see.

I landed, grabbed a wire rail, and looked down. The orphans were milling far below me in obvious confusion. How many were there? Dozens? More? I hurried along the catwalk to the part of the snatch-engines I could reach, a gleaming silver panel covered in little metal switches, and laid my hand on the metal. Poof, gone, sent away to the desert.

I only realized I'd left Wisp down at the bottom of the shaft when he came flying up at me—he was fast, but the orphans noticed him and changed direction, swarming back up the engines, apparently oblivious to the cracklings of electricity or the ventings of scalding steam. No problem, though—I'd just jump *higher.*

When I landed on the next catwalk, two orphans came surging out of the shadows, one an iridescent crab thing, one like a wild boar with eyestalks and open sores filled with teeth. They were on me before I could think, so I just reached out and *shoved*, making the boar disappear—and amazingly not losing a finger to the snapping mouths in its side. I had the good sense *not* to send it to Earth, but instead to the reservoir we'd traveled beneath days before. I suspected if I sent the royal orphans off the Nex, their brothers and sisters would just bring them back immediately with the snatch-engines, but as long as I sent them elsewhere here at the linchpin of the universe, they were unsnatchable.

Seeing what happened to its sibling, the crab-thing hesitated. "Hi," I said. "Maybe you've heard of me. I'm Miranda Candle. I punch people so hard they *disappear*."

I don't know if it understood me or not, but it sure acted pissed-off. It whipped a leg around and hit me on the hip, and went poof as soon as it did, sent to the water with its brother—sister—sibling. I could get used to this.

More orphans reached me, though, crawling onto the catwalk, and I did little short hopping teleports, ending up behind them, beside them, above them, below them, and punching them all away. Nice. Jump-fu. Even with all my hopping, though, the catwalk was soon crowded with gnashing snarling things, and I started to freak out at the way they were pressing in. I touched the catwalk itself and sent it away, and me and all the orphans fell toward the distant floor, suddenly unsupported—except I just jumped up to the next level.

Where there were more orphans. And where I discovered that the jump-engine did a lot of things, but it didn't give me endless energy. I was getting tired, and the nasty beasts just kept coming. I revised my estimate of their numbers from dozens to hundreds and reserved the right to go up from there. The ring on my finger was pulsing with heat, and I wondered if it was possible for me to burn the engine out—if, because I was part of the engine, I might burn *myself* out.

Wisp was trying to help—he possessed the body of one of the bigger orphans, a gorilla-like thing armored in bony plates, with a head covered in long curved beaks, and he turned on the other orphans, knocking them away. But he barely made a dent—and then something bizarre happened. A big scratched-up clear plastic box just *appeared*, popping into empty air from nowhere, surrounding Wisp completely. His motes spewed out of the orphan and bumped into the plastic, but couldn't seem to escape, and I couldn't reach him to send the box away because of the pressure of attacking orphans. The one mote in my ear said, "Miranda, I'm trapped! It's airtight! The orphan I possessed will suffocate, but—I don't think the others *care*."

That's when it started raining stuff. Tires. Buckets. Rocks, rocks, and more rocks. Sheets of scrap metal. Even, for real, an *anvil*. All appearing in bursts of light from the air itself, then falling, victims of gravity. The orphans were snatching *stuff* from other worlds and throwing it down on me. It took all my attention to jump and dodge away from injury. I tried to stay close to the main parts of the engines, because the orphans seemed reluctant to drop heavy junk on delicate machinery, but the little monsters wised up and started guarding the engine more closely, clinging to its surfaces and lashing and slashing at me wherever I appeared. I wasn't hurting them anymore, wasn't sending pieces of the snatch-engine away, wasn't even holding my own.

One time, I zigged when I should have zagged, and a splintery hunk of wood hit my shoulder, knocking me from a catwalk into empty space, and I screamed, too shocked from the pain and the surprise to consciously jump to a place of safety. My automatic self-preservation circuits must have kicked in, because I jumped—

—and found myself back in one of the palace's faintly glowing corridors. I rubbed my aching shoulder and sat on the floor, closing my eyes, wondering what to do next. The engines were too much for me. Maybe with Howlaa in there to help fight the orphans I could have gotten somewhere, but alone? Without even Wisp, anymore?

The walls rippled and opened, revealing another oval-shaped passageway, this one leading downward. "What now? Whatever you want me to do, Miss Palace, I don't think I can manage it."

The light in the walls pulsed rapidly, and I sighed. "I'm going. I hope there's a bed and a buffet down there." I walked along for ages, until my legs got tired, then just started short-hop teleporting as far down the sloping corridor as I could see. Eventually the steep downward slope leveled off and the hallway widened until I encountered metal gates set into the reddened infected flesh of the palace.

But these gates weren't the size of doors. Not even garage-door sized. Not even loading-dock door sized. These doors were three or four stories high, huge bolt-studded metal walls without visible hinges, shut with girder-sized crossbars lumpily welded across the seam. Whatever these doors were meant to hold in was big, and someone really didn't want it getting out. But that wasn't the scariest part.

The scariest parts were all the dents bulging outward, where something on the other side had obviously been pounding on the door trying to get out.

"I'm supposed to go in *there*?"

The palace walls pulsed. I sighed, put my hand on the metal, and stepped through.

And through, and through, and through. It took at least five big steps—the doors were incredibly thick.

Once I emerged on the other side, I couldn't even comprehend what I saw. The snatch-engines had been overwhelming, but they were made up of recognizable things, metal and glass and electricity and machine parts. Now I was in a cathedral-sized space, filled with towering pillars, and bound to those pillars by metal chains was—was—

A whale turned inside-out. A tumor the size of a skyscraper, all pulsing with veins and sprouting weird floral growths that opened and closed and bobbed like flowers in a breeze. A great bulbous shifting thing that moved in and out like a beating heart, that seemed to sigh and breathe.

The air inside the room was humid, like a sauna, and the pillars and chains were slick with moisture. The smell, under the heat, was like a fresh-turned compost heap. The chains—which disappeared *into* the thing, anchored inside that nasty mass of flesh—rattled as it shifted around. I couldn't tell if it was an animal or a plant or something completely different, but it was definitely alive.

The thing moved, body convulsing, and a horrible face started to appear deep in the parting folds, mouth a wet hole, eyes all milky white and red-rimmed, and I realized it was straining against its chains, *reaching for me*.

>A visitor.< The voice was inside my head, almost like my own thoughts, but with a dead monotone delivery I'd only heard inside my mind at my most depressed. >It's been so long since I had a visitor. Come to me.<

I jumped, blindly, just aiming to get somewhere safe.

Chapter 14

I landed in my own backyard.

It was night in Pomegranate Grove, and I wondered how many days had passed, if time went by the same way here as it did on the Nex, and fantasized that maybe only a few hours had gone by here… but the apple tree, in bloom when I left, had lost all its blossoms, and the moon was fatter than before, so I knew at least a few days had gone by. The windows in my house were dark, and I decided it was worth the risk to get some clean clothes and some food from the kitchen before returning to the Nex to do… whatever I could do.

I was really happy to see home, and surprised at myself for being happy. Being away is fun—at least until everything starts to fail and fall apart—but part of the fun of being away is having a home to come back to, maybe.

Tempting as it was just to go sleep in my own bed and accept the inevitable grounding—or worse—that I'd get in the morning when Mom found me, I knew I couldn't stay. For one thing, there was Dad, maybe still alive out there. For another, there was Howlaa and Wisp, who were now *both* captured, because of me. And then there was the Regent. I didn't like him, and didn't want him to win.

Besides, he could reach me with his snatch-engines here, and I didn't think I'd done nearly enough damage to disable those things, even temporarily. The Regent would drag me back to the Nex if I tried to stay, because I had something he wanted. I *was* something he wanted. Wisp and Howlaa's revolution wasn't the great good thing I'd originally imagined—not even really a revolution at all—but now that I had the jump-engine, I had as much reason as they did to want the Regent kicked out of power.

I jumped to the dark of the pantry, surrounded by shelves packed with canned food and dry goods in plastic pest-proof tubs. Mom bought massive quantities of stuff from the warehouse store every month. She'd gotten into hoarding after Dad died, trying to make us feel more secure I guess, even though she hardly cooked. I listened at the door and heard only silence in the kitchen, so I eased the pantry door open and slipped out. There was a light on over the stove, but the rest of the house was dark, Mom and her dumb boyfriend and Cal all asleep upstairs. I went to the fridge and opened it up, wondering what I could eat that wouldn't be missed. It was full of take-out containers—no shock—and I found a box of mu shu pork, which I'm always happy to eat cold. I opened a drawer as quietly as I could and pulled out a couple of chopsticks. The thought of sitting in my own kitchen and having a meal, even a cold greasy take-out meal, was amazing.

After I sat down, I heard a tap-ratt-tat-tap.

I knew the sound. Drumsticks rattling on walls or tables or whatever. My brother Cal is a drummer, and he carries drumsticks with him every-where, rapping on everything he passes—he says he's practicing, but I think he's just equal parts obsessive and annoying. He's in a crappy garage band called Feral Sex Herd. The sound of his tap-tapping made me think of Dad, which was kind of weird, but not really—he's the one who got Cal his first drum kit, and he said drummers can always get gigs, because every teenage kid in the world plays guitar, but there aren't that many decent drummers.

The tap-tapping got louder, and I almost jumped away… but I was so tired of jumping, of running, and maybe I even kind of missed my stupid brother, so I just waited to see what would happen.

Cal came into the kitchen, dressed in boxer shorts and nothing else—he's so gross—and stared at me. "Randy." His bushy eyebrows, just like Dad's, went up and down. "You're eating my breakfast."

"Sorry." I ate another mouthful.

"What the hell happened to your hair?"

I ran my hand through the purple stubble and winced. "The dye's only temporary."

"Uh huh. And why are you dressed like you're in a third-grade dance recital?"

I looked down at my unitard and shrugged. "Didn't have a ton of op-tions. I was going to change."

Cal leaned against the counter, drumsticks tapping on his thighs. "Mom's sleeping in your bed. If you go in there she'll jump on you and never let go."

I winced. "She's pissed."

Cal snorted. "She thinks you're on drugs living under a freeway in Atlanta having sex with strangers for crack. But when she sees you *here*, yeah, she'll go from being scared to being pissed off."

"Didn't she get my note?"

"Yep. Not your best idea, sis. Leaving a note that doesn't make sense on the kitchen table. Mom just flipped out even more knowing you'd been in the house and she'd missed you. That's when she started sleeping in your bed every night. She keeps saying she should've gotten one of those GPS tracker things for your cell phone, which she's been calling every hour on the hour. She can't even get your voicemail."

"Yeah, the phone's been… not working." *Way out of range*, I thought. *Seriously roaming.*

"So where *have* you been? And how much did you get for the necklace?"

I frowned. "What?"

"The necklace you stole from me, I figured you must've pawned it or something, gone on a shopping spree with Jenny Kay. Except she swears she hasn't seen you, and she's worried too. I was *almost* worried about you myself. Anyway, however much money you got, you owe it to me now."

"The necklace wasn't yours either, Cal."

He stopped drumming and crossed his arms. "I bought it. For Clarissa."

Cal's skanky on-again-off-again girlfriend, who everyone knew was really in love with Brandon, the singer in his band, and just hung out with Cal to get close to him. I shook my head. "Right. If you had that kind of money you'd spend it on cymbals or something. Where'd you really find it?"

I'll say this for me and Cal, there's never been a lot of bullcrap between us. He shrugged. "It was just glittering in the dirt out by the fairgrounds. Some rich lady must have dropped it. Finder's keepers, though, Randy."

"I didn't pawn it. I traded it. For this ring." I held out my hand.

"What's that, gold? Randy, that necklace had diamonds on it." He frowned. "Or emeralds? I can't remember."

Because it changed.

"Anyway, you got cheated," he said. "But we can work out some kind of compensation plan, right? Now that you're back, you can start doing my chores for me—"

I just laughed. "Or what? You'll tell Mom I stole the necklace you stole first? You think she'll believe your 'I found it in the dirt' thing?"

"Because you're the trustworthy one, runaway? Please. You're at the top of mom's shitlist. And you don't want to get any farther onto my bad side. I was gonna let you sleep on the couch and deal with Mom in the morning, but I can go wake her up now, if you want."

I shook my head. "I'm not staying, Cal. I just stopped by for a little while. I have to go back out again."

"Are you crazy? Miranda, you're *thirteen*. You can't leave home and, like, seek your fortune. If Mom finds out you were here and I let you go, she'll kill me." His eyebrows went up again. "You *aren't* on drugs, or mixed up in… anything like that… are you? I didn't think you were that dumb. I mean, a little weed, sure, but anything more—"

"No, it's nothing like that. Just don't tell Mom I was here. You never saw me."

"No way, Randy. I don't know what's going on with you, but if you're in some kind of trouble, let Mom help. And if you're not in some kind of trouble yet, you will be. It's not like I never cut a class, but you've missed days of school—miss too many more, and you'll be screwed. You like middle school so much you want to stay an extra year?"

"Cal. I think Dad is still alive."

He came to the table slowly, sat down across from me, and put his drumsticks aside. "Randy. Dad's dead."

"They never found his body. What if he… if something whacked him in the head and he got amnesia or something, and just wandered away from the explosion?"

"You're telling me you've been out looking for Dad? What… *why*?"
"I can't explain right now. But trust me—I'll know for sure soon."

"This is crazy, Randy. I think somebody's scamming you, trying to use you, I don't know what, but there's no way Dad survived. There was nothing left of the restaurant but a hole in the ground."

I didn't dare take Cal to the Nex—no reason to bring him to the Regent's attention, plus he'd waste my time by freaking out—but I wished I could show him *something*. Any demonstration of my new power would just lead to more questions, though, and there's no easy way to say, "Well, there's this other universe, only it's actually *outside* the universe, and it's full of monsters, only they're mostly just people like us, and oh yeah, I'm the last free member of a revolutionary force…" So I fell back on, "Just trust me. I'll be back in a couple of days."

"Cal? Honey, who are you talking to?"

I stiffened at Mom's voice—she was calling from the living room, and I heard her approaching footsteps. When Cal twisted in his chair to answer her, I took advantage of the moment and jumped to my own bedroom.

I heard distant shouting in the kitchen—I guess it had to do with me being there, then suddenly *not*—so I hurried past my rumpled bed to the closet. I had a pretty serious privacy-invasion pang at the thought of Mom in my room, going through my stuff, probably trying to read my e-mail (fortunately my friend Jenny Kay set up some sweet encryption so I could keep my secrets). But there was nothing I could do about that now. I opened the closet and grabbed my go-bag. That was another of Mom's post-Dad life changes, forcing us all to put together little overnight bags to grab in case of fire or terrorist attack or natural disaster, with changes of clothes and nasty dry granola bars and other stuff like that. I scooped up the bag, paused to listen to the ongoing yelling, then sighed. I went to my desk, scribbled a quick note with a sharpie on a piece of printer paper, and left it on the pillow. "Mom—sorry—love you—home soon—don't worry." I didn't think it would help, but it probably wouldn't hurt.

I looked around the room, at the pictures thumbtacked to the walls, my bed, my vanity, my bookshelves, and wished I could stay. Who would've thought I'd miss home? A few nights sleeping in birds nests and lengths of pipe made home seem pretty inviting, even with Mom's dumb boyfriend there half the time.

I jumped back to the Nex, to a corridor deep in the palace, near the big gates that held back the humongous icky *thing* I'd found before.

Going home had actually given me some ideas about what to do next. Maybe I was relying on the jump-engine too much. Cal banged his drumsticks on everything, because to a drummer, everything looks like a drum. To a teleporter, everything looks like a job for teleportation. The problem was, Wisp and Howlaa and me had been calling this thing of ours a revolution, but it wasn't—it was just a jailbreak. The jump-engine could help with a jailbreak, maybe, but a revolution took more than three people with some badass powers. A *real* revolution needed a plan more complicated than punching people until they disappeared.

I'd realized something else at home, or maybe not so much realized as hoped. Hearing Mom's voice made me think about mothers in general, how mothers would supposedly do anything for their kids—whether their kids wanted them to or not. So I got to wondering…

I went to the big metal gates, stepped through them again, and faced the warty gelatinous mountain of flesh chained up on the other side.

"Hey," I said. "Your majesty?"

>*Yes*<, the Queen of Nexington-on-Axis replied.

Chapter 15

Talking to the Queen of Nexington-on-Axis, mother of the royal orphans, secretly imprisoned rightful ruler of the world outside all possible worlds, was pretty freaky. She didn't think in straight lines like a person does, and she didn't always answer my questions in a way that made sense, but after an hour of her dropping images and words into my brain while I ate granola bars and sipped old bottled water, I kind of got the gist. It wasn't much like the story the Regent had told me, but I got the feeling the Queen wouldn't even know how to lie.

The Regent had gained her trust years before, and promised to stop all the various denizens of the Nex from attacking the palace and trying to kill her family (which apparently happened a lot in the old days, which was how a couple of her husbands died). It was a pretty simple deal: He was the public face of the government, and in exchange, the Queen and Kings waited until the citizens died before harvesting any interesting body parts for their own use, and they'd occasionally steal things to help the Regent improve the city, build sewers, homes, enough food, stuff like that. I got the idea the Queen didn't give two craps about the other people living on the Nex, and was happy to let the Regent deal with their problems. The city-state grew, the snatch-engines got fancier, and everything was great. But over the years, all the Queen's husbands sickened and died, and she realized she didn't have anyone left to mate with, and her children were the only children she was going to have for a while… until some of the kids grew up enough to mate with her, which was going to take like hundreds of years.

I know. Totally gross. But they aren't human, and they do things differently than humans do.

>*And then the Regent told me he had killed all my husbands, using subtle poisons and radiations,*< the queen said. >*He told me this while his*

army of Nagalinda and other fierce creatures held my children in a single vast room of the palace, ready to be gassed and burned and flattened. He said he would kill all but the handful of my children he needed to keep the snatch-engines functioning... unless I agreed to this imprisonment, to let everyone believe I was dead, to cede all authority to him. I had no choice. They are my children. I have been here ever since.<

"Why didn't he just kill you?"

>I am the heart of the Nexus. I have always been, and always will be. I am the observer that collapses the probability wave of this improbable world, and allows the Nexus to exist at all. This place is the linchpin of all universes, and I am the linchpin of this place. I cannot be killed, any more than mathematics or entropy or space itself can be killed. I am eternal. And I have been patient.< The queen paused. *>I knew you would come. Or someone like you.<*

Oh, well. I'd never exactly been the Chosen One, but I was the one who showed up, so I got the job.

>Though I did not anticipate it would take this long.<

"How long has it been?"

>Ninety-one thousand, three hundred and sixty-five cycles of the sun.<

I blinked. Math isn't my strongest suit, but back home there are 365 days in a year, and the days here are just a little shorter than days on Earth, so.... more than two hundred *years*? "But the Regent's human! How did he live so long?"

>He found a way to configure the snatch-engines to steal years from the lifespans of other creatures, just a year here or there, but they pile up into forevers. He wishes to be eternal, as I am.<

"If I can find a way to stop the Regent... to protect your children, and free you... what will happen to the people left here, when you're running things again? I don't want them to be hurt."

>If someone else wishes to govern, I will allow it, though I will not allow them into my palace. I will have to take safeguards to ensure this<—she rattled her chains—*>doesn't happen again.<*

I sighed. The whole thing was maybe possible, but it was going to be hard. "I wish I could get Howlaa and Wisp back to help me."

>Then why don't you? With your technology, you can go anywhere.<

"Yeah, but I have to know where I'm *going*."

>Ah. I know the whereabouts of all things in this place. It is my nature to know the location and velocity of every particle in the Nexus. I have been watching your comings and goings with great interest.<

"Whoa, so you know where *Howlaa* is?"

>*Wait.*<

The queen did something I can't quite describe—imagine an ice-cold finger giving you a wet willie, only instead of sticking the finger in your ear, it goes into your *brain*. I knew she could get into my mind, since she was *talking* to my mind directly, but it was weird having my brain rifled through. And I thought my Mom going through my drawers was an invasion of privacy.

>*Ah, this one, the shifting one, yes, I know it. I will show.*<

I got this picture in my head, but not a picture, more a full sensory thing, like a memory, with sounds (buzzing, clanging) and smell (antiseptic) to go with the sight (a chrome-shiny room with a big table in the middle, and strapped to the table, something that writhed). I didn't just see it, I knew where it *was*, in one of those orbital pleasure palaces—which apparently included a lot of unpleasant rooms too.

I could go there. I could get Howlaa out.

"What about Wisp?"

Another brain-rifling, which I was at least braced for this time. >*Mostly here,*< the queen said, and showed me a glass bubble in the same orbital palace, this one full of motes. >*But partly in your ear.*<

I touched my earlobe, remembering the mote Wisp had put there to whisper to me—I guessed he was too far away to talk to me now, but it was kind of comforting, in a weird way, to know a little bit of him was still with me.

I finally asked what I most wanted to ask: "Is my Dad here?"

Another brain touch, another image: a bare room in a deep part of the palace, and my Dad—oh, my Dad, looking a little pudgier but otherwise just the same—pacing back and forth on the little patch of floor beside the bed, head down, frowning. He was alive. He was here. I could save him. I could take him *home*.

>*The Regent will expect you to try and save them. He will have surveillance. He will have snipers. He is waiting for you, Miranda. Do not doubt that.*<

I chewed my lip and did some thinking. I wanted to charge in and save them all, send Dad right back to our living room, break out Howlaa and Wisp, and go in after the Regent… but if I got captured, knocked unconscious and unhooked from the engine, we were all screwed. "I don't think I can do this by myself. I mean… I think the only way to make it happen is to start a revolution." The whole idea was too big, too overwhelming. I'd never organized anything more complicated than a sleepover—how was I supposed to start an uprising?

But the Queen… she'd run this place for who knows how long. Maybe she could help with the planning. I could go anywhere, and she knew where everything *was*, and between the two of us, maybe we could move the world.

>*We will need allies,*< the Queen said.

"Okay. So where do you think I should start?"

She had some pretty big ideas.

I went to the Machine Waste first, because without the steam colossus, our plan—okay, mostly the Queen's plan, but I helped, and the basic *idea* was mine—would fall apart. I jumped from the palace to the radio telescope and opened up my bag, looking for a change of clothes. Even though the Queen was as far from human as Wisp, I still would have felt funny stripping in front of her, but out here in a desert of broken machinery I was less concerned—there might be prying eyes, but they weren't any more interested in my body than a toaster would be. I pulled on an Allison Wonderland concert t-shirt and corduroy pants with frayed bottoms and stuffed my Minion of Mab outfit into the bag. Being in my own clothes again did wonders for my mood. I stood up, cupped my hands around my mouth, and said "Colossus! We need to talk!"

I expected another earth-shaking appearance of the giant machine-god itself, probably rising up from the ground right in front of me, but nothing happened. I figured the boss of the junk-realm had to be listening in on all his territory, so did that mean he was ignoring me, or sneaking up on me, or what?

A skittery mechanical thing came up over the side of the dish, like the horn of an old-fashioned phonograph with a bunch of mechanical crab legs. It rushed at me, and I got ready to jump in case that horn on top was really a cannon or something, but it stopped a couple of feet away, and a scratchy mechanical voice emerged: "Ah, the girl with the jump-engine. Come to sacrifice your body to science?"

The steam colossus's voice was a lot less disturbing when it wasn't highly-amplified super-thunder loud, so I kicked at the colossus's (literally) mobile phone, and it scuttled out of my reach. "I'm here to make a deal with you."

"What do you have to offer me, apart from your vivisected body and the technology therein?"

"I can send you back home," I said.

There was a hiss of dead-air static from the phonograph. Then the steam colossus said, "We should talk in closer physical proximity."

"Why, so you can snatch me up?"

"No, because remote transmissions like this one can be intercepted."

"All right. But if I even think I'm in danger, poof, I'm gone. Where are you?"

"Look to the horizon, in front of you, do you see the platform?"

Off in the distance a structure listed at an angle on spindly legs. "Yeah."

"Jump there."

I focused, I thought, and I jumped, landing on the platform without so much as a wobble. The platform was a rusty, greasy thing of bolted-together slabs of metal, maybe an offshore oil rig or something picked up and dropped in the midst of a field of busted computer monitors.

"PREPARE FOR DESCENT," a voice said from hidden speakers, and the platform shuddered and started to sink. I looked around for something to grab onto and clutched a pole that wasn't too corroded. The platform sank down pretty fast into a hidden shaft, and lights came on at the top of the poles, so I could watch the rock walls slide up past me. After a couple of minutes the platform settled, and I walked off it into a mineshaft tunnel, up a metal ramp, and into what looked like the control room of a spaceship from a science fiction movie. The walls were covered with lights and dials, and a huge glass-and-metal cylinder stood in the middle of the room, with a pulsing floating ball of yellow-gray goop bobbing at the center.

"Welcome to my brain," the steam colossus said, voice coming from the ceiling.

"Hello, brain. So I'm inside your body now?"

"A rare privilege. Only one other human has ever been here—the Regent."

"You made a deal with him, too. What was it? I mean, why didn't you squish him and throw him against a wall when you attacked the palace all those years ago?"

"I see you've been educating yourself in the history of Nexington-on-Axis. The Regent offered me… certain resources, and an autonomous region to rule under my own authority."

"The Machine Waste."

"I sometimes refer to the rest of this cursed place as the Flesh Waste, so I suppose that name is fair."

"So you get all the junk you can use and a place to build more things like yourself in exchange for behaving yourself? And occasionally playing the tough guy on the Regent's behalf?" I sat down with my back against one of the wall panels, because I was tired of standing up and looking at the ceiling.

"In theory. Though the Regent doesn't fulfill all my requests for equipment. He's been hesitant to provide me with sufficient quantities of radioactive material, and he limits my energy sources rather brutally. I think he's afraid I'm going to do something drastic. Which, of course, I *am*. It's just going to take a while at current rates of development. I'd rather assumed I would outlive the Regent in short order, but he's oddly persistent for a fleshthing."

"You don't have any loyalty to the guy, then."

"Loyalty? The concept is meaningless to me."

"Good. Because I'd like to kick him out of his job."

The steam colossus chuckled. "And replace him with who? You? Your friend Howlaa?"

"Nope. The Queen of Nexington-on-Axis."

Another silence. "My voice analysis suggests you believe what you're saying. You have reason to think the Queen yet lives?"

"I talked to her earlier today."

"That is interesting. And improbable, but this is an improbable place. Tell me, then—what is your plan?"

I considered holding back, but if the steam colossus wanted to betray me I was doomed anyway—this couldn't work without his help. So I told him what the Queen and I had worked out.

"Your plan has numerous flaws," it said. "There are many choices governed by emotional demands rather than rational strategic ones. The whole is also rather complex, and complexity can be a problem—the more moving parts a system has, the more prone it is to failure."

I snorted. "You're telling me my plan has too many moving parts? You're a giant steam-powered robot the size of a skyscraper. Hello, kettle? This is pot: you're black!"

"Your colloquialism is tiresome, but your point is taken—sometimes complexity is necessary, and if you insist on the various rescues and repatriations you've described, I suppose such curlicues are unavoidable."

"You think you'd be able to pull off your part of the plan?"

"With negligible effort. The question is whether I will *bother*. You've demonstrated an ability to teleport, but that doesn't mean you're capable of sending *me* back to the place where I'm from. It is an unimaginably distant galaxy."

"I'm sure it is, but from here, all places are equally unimaginably distant, right? I can do it."

"Then take me there now. Prove it."

"No way." The idea was too dangerous. The jump-engine protected me to an extent, but if the steam colossus got what it wanted, it might do its best to kill me, and maybe it could act faster than my jump-engine could respond. I was safe now because the steam colossus wanted to use me, but if I was no longer useful… "But I can send something else. Like a probe, maybe? You were a spaceship, so you must have stuff like that."

"I do, but assuming you can send such a thing to my home space, how do you propose to bring it back? I presume you don't have access to the snatch-engines."

"No, I'll need to be able to lay hands on the probe to bring it back here, which means I'm going to have to go with it." I didn't find the prospect of space travel all that exciting—it always sounded uncomfortable to me, unlike Jenny Kay, who talks about wanting to become a scientist so she can take a trip to the International Space Station or even a Mars base someday. But you do what you have to.

"That will require a probe capable of containing you, and sustaining your life—oxygen, pressure… This will take a little time."

"A little time on my kind of scale, or on yours? Because if you're talking an hour, I'll wait, but if you're talking *months*…."

"Closer to the former. Tell me, how do you propose to reach my galaxy, when you have never been there? I assume the jump-engine has *some* limitations."

"I can tell it to go places based on coordinates."

"Coordinates? That explanation is meaningless. Nexington-on-Axis exists outside the rest of the multiverse, and 'coordinates' are by nature relative, not absolute—they describe the location of a place in relation to *other* places."

"Yeah, it's complicated," I said. "But the Queen is a whiz when it comes to navigation, and she can tell me where to go. She's got a perfect memory of where everything on Nexington-on-Axis came from, and where it is *now*, and she can look for stuff outside, too. How do you think the snatch-engines work? They couldn't grab specific stuff without some way to program the engines, to guide them. The Queen and her kids all have this ability, to know where stuff is." The Queen said they "extrapolated from the original velocities of the moments of creation" but I didn't know exactly what that meant so I didn't repeat it.

"Extraordinary," the steam colossus said. "If you can deliver on your promise, you will be the least useless and objectionable fleshthing I have ever encountered."

"I think you're kind of mean and scary, personally, but you're really freaking big and insanely strong, and that's all I need you to be. So we can help each other. Look, I'm going to take a nap. Wake me when you're ready to go probing."

Something poked me in the ribs, and when I sat up I was face-to-nosecone with a sleek teardrop-shaped thing in gleaming red and black, a little bigger than a coffin, standing on a dozen of those spindly spider-legs the steam colossus seemed to like. It had half a dozen extending multi-jointed arms, one of which had poked me.

"Your chariot awaits," the steam colossus said.

The probe dropped its belly to the floor and the lid slid open with a hiss, revealing a red leather-padded area inside, in a space just about as big as me.

"That looks… claustrophobically cozy."

"It suits your physical parameters. Get in."

"How long should I stay… wherever we're going?"

"The probe will be able to confirm its location using certain astro-nomical landmarks almost instantly, so you needn't stay long. I thought of simply sending you unprotected—you could probably maintain con-sciousness for almost ten seconds if you were exposed to the vacuum of space, which would be ample time for you to take the probe and return. But I suppose you'd be upset if your eardrums burst from the pressure inequality, so I took the trouble of creating a pressurized cabin for you. There won't be more than a few minutes of air, so don't linger."

I climbed into the probe, settling down on the soft cushions, and the lid slid closed over me. "Hey, it's pitch black in here!" I pounded on the lid.

"Yes?"

"How am I supposed to see?"

"Why do you need to see? The probe will see."

I sighed. So much for witnessing a vista never seen before by human eyes and all that. I tried to relax, to pretend I was snuggled in a bed in the dark, but it was hard to forget I was in a metal shell about to be floating in the emptiness of insanely distant space. "I'm ready."

"Then do whatever it is you do."

I placed my hands on the inside of the probe and thought about the string of letters and numbers the Queen had taught me, the coordinates of the place where the steam colossus was snatched. She assured me the jump-engine would understand the coordinate system, since the royal orphans had helped develop that device—it was the same system the snatch-engines used. I'd memorized the coordinates like a little song, and I hummed it under my breath a few times, and then I jumped.

The probe lurched a little, then… nothing. Just hanging there smoothly. I couldn't see or hear anything. "Are we there?" I said. Nothing and nobody answered. After a few more seconds I put my hands back out and jumped us to the steam colossus's brain chamber.

For a moment nothing happened, and I was afraid the jump-engine had failed, that I was stuck in a padded coffin in the depths of space—and then the lid slid back, and I climbed out, in one piece.

"Well?" the steam colossus said.

"Well what?"

"Not *you*," it said, and the probe began to speak.

I thought it would just say "Location confirmed" in a robot voice or something, but the probe's voice was high-pitched and awed. It said "A Wolf-Rayet star shedding mass and venting gases. A globular cluster ringed with blue stragglers. In the distance, a barred spiral galaxy and a dark matter halo. A symbiotic variable star system. An array of galaxies all around them, filaments and voids, filaments and voids."

"And the quark star?" The steam colossus's voice was tense.

"The quark star," the probe said breathlessly. (I guess literally since it has no breath, but it *sounded* breathless.) "Oh, yes, the quark star, the strange star, exotic matter, dark matter. It is there."

"We have an agreement, fleshthing," the steam colossus said. "I will help you, and when we're done, you'll send me back."

"Glad to hear it."

"If you try to cheat me—"

I interrupted. "Please. You freak me out. Why would I want to keep you around, especially if you're all pissed-off from being lied to?" I jumped back to the palace to tell the Queen we were on.

Chapter 16

So then I did the rest of my visitations.

First, I put on my Minion of Mab outfit again, even though it was bedraggled and the wings were droopy, and jumped where the Queen told me—to Fairyland-on-Axis. Apparently it had started life as a warehouse, but the Mablings had turned it into a pretty awesome place. The minions had hauled in tons of dirt and planted trees and bushes and flowers, creating an indoor forest, filled with trees hung with gauzy colorful streamers, mushrooms so huge and perfectly round they looked fake, and even artificial waterfalls. I blended in well enough to walk among the diligent Mablings, who were up on ladders cleaning skylights, on the ground digging in flowerbeds, and up in branches hanging tinkling crystal ornaments. The place was a hippie's dream, and after a little walking I found the white canvas tent where the Mab reigned over her flock. There were Mablings kneeling and bowing all around the open-sided tent, and I stepped around and over them until I got a look at the Mab herself.

She was model-beautiful, blonde, blue-eyed, and dressed all in green, in a low-cut outfit that looked made of living leaves. Her wings were huge, filling the tent, prismatic like a dragonfly's, and her expression was super bored.

"Hey, lady," I said. "You and me need to talk in private."

She stared at me, flicked her fingers, and a couple of the Mablings kneeling at her feet stood up. They were holding pointy swords, fencing foils I guess, and they came at me from either side.

I reached into my bag and pulled out the flower the Queen had sent me to retrieve from the land of mist and mirrors—a green and grassy place full of fog and distant howlings. The flower had red and yellow and blue petals arrayed around a black center, and when she saw it, the Mab gasped. "Out, all of you out, and close the tent!" she shouted, standing up from her throne of branches and water-smoothed rocks.

The Mabling were nothing if not obedient, and they hustled out, pulling ropes to let the sides of the tent fall down as they left. Soon it was just me and the Mab in her torchlit audience chamber, and she rushed at me, snatching the flower from my hand and shoving it into her mouth, chewing it seriously and slowly with her eyes closed, finally shuddering as she swallowed the last gulp. "Years," she murmured. "It's been years… Did the snatch-engines bring it? Do you have more?"

"I can get more," I said. "But wouldn't you rather go back to the source? Head back home?"

She narrowed her eyes. "Fairyland is forever closed to me."

I shook my head. "You and I both know I didn't get that flower from Fairyland, lady. And we both know you aren't a lady. You might fool these girls, but not me. I'll be right back."

I jumped to the land of mist and mirrors. I couldn't see two feet in front of me from the thick fog, the air stank of something harsh and astringent, and the noises were terrible but, fortunately, distant. A patch of the weird flowers grew at my feet, and I plucked another before jumping back.

"Here you go," I said, holding it out, and the Mab grabbed it and did the whole closed-eye-devouring thing again. I talked while she ate. "I can get there, and I can take *you* there… unless you'd rather stay here?"

"If I never see another human girl in wings, it will be too soon," the Mab said. "But I assume you don't offer me this escape as a *kindness*?"

"No. I need a favor first. And it's kind of a weird one…"

I went to see Clan Kil'howlaa next, which wasn't originally part of my plan, but the Queen said it would be a good idea. I was like, "But there's only one of them left, and she speaks *German*."

>You still have a mote of the Bodiless in your ear,< she said. >Use it.<

So that's how I came to be in a tunnel in the dark next to a statue of a horse made of poo, holding a single mote of my friend Wisp's cloud in the palm of my hand. I wished the mote could allow me to talk to Wisp, but he was too far away, or something—there was still a connection, and the mote would still translate for me, but communication with the rest of him wasn't possible.

"English to German, and German to English, okay?" The mote just sort of floated there, not quite touching my palm, like it was subtly repulsed by my physical body. I had no idea if this would work or not. I cleared my throat. "Hey!" I yelled, and the mote in my hand shouted "Achtung!"

The new head of Clan Kil'howlaa emerged, and I spoke to her quickly before she could try to stab me, told her I wasn't working with Wisp and Howlaa anymore, and that I wanted to overthrow the Regent. She was pretty cool about it. The Regent was the one she really hated, since he was the one who'd *sent* Howlaa to the caves to do all those horrible things originally… and, she assumed, this last time, too. I didn't bother to correct her. I felt bad being deceitful, but not too bad, since she *had* punched me in the nose.

"But what can I do?" she asked. "My family is dead, my people gone… how can I help?"

"The god-worms," I said. "You believe one is still alive, right?"

"So I was taught. Deep, asleep, in hibernation, far below ground."

That's what the Queen had told me—most of the god-worms had died in the inhospitable atmosphere of Nexington-on-Axis, but one had crawled into the depths, collapsed the tunnel after it, slowed its metabolism, and gone to sleep. "Can you wake it up?" I asked.

"There is a ritual," she said doubtfully. "It requires all the voices of all the clans speaking as one, which was never possible before, as many were loath to trouble the god… but I am the last of us. Only my voice remains. Perhaps I would be sufficient."

"Then do it. When the Regent is gone, you won't have to live in these tunnels anymore." Seeing the look on her face, I said, "Unless you *want* to. But no one will try to kill you anymore. At least, nobody from the government. Okay?"

"What should I say to the god, if it deigns to hear me?" She trembled a little, freaked out by the idea of talking to her god.

I hoped the god-worm would answer, though I worried the "ritual" was just wishful thinking. The god-worm's presence wasn't strictly necessary, but it would really help. "Here's what you say," I began.

I jumped to Merrill's creepy farmhouse, right to the midst of his inner sanctum, since Howlaa said he liked to booby-trap the place in case of visitors from the Regent. Merrill was asleep in a recliner with a newspaper written in Greek or something open across his chest. At least, I thought he was asleep until I noticed the nose of the shotgun pointing at me from under the newspaper. I held up my hands. "I come in peace."

He grunted. "You were here with Howlaa. How'd you get in without triggering my alarms?"

"I'm good at getting in and out of places." I jumped right behind him, leaning over the chair and grinning down into his shocked face. His breath smelled like rubbing alcohol and moldy peaches, so I didn't stay that close for long. "I can get *you* out of this place, too."

"Oh yeah? What makes you think I want to go anywhere?" "I'm talking about sending you *home*. Back to Earth."

He snorted. "The Earth I come from isn't a place you'd want to go back to, kid. I don't think it's the same one you're from, unless you were indentured as a duct-cleaner to the Cog Lords? I spent all my days servicing the machinery of our clockwork overlords. Being enslaved to a *human* like the Regent is actually a step up."

"So if you could go anywhere, where would you want to go?"

"Back to my apartment in the city center would be nice, with my old security clearances and access to all the equipment I could use, so I don't have to make do with the crap they left me out here in the hinterlands. I swear, you try to make a little extra money on the side peddling redundant extra parts to the cyborg community and the reaction is *all* out of proportion—"

"Look, I can guarantee you all that stuff, okay?"

He wasn't pointing the shotgun directly at me anymore, but he definitely wasn't thrilled with my company either. "How exactly are you planning to do that, little miss fugitive? I'd be better off turning you in to the Regent in exchange for the restoration of some privileges." "That would be harder than you think." I explained about the jump-engine, which required yet another demonstration of its powers. At least jumping to the city center and bringing him back a scone from the café he loved best gave me a chance to grab a cup of fancy coffee too, though I had to barter the water-purifying tablets from my emergency go-bag.

"To topple the Regent," he said, between bites of scone. "It's crazy, but so was his rise to power. What do you want from me? I can't go far without the Regent noticing—I can limit his surveillance here, but I'm pretty well boxed in."

"I just need you to provide a safe haven for some mutual friends."

I jumped back to the city center, this time to room 112 at the saloon, where Templeton was in bed being serviced by a geargirl with multiple robotic arms, wearing smoked-glass goggles and greasy overalls. She was working on one of the servos in his knees with a little welding torch. Neither noticed me at first, so I cleared my throat. She stood, turned up the flame on her torch, and stepped toward me, pincer-ended arms fanning out in a scary array.

"It's all right." Templeton propped himself up in the bed, which had to be reinforced with metal or something to hold his weight. "She's a friend of an acquaintance."

The geargirl shrugged, turned off the torch, and stepped out into the hallway.

"The rumor is Howlaa got snatched at a restaurant not far from here. Guess you got away? Not surprising. You'd have to be the world's biggest idiot to get caught using the snatch-engine."

"I'm going to set Howlaa free, too."

"That's just the kind of thinking that'll get you captured. Not that I care. The inside of this room looks the same to me whether *you're* free or not."

"I'm going to stop the Regent," I said. "I have a plan."

"The plan of a thirteen-year-old girl with more power than sense? I'm sure it's *wonderful*."

I almost blurted out that it wasn't just my plan, but also the *Queen's*… except I didn't really trust Templeton. I figured he'd sell me out at the first opportunity if he thought it would help him. I got to the point. "I'm not asking you to do anything, not yet. But if things work out, and we do knock the Regent off his throne, I'll need your help with the jump-engine."

"Is it malfunctioning?"

"No, but… I'd like to be able to take it off. Preferably without dying in the process."

"Power over all of space doesn't appeal to you? You're a weird girl, Miranda."

"I didn't say I don't want it. I do, believe me. Even if my life ever goes back to normal, the ability to go places in an instant… it's pretty appealing. But I've got other priorities."

"Whatever." Templeton waved his hand at me. "If you defeat the Regent and get me out from under house arrest, sure, I'll help you with the ring. And if magical ponies come running down the street, I'll save one for you. And if I start to crap gold nuggets, I'll put aside a few for your college fund. And if I vomit rose petals, I'll—"

"Asshole," I said, and jumped away.

I landed in my bedroom. It was morning on a workday, and Mom usually left before dawn, so I made a calculated bet she wouldn't still be in my bed. She wasn't—I had the room to myself. I looked out my window, and Cal was just getting into his car in the driveway. Perfect. I waited for him to shut the door and put on his seatbelt, then jumped—I didn't want to startle him while he was driving.

I appeared in his passenger seat. "Hey, Cal."

He startled and banged his head against the roof of the car. I tried not to smirk. "Jesus, Miranda, what the hell—where did you come from?"

"I need you to do something for me, Cal. Only not really for me. For Dad."

His eyes narrowed. "Don't start that shit with me, Miranda—"

I touched his wrist. I jumped us to the treehouse in the back yard. He staggered away from me, bumping his head on the low ceiling, then sitting and putting his back to the wall. "How did you do that? What's happening?"

"You're going to be late for school this morning, bro," I said. "Sit down. I've got a lot to tell you, and a favor to ask."

Convincing Cal took a lot longer than I expected, which was something I *should* have expected, if that makes any sense. I didn't dare jump him to Nexington-on-Axis, but I took him back to the little beach in Hawaii where we'd spent so many mornings on our last real family vacation. That made him believe, though he wasn't gracious about it. I'd hoped to grab some food, but it looked like I'd have to go through the night's events fuelled only by dry granola bars. Those are the sacrifices we revolutionaries have to make.

I jumped to the queen, yawned, and caught a few hours of sleep in her shadow. When I woke up and drank some water, I said, "I'm almost ready. Just one last visit."

>I advise against this,< she said. >It will accomplish nothing.<

"Maybe, but I need to try. You'll show me where he is?"

The queen gave me a vision, of an old man in a simple book-lined room, and I jumped there.

"I've come to give you one last chance," I said, leaning against one of the Regent's bookshelves.

The Regent closed the book he was holding, put it down on the desk, removed his reading glasses, and said, "Interesting."

"You're wondering how I found you—how I knew where to jump."

He nodded.

"Maybe I've got more resources than you realize."

"Apparently. Though I still think I have the advantage in this situation." His chair creaked as he leaned back and crossed his legs. "You're offering me one last chance—to do what, exactly?"

"A few things. To send my father home. To free Wisp and Howlaa. To use the power of the jump-engine to send *anyone* who wants to leave here back to their own homes. To make Nexington-on-Axis something other than a prison. To basically be a better leader and less of a bastard."

"Mmm. And you feel qualified to criticize my leadership? Your, what, dozen years of life provide you with the appropriate knowledge and insight?"

"I know you have a lot more stolen lifetimes' worth of experience than I do, but experience doesn't change what's right and what's wrong. You know you're wrong. You just don't care because you're the one on top."

"Right or wrong—and I would argue that those terms, as you frame them, are laughably irrelevant—I am indeed on top, and that's where I intend to remain. I've been polite with you, Miranda, but really—your co-conspirators are captured, and your father is in my power. Surrender yourself now or I'll have all of them eliminated. The royal orphans can pick over their corpses for useful body augmentations. Do you understand? I am no longer being patient with you."

"Why do you call them orphans?" I said. "When we both know their mother is still alive?"

I waited just long enough to see his eyes widen before I jumped away.

Everybody deserves one last chance. I really wished he'd taken it. That would have been easier, cleaner. My way, I was afraid people were going to get hurt.

The Regent's people, mostly.

Chapter 17

I jumped to the Mab's warehouse at the appointed time, and everything was just like she promised, two rows of Mablings in winged unitards lined up on either side of a path leading to the Mab's throne. I walked between the silent rows of four dozen girls, then knelt before the Mab, which wasn't fun, but it was part of the deal. "My lady," I said. "I thank you for your boon."

"Arise, daughter." The Mab snapped her fingers. A couple of attendants came and helped me out of my clothes, then dressed me in fresh Mabling-wear—my old outfit was too bedraggled, and I needed to look just like all the others.

"You ready?" I said, and the row of Mablings shouted "Ready!" They all held out their hands. I took a breath, then ran down the path with my own hands out, slapping the palms of every girl on either side as I ran. With each slap, the girls I touched disappeared, and when I reached the end of the line and sent the last one away, the Mab approached me.

"Ready to go home?" I said.

"You should come with me, Miranda." She smiled, and her face lit up like it was glowing from the inside, her hard angles softening, her eyes becoming deep and gentle. She touched my cheek, and I let myself lean into her, remembering things I couldn't possibly remember, moments when I was just a tiny baby held in my Dad's arms, utterly safe and protected and loved. The Mab kept speaking, soft murmurings: "I will take you into my home, a palace of woven grass and smoke, and you will rule there by my side, a princess, honored, adored, appreciated, finally truly appreciated for all you have to offer, an end to fighting and striving, an eternity of comfort and joy…" I closed my eyes and breathed in, the scent of her all sweetly comforting and familiar, like the kitchen when my Dad embarked on a grand culinary experiment, all spices and warmth…

Then the little mote in my ear began to speak—to *translate*—and I heard what the Mab was really saying:

"Eat you, I'll *eat* you and take your ring, that pretty ring will be mine, I'll make your fingerbones into a necklace, I'll tear you—"

She'd almost bewitched me, enchanted me, ensorcelled me, wrapped me up in her mists and shadows. Thank goodness for that little piece of Wisp in my ear, or I would've been lost. I slapped her hands away, then reached out and shoved her in the chest.

In the instant before I sent her back to the land of mist and mirrors, her illusion dropped. Her true form was like a spiderweb wet with morning dew, twisting and wriggling, and when she disappeared, my hand came away damp. I wiped whatever it was—sweat, slime, substance?—off on one of my wings, counted to ten to calm myself down a bit, and then jumped myself.

I landed in total chaos, which was exactly what I wanted. We were in one of the orbital palaces, in the room where Howlaa was being held and experimented upon, and the Mablings were totally wrecking up the place. The doctors fled into a hallway, pursued by hooting Mablings who lashed them with wooden switches decorated like wands. A handful of other girls smashed the surveillance cameras and overturned cabinets. Some of them dropped to the floor, tasered or tranquilized by automated defenses prepared for me, but I was untouched—just one of the multitude.

I went to Howlaa, and she pulled herself together into the female form I'd first seen her in. She looked around wildly—I was close to her, but there were ten other girls just as close—and I didn't do anything to call attention to myself. I just touched her wrist, and jumped us out of there. I thought the Mablings would be okay, mostly—the Regent would have bigger things to worry about soon, and a horde of unruly girls in fairy costumes would be the least of it. I was still worried and guilty, though, because some of them had already been knocked unconscious, and others might end up in ever worse shape.

Howlaa and I landed in Merrill's basement, and Merrill himself nodded at us lazily. "We're thoroughly shielded down here. No way we're under surveillance."

Howlaa shook her head. "Randy, what did you *do*?"

"I started a revolution," I said. "I have to go get Wisp now." I bounced back to the orbital palace, which was still ringing with chaos and shouting, and found Wisp in his glass bubble in an empty room; I guess there was no fun or glory in vivisecting a ball of gnat-sized particles. I touched the glass ball, and sent it away (dropping it in the middle of the snatch-engines, and hoping it would hit a royal orphan on the head). Wisp fuzzed and wobbled and said "Miranda?" The mote in my ear slid out and zipped back to the main body. "I've been able to hear you all this time, with the particle in your ear, though I was unable to communicate. This plan of yours—it's extra*ordinary*."

"Good, then you can explain it to Howlaa, because I won't have time. Come on, in you go." I opened my mouth, and Wisp flew in, avoiding going up my nostrils this time, which was good, since that tickled. I jumped back to Merrill's basement, and Wisp came streaming out again.

"Looks like you're the new boss, Randy," Howlaa said. "What do I do?"

"Just sit tight," I said. "Everything's under control, and you'll be safe here—"

"We don't care about *safe*," Wisp said. "We want to be *involved*."

I looked at Merrill, who shrugged—he'd put together the safehouse, so his part of the bargain was over. It wasn't his fault if the fugitives didn't want to lay low. "But, guys, what you've been through, are you sure you want—"

"I have only been through boredom, and worry," Wisp said. "And Howlaa's profession has exposed her to more than a little in the way of torture."

"I find that getting nasty revenge helps my healing process," Howlaa said.

"Okay, then. You can come with me to get my Dad."

"Just to be safe," Howlaa said, and transformed into the Rendigo.

We jumped, and once again, Howlaa caught a projectile meant for me—but this time it was a bullet, not a tranquilizer. There were three Nagalinda guards armed with handguns. No fancy ray guns here, just big pistols. My Dad was tied up facedown on the bed, and he screamed when the guns fired—it must be even scarier to hear gunshots when you can't see what's going on.

Howlaa shrugged off the bullets and swatted the guards aside, knocking them down and unconscious. She transformed into her human form again. "Move fast, Randy, we'll have more company soon."

I untied my Dad's hands, and he rolled over on the narrow bed. Up close he looked older than I remembered, a little fatter, and his eyes were shadowed, but he still *smelled* like my Dad, like herbs and baking bread, and I threw my arms around his neck and hugged him tighter than I had since I was a little kid.

"Who—what—Miranda?" he whispered. "Is that you?"

I realized I was still in the Mabling outfit, which wasn't exactly my usual fashion, and there was the purple hair too, so I said, "Yes, it's me, I'm here, I'm going to take you home."

"Home? But what—but how—"

"*Randy*," Howlaa growled, and I nodded.

"Okay," I said. "Meet me in the audience chamber later, guys?"

I grabbed my Dad's hand, and we jumped.

We landed in the treehouse behind our house, where Cal sat staring through a square window cut out from the plywood. Dad built that treehouse when we were little kids.

"Holy shit and fuck me sideways," Cal said.

"Language, Cal," Dad said, and then we were all silent for a moment, until Dad started laughing and crying all at once and Cal threw his arms around him in an embrace that was almost like a wrestling move, it had so much back-slapping and bear-hugging.

I kissed Dad's stubbly cheek and said, "Welcome home."

"I can't believe you were telling the truth," Cal said. "Dad, were you really in this other *world*?"

"I was. Sometimes I thought it was a nightmare, but it was real."

"Maybe we should come up with a simpler story to tell Mom," I said. "Like maybe the explosion gave you amnesia, you've been wandering around working odd jobs, I saw you a few days ago and I spent the past few days tracking you down. Something like that? We can tell her the truth later if you want, but for now… I think just seeing you is going to be enough for one night."

"I guess you're right," Dad said. "But Miranda—*how*? How did you get there? How did you find me? How did you bring me back?"

"Cal will explain."

"I barely understand it myself. I thought it was total bullshit!" Cal winced at his own curse word. "Sorry, Dad. You explain it, Miranda."

"I would. But I don't think I'm going to be here much—"

And then I got snatched up and stolen away.

The Regent paced up and down in a long observation room, with big windows looking down on the tops of the snatch-engines, all crackling with strange lightning. "*You*," he said. "You think you've accomplished anything? Fomenting a little unrest in the provinces? Bah. I've heard reports of a god-worm, of all things, laying waste to my forces, but I assume that's just Howlaa in some oversized snakelike form. As for loosing a couple of prisoners? It's trivial, Miranda. You're just a child playing at revolution. I'm tuning the engines now to snatch up your father, your brother, your mother, your mother's boyfriend, your friend Jenny, maybe your whole *town*, and I'll drop it in the middle of the Landlock Sea and let them all drown if you don't—"

"Shushit," I said, putting a finger to my lips. "It's going to happen soon. Is the sun turned off yet?"

"What? I don't think you understand the enormity of—"

The whole palace shook, and the upper floors of the palace were torn away, rubble showering down, exposing us to the just-darkened sky above. I felt bad about this part, too—the palace was a living thing, after all, and it had helped me—but it was temporary damage to provide greater freedom, and the Queen said the palace would heal just fine in time. Most of the parts inhabited by the Regent were dead flesh anyway.

The steam colossus leaned down, put its complex face into the hole above us, and regarded the shocked Regent.

"HELLO, GERALD," it said. "I REGRET TO INFORM YOU THAT OUR RELATIONSHIP HAS COME TO AN END."

Then it punched the snatch-engines to pieces with one house-sized fist. Royal orphans went scurrying up the steam colossus's arm, but it flicked them away and then strode off.

"Let's go see the queen," I said, and grabbed the Regent's arm.

>*Abdication and exile are your only options,*< the queen said. >*Unless you'd like Miranda to send you to deep space? My children will be unable to save you now that the engines have been disabled, and even your formidable personal physical protections will not keep you from going mad alone in the cold and the dark.*<

"I recognize the position I'm in," the Regent said, staring downward.

"I gave you a chance," I said. "It didn't have to be this way."

He laughed and shook his head. "You have no idea what you've done, Miranda. This beast, this monster, this *entity* we call a queen could not be less interested in the lives of humans or any other sentients here. They will all die in starvation and squalor in the wake of her neglect. You're a fool."

>*I will not attempt to rule the inhabitants of this place.*<

"Oh, anarchy then, that's *wonderful*."

"Not anarchy, either," I said. "Just a change in leadership."

I watched as the Regent unlocked the Queen's complex chains, and then I walked with him up a sloping corridor toward his audience chamber. "She'll execute me," he said. "You must know that."

"I thought she was utterly indifferent to humans?"

"I'm a *special* human."

"No execution. I'll give you a ticket off this rock. Or asteroid. Or plane. A one-way ticket."

"You'd set me free? To plot my plots and plan my plans? I don't object, but it's not very smart."

"Please. We both know that, without the orphans to steal extra years for you, you're not going to live forever anymore."

"True enough. I wonder if France is much like I left her…"

"Oh, you don't get to *choose* where I send you. And there's no way I'm sending you to France—at least not the France on the Earth where I'm from. I'm not sharing a planet with you. But I'll send you someplace with an atmosphere you can breathe and food you can eat, fear not."

"Oh, the cruelty of the young. I civilized this place. I made it into a city-state, when it was just horror and wilderness. And you come along and—"

"Whatever," I said. "You brought this on yourself. Like I said. I gave you a chance to do the right thing."

We reached the ruined base of the snatch-engines, where dozens of royal orphans—newly un-orphaned—were scurrying about trying to repair the considerable damage the steam colossus had done. The Regent whistled, and the native children of Nexington-on-Axis lifted their heads and antennae and sensory structures.

"My darlings," he said. "My boys and girls and otherwise, I have great news for you. Your mother, long thought dead, has awakened from her slumber, and she is alive. She cannot wait to see you." He glanced at me. "That little speech was for your benefit, by the way. I communicate with them telepathically."

The princes and princesses (and otherwise) of Nexington-on-Axis streamed past us, their hatred of me apparently forgotten in the news that their dead parent was actually alive. I could understand that.

"I suppose that's it for me, then," he said.

"I'm guessing you regret ever creating this thing, huh?" I held out my hand and admired the golden ring.

"It was, in retrospect, not my savviest move."

"Live and learn," I said. Then I punched him in the chest and made him disappear.

I just wanted to go home, but I had too much else to do first. I found Howlaa and Wisp waiting for me in the audience chamber, and Howlaa picked me up in a giant hug. "You!" she shouted. "You are the least worthless human I've *ever* met!"

"I've got a question for you two," I said. "Now that the Regent's gone… are you still so desperate to leave Nexington-on-Axis?"

"It *does* seem more hospitable now," Wisp said.

"Even smells better," Howlaa agreed.

"God. Because you guys are in charge of the place."

I'd never seen Howlaa look afraid before. It looked pretty funny. "Miranda, I'm the *worst* choice," she said.

"I concur," Wisp said.

"Too bad. The Queen has spoken, and she's giving authority over all the sentient denizens of Nexington-on-Axis—excluding her family—to *you*. Except for the Machine Waste, which will belong to second-generation steam colossi. And some of the provinces, which are now an autonomous zone run by the god-worm."

Howlaa gaped.

"Yeah," I said. "I wanted some big distractions to keep the Regent off balance during the jailbreak, so I got the last Underdweller to wake up her god and start raising hell in the outskirts. Well, it was the Queen's idea, but I did all the talking."

"A god-worm. I'll have to get out there and taste its blood," Howlaa said. "But Randy, really, we're lousy choices. You, though—you could be queen. We'll get you a crown and everything. Tiara. Thing."

"As if. I'm going home to spend some time with my Dad. Besides, you'll have help. And once I figure out how to get this ring off my finger—and you find out who you want to wear it *after* me—you'll have the power of the jump-engine, and this place won't be a prison anymore. Should be a much nicer place to rule. Besides, you don't have to run the place like the Regent did. Maybe let people vote for their own leaders. I'll loan you my civics textbook so you can see how it's done."

"Well, Wisp, you promised me freedom, and instead I've got another *job*," Howlaa said.

"This one will involve rather less brutal violence, at least," Wisp said.

"Exactly. There's no upside. It's all bad news."

"You will have access to the fullness of the Regent's wine cellar, however. And his beer cellar. And his bar."

"There's a ray of light after all," Howlaa said.

I yawned. No time to rest, though. "I'll give you guys a little while to process your thoughts and feelings or whatever. I've got some business to do."

"AH, MIRANDA." The steam colossus was sitting—who knew it could sit?—on a hill overlooking an algae-slick green sea, part of a nature preserve not far from the city center. Its footsteps had destroyed large chunks of that nature, and its smoke was already making the air stink. I sat on a rock next to one of its many knees. "I WILL NOT MISS THIS PLACE AT ALL."

"What will you do when you get back to outer space?" I asked, wondering just what exactly I was setting loose in the universe.

"I WILL COMPLETE MY ORIGINAL MISSION. IF YOU ARE VERY LUCKY, YOU WILL NEVER FIND OUT WHAT THAT MISSION WAS."

"Cryptic it is, then. I appreciate your help."

"IT WAS NOT HELP. IT WAS A TRANSACTION."

"Okay. Nice doing business with you."

His sensor array swiveled. "YES. I SUPPOSE IT WAS. I WISH TO GO NOW."

I touched a tiny part of its warm metal knee, and the ring on my finger tightened and hummed—I guess moving something that big took more effort than usual—and the steam colossus vanished. I squeezed my eyes shut in a sudden gust of wind, air rushing to fill the void where the giant space-monster had been.

I couldn't help but feel like I'd just made Nexington-on-Axis a better place. Again. I was on a roll.

Next I went to visit Templeton, who was staring out his window.

"You did it," he said. "I can't *believe* it. The Regent is gone, the Queen is alive, she's making pronouncements about Howlaa and Wisp taking over in the Regent's place, she's sealing off the palace, people are either rioting or celebrating in the streets, I can't tell which… I don't *believe* it."

"Believe it. The Regent is gone, gone, gone."

"Where did you send him?"

"To a version of Earth governed by the Cog Lords. The Queen told me the coordinates. We'll see how he likes living under a dictatorship. Now, can you get this ring off me?"

"It was never meant to be permanently bound to one individual," Templeton said. "Howlaa and Wisp just stole an unfinished prototype. I'm sure there are plans in the lab to finish the device. Now that I can walk out of this room without imploding, I'll get right on it. Come see me in the lab in a couple of days." His servos whirred in a moment's silence, then he said, "You did good, Miranda."

"Coming from you, I'll try not to take that as an insult." I jumped home.

Chapter 18

I landed in the backyard, for safety's sake. There was a lot of yelling coming from the house. Cal was in the driveway, leaning on the side of his car. I walked over to him. "So," I said. "I guess they had the big reunion. What'd I miss?"

"Well, Mom's boyfriend was over, and when Dad found out he and Mom were together, the two of them almost got into a fistfight."

I groaned. "I was wondering how that first meeting would go."

"Ross took off, said he knew we all had a lot to talk about, but really he was just scared of getting the crap beaten out of him. I mean, Dad's got fifty pounds on the guy."

"Jeez. I didn't even... All I could think about was getting Dad home, you know? I didn't think about how crazy it would make everything afterward."

Cal laughed. "Nobody ever said happy endings were easy, Randy. Mom is grilling Dad like a steak in there. You should go take some of the heat off him." He clapped me on the shoulder. "I'm pretty sure you're going to be grounded until after *college* graduation. Maybe longer when Mom sees your haircut."

Two days later things were just as complicated, but we'd done the tearful reunion thing and Dad cooked us all a huge meal—Mom's boyfriend was there too, which was awkward, but whatever. I was totally grounded—even though I'd brought Dad home, I wasn't off the hook for being AWOL for the best part of a week—but late one night I jumped back to Nexington-on-Axis. The palace was barely recognizable, just a dome of faintly-glowing stone without so much as a window or a door. The Queen had been serious about closing the place off to outsiders, and I guess the palace was happy to go along with her wishes.

Howlaa and Wisp had set up their government in the saloon, and I found them there, at a big table surrounded by lizard-people and Nagalinda and humans and cyborgs, everybody arguing, with Wisp floating in the middle and translating. Various bummed-out Mablings sat around the bar drinking, their whole worldview turned over when their mistress ran away.

"The hero of the revolution!" Howlaa called, and everyone cheered, which was pretty freaky—I haven't gotten that much applause since I won the third-grade spelling bee at the county fair. People slapped me on the back and shoved drinks into my hands, which I mostly put back down again, because the last thing I needed was Mom realizing I had a hangover in the morning. She didn't know I was technically un-ground-able, and I liked it that way.

Howlaa shooed everybody off, and he and Wisp took me into a curtained-off private booth. "So how're things going?" I asked.

"Chaotic," Wisp said. "But the Queen says repairs on the snatch-engines are coming along nicely, and she's willing to allot us one-sixteenth of her children's time to import the things we need. Once we have your jump-engine, we won't be as dependent on the Queen, which I think will suit *all* of us better. I wonder if the Regent was trying to develop independence from the royal family all along?"

"Probably trying to make it so he could kill *all* of them," Howlaa said. "Don't give him too much credit." She sighed. "You know, Randy, I thought once word got out that we could send people away, this place would become a ghost town, but enough people want to stay that we'll definitely need a real system of government. Though for now the government of, 'Because I said so and I can beat you all up' seems to be working."

"Generally speaking, second and third-generation Nexingtons have no desire to repatriate to their ancestral homes," Wisp said. "You have no *idea* what you've gotten us into, Miranda. Putting the Nex back on track, emptying the prison camps, creating some sort of reasonable governmental structure—it's a huge undertaking."

"Nobody ever said happy endings were easy," I said, and didn't bother crediting the line to Cal. "Has Templeton figured out how to get this ring off me yet?"

"Let's go see," Howlaa said.

Templeton's lab was more machine shop than operating room, all greasy tables and rattly shelves heaped with a mini-Machine Waste's worth of junk. "Miranda!" he called. A lot of his body was gleaming with gold fittings now; he'd spent some time doing upgrades. "Come here, sit down." I took a chair at a table heaped with schematics and wire and weirdly-shaped tools that seemed to curve out of this dimension and into another. Templeton sat across from me, took my hand in his, and leaned over, putting his face half an inch from my knuckle. A lens came telescoping out of his face, and then one of the ends of his fingers split up into a dozen hair-thin micro-manipulators and began tugging and twisting at the ring. "Turn your face away," he said, just in time for me to get nearly blinded by a flash of purple light. The ring began to hum and twist and heat up on my hand, and I tried to pull away, but Templeton grabbed my wrist with his other metal hand, and a noise like a dentist's drill rose from the ring.

"If you hurt her, I'll break you down for scrap," Howlaa said, stepping forward.

The drilling sound stopped. Templeton sat up. "There, it's done. It can be taken on and off, though I wouldn't do it too often in rapid succession. The ring, please?"

I touched the ring, which felt tight but not super tight, and slid it off, holding it in the palm of my hand. I passed it over—but to Howlaa, not Templeton. Howlaa couldn't use it herself, but I doubted Templeton would be her choice for official Ringbearer for the new government.

"Do you feel any different, Miranda?" Wisp said.

"I don't know." I tried to jump across the room. Nothing, not so much as a twitched mental muscle. My jumping days were over. I sighed. "I'm really going to miss that thing. You know somebody who can use that ring to send me home?"

"Merrill will," Howlaa said. "He won't do as a permanent ringbearer—too unreliable—but he's delighted you sent the Regent to his own oppressive Earthly home, and he doesn't want to leave the Nex, so we can trust him to wear it for a few moments."

"I guess… that'll be goodbye, then," I said. "I feel like I've known you two forever. I'm going to miss you a lot."

"You've literally changed our world, Miranda," Wisp said. "We can't thank you enough."

"You showed me it's possible to kick ass with your *brain*," Howlaa said. "We're going to miss you, too."

"Vomiting imminent," Templeton said.

So they sent me home.

About a month after I left the Nex for the last time, life had settled down, but wasn't exactly what you'd call normal. Mom and her boyfriend were "on hold" while she tried to "figure some stuff out," which was annoying, because I'd figured they'd insta-break-up once Mom found out she wasn't a widow. But, like Cal said: not easy.

Dad had finally convinced the government he was still alive, and he was working at a restaurant and living with us, though he and Mom weren't sharing a bedroom or anything. She kept poking holes in his amnesia story, no matter how much Cal and I tried to cover for him, and she was convinced he'd walked out on us and only come back years later out of guilt or desperation. She went back and forth on whether I was his accomplice or if he was lying to me, too. I knew we were going to have to tell Mom the *real* truth sometime, but the problem was, I didn't have a jump-engine anymore to prove any of the crazy story to her. Which made things kind of difficult.

I was still mostly grounded, but Mom had started letting me go to the library to do some studying, which was how I got some time along with my friend Jenny Kay at last. I wanted to tell her all about Nexington-on-Axis, but knew she'd never buy it without proof. She's an Occam's Razor kind of girl, and she'd just assume I was crazy if I didn't have any evidence to the contrary. So I just fed her the story about seeing Dad on the street and trying to track him down, and she seemed satisfied with that, though I wasn't thrilled with lying to my best friend.

I was in the library with Jenny when Howlaa Moor strolled in—along with the blonde Underdweller who'd punched me in the nose. She wore a golden ring on her finger, and a green dress, and her face tattoos were gone, and she'd even had a bath in the recent past. Howlaa wore a long trenchcoat made of shadowcloth.

"Randy," Howlaa said, too loud, but she doesn't really know how libraries work, probably. "Your father said I'd find you here."

"Who's this?" Jenny's voice was a little sharp but mostly curious, because she's full of the curious.

"Jenny, this is my friend Howlaa."

"Interesting name," she said. "Where do you know Randy from?"

"My reputation doesn't precede me?" Howlaa said. "Randy, I'm hurt. You haven't told—"

I made cutting-my-throat gestures and Howlaa shut up. "Ah, right. Well. Nice to meet you, the famous Jenny. *I've* heard of *you*. And Miranda, you remember our friend Ermintrude? We call her Trudy."

"Guten tag," the Underdweller said, looking around the library like she expected to be attacked by books at any moment.

"I guess she's, ah, mellowed a little since we last met?" I said.

"She's the god-worm's ambassador to the city center," Howlaa said. "We worked out our differences, and she's got a wide streak of loyalty, so she's the perfect ringmaiden."

"Are you all talking in some sort of code?" Jenny Kay said, not quite patiently.

"I won't keep you," Howlaa said. "I just wanted to give you… this." She set a small silver ring on the table in front of me, where it clicked gently against the wood. "First new one we've made, and everyone agreed, you should be the one to have it. Wisp sends his whiny love—he wanted to be here in person, but figured he'd be too conspicuous. *A votre san*, Miranda. Come see us sometime." She turned on her heel and strode out of the library, and Trudy sighed a long-suffering sigh and went after her. I could see how being Howlaa's chauffeur would get old.

"What on Earth was all *that* about?" Jenny Kay said.

"Nothing on Earth." I picked up the silver ring, and slipped it onto my index finger. It tightened a little and tingled. I took Jenny Kay's hand. "Nothing on Earth at all." I looked around, and we were unobserved, no-body in our little corner of the library.

I had two hours before I had to be home. Plenty of space and time.

"Come on, Jenny," I said. "I've got something you'll have to see to believe."

The End

Dream
Engine

Dream Engine

The Stolen State, The Magpie City, The Nex, The Ax—
this is the place where I live, and hover, and chafe in my service; the place
where I take my small bodiless pleasures where I may. Nexington-on-Axis
is the proper name, the one the Regent uses in his infrequent public ad-
dresses, but most of the residents call it other things, and my—prisoner?
partner? charge? trust?—my *associate*, Howlaa Moor, calls it The Cage, at
least when zie is feeling sorry for zimself.

The day the fat man began his killing spree, I woke early, while Howlaa slept on, in a human form that snored. I looked down on the streets
of our neighborhood, home to low-level government servants and the
wretchedly poor. The sky was bleak, and rain filled the potholes. The royal
orphans had snatched a storm from somewhere, which was good, as the
district's roof gardens needed rain.

I saw a messenger approach through the cratered street. I didn't recognize his species—he was bipedal, with a tail, and his skin glistened like
a salamander's, though his gait was birdlike—but I recognized the red
plume jutting from his headband, which allowed him to go unmolested
through this rough quarter.

"Howlaa," I said. "Wake. A messenger approaches."

Howlaa stirred on the heaped bedding, furs and silks piled indis-
criminately with burlap and canvas and even coarser fabrics, because
Howlaa's kind enjoy having as much tactile variety as possible. And, I
suspect, because Howlaa likes to taunt me with reminders of the physical
sensations I can not experience.

"Shushit, Wisp," Howlaa said. My name is not Wisp, but that is what
zie calls me, and I have long since given up on changing the habit. "The
messenger could be coming for anyone. There are four score civil servants
on this block alone. Let me sleep." Howlaa picked up a piece of half-eaten

globe-fruit and hurled it at me. It passed through me without effect, of course, but it annoyed me, which was Howlaa's intent.

"The messenger has a *red plume*, skinshifter," I said, making my voice resonate, making it creep and rattle in tissues and bones, so sleep or shutting-me-out would be impossible.

"Ah. Blood business, then." Howlaa threw off furs, rose, and stretched, arms growing more joints and bends as zie moved, unfolding like origami in flesh. I could not help a little subvocal gasp of wonder as zir skin rippled and shifted and settled into Howlaa's chosen morning shape. I have no body, and am filled with wonder at Howlaa's mastery of physical form.

Howlaa settled into the form of a male Nagalinda, a biped with long limbs, a broad face with opalescent eyes, and a lipless mouth full of triangular teeth. Nagalinda are fearsome creatures with a reputation for viciousness, though I have found them no more uniformly monstrous than any other species; their cultural penchant for devouring their enemies has earned them a certain amount of notoriety even in the Ax, though. Howlaa liked to take on such forms to terrify government messengers if zie could. Such behavior was insubordinate, but it was such a small rebellion that the Regent didn't even bother to reprimand Howlaa for it—and having such willfully rude behavior so completely disregarded only served to annoy Howlaa further.

The Regent knew how to control us, which levers to tug and which leads to jerk, which is why he was the Regent, and we were in his employ. I often think the Regent controls the city as skillfully as Howlaa controls zir own form, and it is a pretty analogy, for the Ax is almost as mutable as Howlaa's body.

The buzzer buzzed. "Why don't you get that?" Howlaa said, grinning. "Oh, yes, right, no hands, makes opening the door tricky. I'll get it, then."

Howlaa opened the door to the messenger, who didn't find the Nagalinda form especially terrifying. The messenger was too frightened of the fat man and the Regent to spare any fear for Howlaa.

I floated. Howlaa ambled. The messenger hurried ahead, hurried back, hurried ahead again, like an anxious pet. Howlaa could not be rushed, and I went at the pace Howlaa chose, of necessity, but I sympathized with the messenger's discomfort. Being bound so closely to the Regent's will made even tardiness cause for bone-deep anxiety.

"He's a fat human, with no shirt on, carrying a giant battle-axe, and he chopped up a brace of Beetleboys armed with dung-muskets?" Howlaa's voice was blandly curious, but I knew zie was incredulous, just as I was.

"So the messenger reports," I said.

"And then he disappeared, in full view of everyone in Moth Moon Market?"

"Why do you repeat things?" I asked.

"I just wondered if it would sound more plausible coming from my own mouth. But even my vast reserves of personal conviction fail to lend the story weight. Perhaps the Regent made it all up, and plans to execute me when I arrive." Howlaa sounded almost hopeful. "Would you tell me, little Wisp, if that were his plan?"

Howlaa imagines I have a closer relationship with the Regent than I do, and has always believed I willingly became a civil servant. Howlaa does not know I am bound to community service for my past crimes, just as Howlaa is, and I allow this misconception because it allows me to act superior and, on occasion, even condescend, which is one of the small pleasures available to we bodiless ones. "I think you are still too valuable and tractable for the Regent to kill," I said.

"Perhaps. But I find the whole tale rather unlikely."

Howlaa walked along with zir mouth open, letting the rain fall into zir mouth, tasting the weather of other worlds, looking at the clouds.

I looked everywhere at once, because it is my duty and burden to look, and record, and, when called upon, to bear witness. I never sleep, but every day I go into a small dark closet and look at the darkness for hours, to escape my own senses. So I saw everything in the streets we passed, for the thousandth time, and though details were changed, the essential nature of the neighborhood was the same. The buildings were mostly brute and functional, structures stolen from dockyards, ghettoes, and public housing projects, taken from the worst parts of the thousand thousand worlds that grind around and above Nexington-on-Axis in the complicated gearwork that supports the structure of all the universes. We live in the pivot, and all times and places turns past us eventually, and we residents of the Ax grab what we can from those worlds in the moment of their passing—and so our city grows, and our traders trade, and our government prospers. It is kleptocracy on a grand scale.

But sometimes we grasp too hastily, and the great snatch-engines tended by the Regent's brood of royal orphans become overzealous in their cross-dimensional thieving, and we take things we didn't want after all, things the other worlds must be glad to have lost. Unfortunate imports of that sort can be a problem, because they sometimes disrupt the profitable chaos of the city, which the Regent cannot allow. Solving such problems is Howlaa's job.

We passed out of our neighborhood into a more flamboyant one, filled with emptied crypts, tombs, and other oddments of necropoli, from chipped marble angels to fragments of ornamental wrought iron. To counteract this funereal air, the residents had decorated their few square blocks as brightly and ostentatiously as possible, so that great papier-mâché birds clung to railings, and tombs were painted yellow and red and blue. In the central plaza, where the pavement was made of ancient headstones laid flat, a midday market was well underway. The pale vendors sold the usual trinkets, obtained with privately-owned low-yield snatch-engines, along with the district's sole specialty, the exotic mushrooms grown in cadaver-earth deep in the underground catacombs. Citizens shied away from the red-plumed messenger, bearer of bloody news, and shied further away at the sight of Howlaa, because Nagalinda seldom strayed from their own part of the city, except on errands of menace.

As we neared the edge of the plaza there was a great crack and whoosh, and a wind whipped through the square, eddying the weakly-linked charged particles that made up my barely-physical form.

A naked man appeared in the center of the square. He did not rise from a hidden trapdoor, did not drop from a passing airship, did not slip in from an adjoining alley. Anyone else might have thought he'd arrived by such an avenue, but I see in all directions, to the limits of vision, and the man was simply *there*.

Such magics were not unheard of, but they were never associated with someone like this. He appeared human, about six-feet tall, bare-chested and obese, pale skin smeared with blood. He was bald, and his features were brutish, almost like a child's clay figure of a man.

He held an absurd sword in his right hand, the blade as long as he was tall, but curved like a scimitar in a theatrical production about air-pirates, and it appeared to be made of *gold*, an impractical metal for weaponry. When he smiled, his lips peeled back to show an amazing array of yellow stump-teeth. He reared back his right arm and swung the sword, striking a merrow-woman swaddled all over in wet towels, nearly severing her arm. The square plunged into chaos, with vendors, customers, and passers-by screaming and fleeing in all directions, while the fat man kept swinging his sword, moving no more than a step or two in any direction, chopping people down as they ran.

"The reports were accurate after all," Howlaa said. "I'll go sort this." The messenger stood behind us, whimpering, tugging at Howlaa's arm, trying to get zim to leave.

"*No*," I said. "We were ordered to report to the Regent, and that's what we'll do."

Howlaa spoke with exaggerated patience. "The Regent will only tell me to find and kill this man. Why not spare myself the walk, and kill him *now*? Or do you think the Regent would prefer that I let him kill more of the city's residents?"

We both knew the Regent was uninterested in the well-being of individual citizens—more residents were just a snatch-and-grab away, after all—but I could tell Howlaa would not be swayed. I considered invoking my sole real power over Howlaa, but I was under orders to take that extreme step only in the event that Howlaa tried to escape the Ax or harm one of the royal orphans. "I do not condone this," I said.

"I don't care." Howlaa strode into the still-flurrying mass of people. In a few moments zie was within range of the fat man's swinging sword. Howlaa ducked under the man's wild swings, and reached up with a long arm to grab the man's wrist. By now most of the people able to escape the square had done so, and I had a clear view of the action.

The fat man looked down at Howlaa as if zie were a minor annoyance, then shook his arm as if to displace a biting fly.

Howlaa flew through the air and struck a red-and-white striped crypt headfirst, landing in a heap.

The fat man caught sight of the messenger—who was now rather pointlessly trying to cower behind *me*—and sauntered over. The fat man was extraordinarily bow-legged, his chest hair was gray, and his genitals were entirely hidden under the generous flop of his belly-rolls.

As always in these situations, I wondered what it would be like to fear for my physical existence, and regretted that I would never know.

Behind the fat man, Howlaa rose, rippled, and transformed, taking on zir most fearsome shape, a creature I had never otherwise encountered, that Howlaa called a Rendigo. It was reptilian, armored in sharpened bony plates, with a long snout reminiscent of the were-crocodiles that lived in the sewer labyrinths below the Regent's palace. The Rendigo's four arms were useless for anything but killing, paws gauntleted in razor scales, with claws that dripped blinding toxins, and its four legs were capable of great speed and leaps. Howlaa seldom resorted to this form, because it came with a heavy freight of biochemical killing rage that could be hard to shake off afterward. Howlaa leapt at the fat man, landing on his back with unimaginable force, poison-wet claws flashing.

The fat man swiveled at the waist and flung Howlaa off his back, not even breaking stride, raising his sword over the messenger. The fat man was uninjured; all the blood and nastiness that streaked his body came from his victims. His sword passed through me and cleaved the messenger nearly in two.

The fat man smiled, looking at his work, then frowned, and blinked. His body flickered, becoming transparent in places, and he moaned before disappearing.

Howlaa, back in Nagalinda form, crouched and vomited out a sizzling stream of Rendigo venom and biochemical rage-agents.

Howlaa wiped zir mouth, then stood up, glancing at the dead messenger. "Let's try it your way, Wisp. On to the Regent's palace. Perhaps he has an idea for… another approach to the problem."

I thought about saying "I told you so." I couldn't think of any reason to refrain. "I told you so," I said.

"Shushit," Howlaa said, preoccupied, thinking, doing what zie did best, assessing complex problems and trying to figure out the easiest way to kill the source of those problems, so I let zim be, and didn't taunt further.

Before we entered the Palace, Howlaa took on one of zir common working shapes, that of a human woman with a trim assassin-athlete's body, short dark hair, and deceptively innocent-looking brown eyes. The Regent—who had begun his life as human, though long contact with the royal orphans had wrought certain changes in him physiologically and otherwise—found this form attractive, as I had often sensed from fluctuations in his body heat. I'd made the mistake of sharing that information with Howlaa once, and now Howlaa wore this shape every time we met with the Regent, in hopes of discomforting him. I thought it was a wasted effort, as the Regent simply looked, and enjoyed, and was untroubled by Howlaa's unavailability.

We went up the cloudy white stone steps of the palace, which had been a great king's residence in some world far away, and was unlike any other architecture in Nexington-on-Axis. Some said the palace was alive, a growing thing, which seemed borne out by the ever-shifting arrangement of minarets and spires, the way the hallways meandered organically, and walls that appeared and disappeared. Others said it was not alive but simply magical. I had been reliably informed that the palace, unable to grow *out* because of the press of other government buildings on all sides, was growing *down*, adding a new sub-basement every five years or so. No one knew where the excavated dirt went, or where the building materials came from—no one, that is, except possibly the royal orphans, who were not likely to share the knowledge with anyone.

Two armored Nagalinda guards escorted us into the palace. That was a better reason for Howlaa to change shape—Nagalinda didn't like seeing skinshifters wearing their forms, because it meant that at some point the skinshifter had ingested some portion of a Nagalinda's body, and while their species enjoyed eating their enemies, they didn't tolerate being eaten by others.

We were escorted, not to the audience room, but into one of the sub-basements. We were working members of the government, and received no pomp or ceremony. As we walked, the Nagalinda guards muttered to one another, complaining of bad dreams that had kept them up all night. I hadn't even realized that Nagalinda *could* dream.

We reached the underground heart of the palace, where the Regent stood at a railing looking down into the great pit that held the royal snatch-engines. He was tall, dressed in simple linen, white-haired, old but not elderly. We joined him, waiting to be spoken to, and as always I was staggered at the scale of the machinery that brought new buildings and land and large flora and fauna to the Ax.

The snatch-engines were towering coils of copper and silver and gleaming adamant, baroque machines that wheezed and rumbled and squealed, with huge gears turning, stacks venting steam, and catwalks criss-crossing down to the unseen bottom of the engine-shaft. The royal orphans scuttled along the catwalks and on the machinery itself, their bodies feathered and insect-like, scaled and horned, multi-legged, some winged, all of them chittering and squeaking to one another, making subtle and gross refinements to the engines their long-dead parents, the Queen and Kings of Nexington-on-Axis, had built so many centuries ago. The orphans all had the inherent ability to steal things from passing worlds, but the engines augmented their powers by many orders of magnitude. The Queen and Kings had been able to communicate with other species, it was said, though they'd seldom bothered to do so; their orphans, each unlike its siblings except for the bizarre chimera-like make-up of their bodies, communicated with no one except the Regent.

"I understand you attempted to stop the killer on your way here," the Regent said, turning to face us. While his eyes were alert, his bearing was less upright than usual. He looked tired. "That was profoundly stupid."

"I've never encountered anything my Rendigo form couldn't kill," Howlaa said.

"I don't think *that's* a true statement anymore. You should have come to me first. I have something that might help you." The Regent stifled a yawn, then snapped his fingers. One of the royal orphans—a trundling thing with translucent skin through which deep blue organs could be seen—scrambled up to the railing, carrying a smoked-glass vial in one tiny hand. The Regent bowed formally, took the vial, and shooed the orphan away. "This is the blood of a questing beast. You may drink it."

"A questing beast!" I said. "How did you ever capture one?"

"We have our secrets," the Regent said.

Howlaa snorted. "Even questing beasts die sometime, Wisp. The snatch-engines probably grabbed the corpse of one." Howlaa was pretending to be unimpressed, but I saw zir hands shake as they took the vial.

Questing beasts were near-legendary apex predators, the only creatures able to hunt extra-dimensional creatures. They could pursue prey across dimensions, grasping their victims with tendrils of math and magic, and chasing them forever, even across branching worlds.

"Wherever the killer disappears to, you'll be able to follow him, once you shift into the skin of a questing beast," the Regent said.

"Yes, I've grasped the implications," Howlaa said.

"Then you've also grasped the possible avenues of escape this skin will provide you," the Regent said. "But if you think of leaving this world for frivolous reasons, or of not returning when your mission is complete, there will be… consequences."

"I know," Howlaa said, squeezing the vial. "That's what my little Wisp is for."

"I will be vigilant, Regent," I said.

"Oh, indeed, I'm sure," the Regent said. "Away, then. Go into the city. The killer seems to favor marketplaces and restaurants, places with a high concentration of victims—he has appeared in five such locations since yesterday. Take this." He passed Howlaa a misshapen sapphire, cloudy and cracked, dangling on a thin metal chain. "If any civil servant sees the killer, they will notify you through this, and, once you drink the blood of the questing beast, you will be able to 'port yourself to the location instantly."

Howlaa nodded. I would go wherever Howlaa did, for my particulate substance was inextricably entangled with zir gross anatomy. Howlaa uncapped the vial and drank the blood. Zir body, through the arcane processes of the skinshifter race, sequenced the genetic information of the questing beast, the macro-in-the-micro implicit in the blood, and incorporated the properties of the beast. Howlaa shivered, closed zir eyes, swallowed, and whined deep in zir throat. Then, with a little sigh of pleasure, Howlaa opened zir eyes and said, voice only slightly trembling, "Let's go, Wisp. On with the hunt."

The killer did not reappear that day. Howlaa and I went to the Western Outskirts, one of the few safe open spaces in the Ax, so zie could practice being the questing beast. It's dangerous to loiter in empty lots in the city proper, because the royal snatch-engines are configured to look for buildings that can fill available gaps. Thus, a space that is at one moment a weed-filled lot can in another instant be occupied by an apartment building full of bewildered humans, or a plaster-hive of angrily jostled buzz-men, or stranger things—and anyone who happened to be standing in the empty lot when the building appeared would be flattened. But the Western Outskirts are set aside for outdoor recreations, acre upon acre of playing fields, ramshackle wooden sky-diving platforms, lakes of various liquids for swimming or bathing or dueling, obstacle courses, consensual-cannibalism hunting grounds, and similar public spaces. Howlaa chose an empty field marked off with white lines for some unknown game, and transformed into the questing beast.

As one of the bodiless, dedicated to observation, it shames me to admit I could make little sense of Howlaa's new form; too much of zir body occupied non-visible dimensions. I saw limbs, golden fur, the impression of claws, something flickering that might have been a tail pendulum-swinging in and out of phase, but nothing my vision could settle on or hold. Looking at Howlaa in this form agitated me. If I had a stomach, I might have found it nauseating.

Howlaa flickered back to female human form and spent some minutes curled on the ground, moaning. "Coming back to this body is a bit of a shock," zie said after a while. "But I think I get the general idea. I can go anywhere just by finding the right trail of scent."

"But you *won't* go anywhere. You won't try to escape."

Howlaa threw a clod of dirt at me. "Correct, Wisp, I won't. But not because you'd try to stop me—"

"I *would* stop you."

"—only because I don't like being tossed aside in a fight. I'm going to follow this fat bastard, and I'm going to *chew* on him. You can't lose a questing beast once it gets its claws in you."

"So... now we wait."

"Now *you* wait. I'm going to drink. One of the advantages of wearing a human skin is that something as cheap and plentiful as alcohol provides such a fine buzz."

"Is this the best time to become intoxicated?" We bodiless have a reputation for being prudish and judgmental, which is not unwarranted. I can never get drunk, can never pleasantly impair my own faculties, and I am resentful of (and confused by) those bodied creatures that can.

"Which time? This time, when I might be killed by a fat man with a golden sword tomorrow? Yes, I'd say that's the best time for intoxication."

The next morning, we went to a den of vile iniquity near the palace. While Howlaa drank, I observed, and listened. I learned that a plague of nightmares was troubling the city center, and many of the bar's patrons had gone to stay with relatives in more far-flung districts in order to get some sleep. At least Howlaa and I wouldn't be called upon to deal with *that* crisis—bad dreams were rather too metaphysical a problem for Howlaa's methods to solve.

After a morning of Howlaa's hard drinking, the sing-charm the Regent had given us began to sound. Howlaa was underneath a table, talking to zimself, and seemed oblivious to the gem's keening, though everyone else in the bar heard, and went silent.

"Howlaa," I said, rumbling my voice in zir bones. Howlaa scowled, then skinshifted into a Nagalinda form, becoming instantly sober. Nagalinda process alcohol as easily as humans process water.

"Off we go," Howlaa said, and rushed into the street, transforming into the questing beast once zie was far enough away to avoid inadvertently snagging any of the bar patrons with extra-dimensional tendrils.

We *traveled*, the city folding and flickering around us, buildings bleeding light, darkness pressing in from odd angles until I was hopelessly disoriented. Seconds later we were in the middle of the Landlock Sea, on a floating wooden platform so large it barely seemed to move. The sea-market nearby was in chaos, fishermen and hunters of various species—Manipogos, Hydrans, Mhorags, others—running wildly for boats and bridges or diving into the water to get away from the fat man, who was now armed with a golden trident. He speared people, laughing, and

Howlaa went for him and grappled, flashing tendrils wrapping around the fat man's bulk, barely-seen limbs knocking aside his weapon. The fat man stumbled, staggered, and fell to his knees. Howlaa's ferocious lashings didn't penetrate the man's impossibly durable flesh, but at least he'd been prevented from further acts of murder.

Then the man vanished, and Howlaa with him, and I was pulled along in their wake, on my way to wherever the fat man went when he wasn't killing residents of the Ax for sport.

For a moment, I looked down on the Ax, which spun as sedately as a gear in a great machine, and other universes flashed past, their edges blue- and red-shifting as they went by at tremendous speeds, briefly touching the Ax, sparks flying at the contact, the royal snatch-engines making their cross-dimensional depredations. Then we plummeted into an oncoming blur of blue-green-white, and after a period of blackness, I found myself in another world.

"*Wisp*," Howlaa hissed as I came back into focus. I had never been unconscious before—even my "sleep" is just a blessed respite from sensory input, not a loss of consciousness—and I did not like the sensation. Our passage from the Ax to this other plane had agitated my particles so severely that I'd lost cohesion, and, thus, awareness.

Now that my faculties were in control of me again, I saw a star-flecked night sky above, and Howlaa in human-female form, crouching by bushes beside a brick wall. I did not see the fat man anywhere.

"What—" I began.

"Quiet," Howlaa whispered, looking around nervously. I looked, but saw nothing to worry about. Grass, flowerbeds, and beside us a single-story brick house of a sort sometimes seen in the blander sections of the Middling Residential District. "The fat man got away," Howlaa said. "Only he actually *melted* away, or misted away, or… My tentacles didn't slip. He didn't slip through them. He just *disappeared*. Nothing can escape a questing beast."

"Perhaps the legends exaggerate the beast's powers," I said.

"Perhaps you'd best shushit and *listen*, Wisp. There's an open window just over there, and I can *almost* hear…"

I did not have to settle for almost. I floated above the bushes a few feet to the window, which opened onto a bedroom occupied by two humans, neither of them the fat man. The man and woman were both in bed, illuminated by a single bedside lamp. The man, who was pigeon-chested and had thinning hair, gestured excitedly, and the woman, an exhausted-looking blonde, lay propped on one elbow, looking at him through half-closed eyelids.

I listened, and because Howlaa is (I grudgingly admit) better at data analysis than I am, I let zir listen, too, by extending a portion of my attenuated substance down toward zim, a probing presence that Howlaa sensed and accepted. My vision blurred, and sounds took on strange echoes, but then I found my focus and stopped picking up residuals of Howlaa's sensory input—but zie would see and hear everything as clearly as I did.

"It's amazing," the man was saying. "They get more real all the time. I know you think it's stupid, but lucid dreaming is *amazing*, I'm so glad I took that seminar. It's like living a whole other life while I'm asleep!"

"What did you do this time?" She leaned back and closed her eyes.

The man hesitated. "I was in a sort of fish-market. There were fish-people, mermaids, selkies, things like that, and ordinary people, too, all buying and selling things. There was a lake, or an inland sea, and we were all on a wooden platform floating on the water…"

"You get seasick just stepping over a puddle," she said.

He looked at her, mouth a tense line, eyes narrowed, and I think if she had seen his expression she would have leapt from the bed in fear for her life. Unless long association with this man had dulled her awareness to the dark currents in him I saw so clearly.

"My dream body doesn't get sick," he said. "It's part of my positive visualization technique. My dream body is impervious to harm."

"And I bet you look like a movie star, too."

Another hesitation, this one accompanied by a troubled frown. "Something like that."

I wondered what his dream self *really* looked like—his father? An old enemy? A figure from a childhood nightmare that he could not escape, but was eventually able to embody?

He continued. "The only problem is, I can't seem to control where I *go*. The teacher at the seminar said that was the best part, being able to go to the mountains or the beach or outer space as easily as thinking it. But I just find myself in this city full of strange people and creatures, and…"

"Do you fuck any of those strange people?" she asked.

"No. It's not like that."

"What good's having control of your dreams if you can't wish yourself into a sex dream? Seems like *that* would be the best part."

"I want to go back to sleep," he said. "I want to try again."

"You don't have to ask my permission. I was sleeping fine until you sat up and started yelling. Doesn't sound like lucid dreaming is doing you much good—you're still having nightmares."

"The nightmares are different now," he said. "I'm in control." But she just turned over and pulled the sheet up to her neck.

"He's the fat man," Howlaa said, speaking silently into me, able to share thoughts as easily as we shared senses. "He goes to the Ax in his dreams, and he kills us for pleasure. That's why the questing beast couldn't hold the killer, why he melted away, because he has no substance beyond the borders of the Ax."

"Madness," I said, though Howlaa's intuitive leaps had proven right more often than my resultant skepticism.

"No, I think I've figured it. The Regent has consulted with many oneiromancers, lucid dreamers, and archetype-hunters over the years—I know, because I was sent to kidnap and press-gang many of them into civil service. I never knew why he wanted them before. I think that, with the Regent's help, the royal orphans have constructed a machine to steal dreams. A *dream* engine, that grabs mental figments and makes them real. But they locked on to this mad man's dream, and now his dream-self will keep coming, and killing, until this world spirals too far from the Ax for the engine to reach, which could take years."

"A dream engine," I repeated. "The activity of such a machine might explain the plague of nightmares in the city center."

"I doubt the Regent would worry overmuch about properly shielding any strange radiations," Howlaa said. "This is a new low for him. It's not enough that he grows rich through the orphan's thefts—now he wants to pillage our dreams, too."

The man lay on his back, staring at the ceiling. Despite his words, he did not seem eager to sleep again. If Howlaa was right, the man had just been chased out of his fantasy of infinite strength by the monstrous questing-beast, which would be enough to give any dreamer pause.

"If you're right, we have to kill him," I said.

"Or not," Howlaa said.

Howlaa severed our connection, swirling my motes, and so it took me a moment to realize zie was transforming into the questing beast again—and I knew why. To jump away from this world, to another plane, adjacent to this one but not necessarily adjacent to the Ax. A few dimensional leaps, a little time, and Howlaa would be far beyond the Ax's influence, beyond the grasp of even the greatest snatch-engines.

But I still had a chance, this brief moment between transformations, to strike, and I did. I performed the one act that Howlaa could not resist, the power I was given permission to use only in circumstances as extreme as these.

I took possession of Howlaa's body.

Howlaa fought, and I batted zir efforts aside, then simply reveled in having a body, especially a body as sensitive as the questing beast's, seeing into higher dimensions, seeing colors that only exist between worlds. I wanted to fly through suns, roll across jagged stones, immerse myself in lava, *feel feel feel* this forever.

Howlaa was laughing at me, a tinny internal sound. "Shushit," I said, not speaking aloud. I didn't even know if this body had vocal cords. "You didn't escape. You failed. We're going to kill this man, and then return to the Ax."

"Go on then," Howlaa said. "Best of luck."

I attempted to take a step forward, and everything blurred. My head rang with odd chimes, and bizarre scents assailed me. I had never been in a body so sensitive to smell—each scent was like a line attached to me, tugging me in one direction or another. I paused, and the chaos of sensory input lessened. I took another step toward the dream-killer's window, and this time a whole new set of sensations struck me, making me fall to the ground.

"This form will not do," I said.

"Why not? Because you have no finesse, Wisp? Because you can control gross motor functions, but the intricacies are lost to you? In the questing beast's form, even the most trivial movement is intricate. Then why not take another form, a simpler one?"

I felt rage—glandular rage, pumping up from somewhere in this body, a biological response to a mental state. I never get used to that, the feedback loop of mind and body that the corporeal undergo constantly, and I tried to dismiss its effects. I couldn't shift into another form. That was far too intricate a task for my understanding of how to control a body. If Howlaa had been in a human form, I could have broken into the man's house, stabbed him with a knife, and walked out again—such simple physical manipulation was within my powers. But as the questing beast...

"We have reached an impasse," I said.

"And what do you propose?"

"Kill this man," I said. "And I will not report your attempt to escape."

Howlaa laughed. "Oh, please, don't report me. What will they do? Sentence me to another lifetime of servitude?"

"Just kill him! That's why we came."

"I came to kill an invulnerable fat man with the golden weapons, Wisp, not a mentally disturbed human in his bed."

"They are the same!"

"They are not the same. This man is mad, but he is not the killer—he simply dreams of killing."

"But… his dreams are evil…"

"You would hold us responsible for our dreams now? If so, I am a regicide a thousand times over, for in my dreams, I rip the Regent and his orphans to wet bits every night. The Regent is the guilty party in this—he has made a machine that steals dreams, and he brought the killer to our city."

"What do you recommend?"

"Fixing this problem at the source. Which is what I was trying to do when you so rudely possessed me."

"You were trying to escape." I said.

"No, Wisp, I was trying to return to Nexington-on-Axis. Sorry I didn't consult you—my understanding was that you're an observer, here to lend me support."

"I am here to make sure you serve your duty," I replied, wondering if zie was telling the truth.

"I will. But my duty is not to the Regent. I serve the welfare of Nexington-on-Axis. Come, Wisp, and I'll show you I do have a sense of responsibility. Such a strong one, in fact, that I won't kill an innocent madman for the Regent's crimes."

I gave up control of Howlaa's body, and with more shifting, we returned to the Ax.

We appeared in the Regent's private chambers, which should have been impossible, as there were safeguards against teleportation there. The Regent sat in a wingback chair, holding a ledger in his lap, and he raised his eyebrows when we appeared.

Howlaa shifted to female human form, only swaying a bit on zir feet in the aftermath of being the beast. "Huh," zie said. "I wondered if that would work. It's said nothing can stop a questing beast from coming and going as it pleases."

"Mmm," the Regent said. "I trust you solved our problem, and disposed of the fat man? I'll see you get something extra in your next pay allotment. Now, go away. I'm busy." He looked back down at his ledger.

Howlaa cleared zir throat. "Regent. I require your assistance in the fulfillment of my duties."

The Regent looked up. "You didn't kill the fat man?"

"My investigation is ongoing. I need to see the new snatch-engine, the one that steals dreams, and I may have some questions regarding its operation."

The Regent set his ledger aside and stared at Howlaa for a long moment. "Well," he said. "You are not famed for your powers of deduction, Howlaa Moor, but for your powers of destruction. I had not expected you to make inquiries, and I did not ask you to. You are dismissed from this case. I will assign someone else to deal with the fat man."

"Respectfully, sir, you may not interfere with any legitimate inquiries I care to make in an ongoing investigation. My contract prohibits such interference. Again, please have me escorted to the new snatch-engine, and provide someone knowledgeable to answer any questions I might have. Or do you believe this line of inquiry is without cause? If so, I would be happy to bring my evidence before the magisters." Howlaa smiled.

I was in awe at zir audacity. To confront the Regent this way! And zie had no evidence, just intuition and inference. If the Regent called the bluff... But no. He didn't want any evidence Howlaa might possess brought before the magisters and, indirectly, the citizens of the Ax.

"I am the Regent, Moor. You take orders from me."

"Indeed. But my contract states that I serve the city, and not the ruler. You may not lawfully inhibit me. Break my contract, if you like, and I'll not trouble you again. Otherwise, you are obliged to cooperate."

"I could have you executed for treason."

Howlaa bowed. "You are welcome to try, sir." Skinshifters *could* be executed, but it was difficult, since a long-lived member of the species would have forms resistant to most obvious methods of execution. "But if you choose not to execute me or break my contract, then I must ask, for the third time, that you take me to the dream engine and provide –"

"Yes," the Regent snapped. "Fine."

I was astonished. Howlaa's bluff had succeeded. Zie was too valuable for the Regent to dismiss from duty or kill, and his own laws prevented any other action.

The Regent couldn't simply disregard these laws, for they were the source of his power. Without his laws, there would be no city of Nexington-on-Axis, just a giant junkheap full of things snatched at random by the orphans, indiscriminate slaves to their magpie impulses. "But I am about to show you a state secret."

"That's fine," Howlaa said. "My contract gives me any necessary clearances to fulfill my duties –"

"I *know* what your contract says, Moor. I wrote it myself, so you would be forced to serve the city in perpetuity, even in the event of my death. Now shut up about it. I'm taking you where you want to go. If you speak a word about this device to anyone, you *will* be executed for treason. We have methods designed for your kind. There's a special chamber in one of the basements for disposing of skinshifters."

"I serve the state," Howlaa said. "I will not betray it."

I wondered what kind of execution chamber the Regent had that could hold a questing beast, since the safeguards on his private chambers had been insufficient to keep the beast out. I didn't think the Regent realized what kind of power he was giving Howlaa by letting zim drink the questing beast's blood.

We set off down the shifting opalescent corridors of the palace, and the walls groaned around us as they moved.

"You think the killer is a dream-being, snatched here by the experimental engine," the Regent said as we walked.

"I'll submit my report when my investigation is complete," Howlaa said. "Along with my recommendations for how to rectify the problem."

The Regent scowled, but kept walking. Finally we reached a door of black iron. The stone around it was discolored and cracked—the substance of the palace apparently had an allergy to iron, but the heavy metal had certain shielding properties that made its use necessary on occasion. The Regent knocked, a complex rhythm, his unbreakable adamant signet ring clanging against the metal with each rap.

The door swung open silently, and the Regent ushered us into the dimly-lit place beyond.

"This is the dream engine," the Regent said. "Not what you expected, I wager."

"No," Howlaa murmured. "It's not."

Unlike the snatch-engines, there were no gears here, no oiled pistons, no sparking ladders of electricity, no bell-shaped domes of glass, no miles of copper pipes for coolant. There was only a throbbing organic mass in a web of wires, a red-and-green slick thing with no visible eyes or limbs, though it did have vestigial wings, prismatic like a dragonfly's, which drooped to the floor. A royal orphan, pinned in a web of wires.

Howlaa crossed zir arms. "So it's psychic, then."

The Regent smiled. "In a way. It sees dreams. More importantly, it *covets* dreams. And what the royal orphans covet, they get. Much of the process of governing Nexington-on-Axis is making sure the orphans want things the city *needs*. They don't care what happens to the things they snatch. They simply live for the process of snatching. This one is no different, except for the sorts of thing it snatches."

"You haven't been successful making this one want things the city needs, since it pulled a madman's murderous dream to this world."

"You're certain of that?" the Regent said.

Howlaa just nodded, and the Regent sighed. "I'll have to spend some time tuning the process. It's still experimental. I trust you found and killed the dreamer, to prevent another incident?"

"I did not," Howlaa said. "If I had known for certain about the existence of this dream engine, I would have tried, but I only had suspicions. When I grabbed the fat man, I was carried to another world, surrounded by houses filled with sleeping humans, with no sign of the fat man anywhere. That's when I began to suspect that I'd grabbed a dream-figment—I remembered your studies with various experts on dreaming, Platonic ideals, the collective unconscious, things of that nature."

"You have quite a memory," the Regent said.

"I drank the blood of an elephant once," Howlaa said, and I almost laughed. "Since I wasn't *sure* the killer was a dream-thing, I came back here to inquire further."

"We should talk in the hall," the Regent said abruptly. "Vibrations disturb the engine." Indeed, the vestigial wings were flickering, weakly, and we left the room. Once in the hall, the Regent said "How do you intend to proceed?"

"When the killer appears again, I'll grab him, and when he sweeps me back to the human world with him again… well, I think it's safe to assume that the dangerous dreamer will be somewhere in the general vicinity of the place where I land. I'll simply kill everyone within a mile or so. It will take time, but I have some forms that are suited to the task."

I was stunned. I knew Howlaa was lying. We knew very well who the dreamer was, and Howlaa had shown no inclination to kill him. So what *was* zie planning?

"Very good," the Regent said. " But if you mention a *word* about the contents of that room, I'll have you flayed into your component atoms. Understood?"

"The authorities appreciate your cooperation," Howlaa said. The Regent sniffed and walked away.

"Come, Wisp. Back to our eternal vigilance."

"Back to the bar, you mean."

"Just so." Howlaa grimaced, touching zir stomach. "Shit. I've got a pain in my gut."

"Are you all right?"

"Probably something I ate in another form, that doesn't agree with this one. I'll be all right." Howlaa shivered, stretched, and became the questing beast. We traveled.

I tried to get some sense out of Howlaa at the bar, before zie drank too many red bulldozers, primal screams, and gravity wells to maintain a coherent conversation. I slipped a tendril into zir mind and said "What is your plan?"

"Assume what I told the Regent is true," Howlaa said, smiling at the human bartender, who looked appreciatively at Howlaa's human breasts as she mixed drinks. "If things work out, it won't matter, but if things go badly, you'll need all the plausible deniability you can get. No reason for you to go down with me if I fail. This way you can honestly claim ignorance of my plans."

"You want to protect me from getting in trouble with the Regent?" I said, almost touched.

Zie laughed aloud and gulped a fizzing reddish concoction. "No, Wisp. But on the off chance that they imprison me instead of putting me to death, I don't want to be stuck in a cell with you forever."

After that, zie wouldn't talk to me at all, but had fun as only Howlaa on the eve of potential death can.

Zie vomited more often than usual, though.

A day passed, and Howlaa was sober and bored at home, playing five-deck solitaire while I made desultory suggestions, before the fat man reappeared. The singing gem keened at mid-day. Howlaa cocked zir head, taking information from the gem.

Zie became the questing beast, and we were away.

This time we landed in the city center. The fat man sat on the obsidian steps of the Courthouse of Lesser Infractions, face turned up to the sun, smiling up at the light. He held a golden scythe across his knees, and blood and bodies lay strewn all over the steps around him, many wearing the star-patterned robes of magisters.

Howlaa did not hesitate, but traveled again, this time appearing directly in front of the fat man and lashing out with barely-visible hooked appendages to grasp the killer. Then Howlaa traveled again. We reappeared in the racing precinct, startling the spectators and scattering the thoroughbred chimeras. The fat man struggled in the hoof-churned mud, his weapon gone.

I had barely overcome my disorientation before Howlaa traveled again. I knew it was Howlaa controlling the movement, for the sensation was quite different from the swirling transcendence that came when the fat man dragged us to that other world. This time we appeared in another populated area, the vaulted gray halls of the Chapel of Blessed Increase in the monastic quarter. We flickered again, Howlaa and the fat man still locked in struggle, and flashed briefly through another dozen places around the city, all filled with startled citizens—in the adder's pit, the ladder to the stars, the moss forest, the monster farm, the glass park, the burning island. We even passed through the Regent's inner chamber, briefly, though he was not there, and through other rooms in the palace, courtrooms, dungeons, and chambers of government. There was a fair amount of incidental damage in many of these instances, as the fat man rolled around, kicked, and thrashed.

Then we appeared in the dream engine's chamber, and everything in my full-circle visual field wobbled and ran, either as an aftereffect of all that spatial violation, or because bringing a dream into such proximity with the dream engine set up unstable resonances.

Howlaa and the fat man thrashed right into the pulsing royal orphan in its tangle of wires. The orphan's wings fluttered as it broke free from the mountings, and the ovoid body fell to the floor with a sick, liquid sound, like a piece of rotten fruit dropping onto pavement. The fat man broke free of Howlaa—though that wasn't possible, so Howlaa must have *let* him go. He attacked Howlaa, who flickered and reappeared on the far side of the weakly pulsing royal orphan. The fat man roared and strode forward, a new weapon suddenly in his hand, a six-foot polearm covered in barbs and hooks. He tread on the royal orphan, which popped and deflated, a wet, ripe odor filling the room. The fat man swung at the unmoving Howlaa, but the weapon disappeared in mid-arc. The fat man stumbled, falling to one knee, then moaned and came apart. It was like seeing a shadow-sculpture dissolve at the wave of an artist's hand, his substance darkening, becoming transparent, and finally melting away.

Howlaa became human, fell to zir knees, and shivered. "Feel sick," zie said, grimacing.

I was terrified. The Regent might kill us for this. We'd stopped the fat man, yes, but at the cost of a royal orphan's life. "We have to go, Howlaa," I said. "Become the questing beast. I won't try to stop you—let's flee across the worlds. We have to get away."

But Howlaa did not hear, for zie was vomiting now, violently, zir whole body heaving, red and milky white and translucent syrupy stuff coming from zir mouth, mingling with the ichor from the dead orphan on the floor.

The door opened. The Regent and two Nagalinda guards entered. "No!" the Regent cried. "No, no, no!" The guards seized Howlaa, who was still vomiting, and dragged zim away. I floated along inexorably behind. The Regent stayed, kneeling by the dead orphan, gently touching its unmoving rainbow wings.

"Feeling better, traitor?," the Regent said. Howlaa sat, pale and still unwell, on a hard wooden bench before the Regent's desk.

"A bit," Howlaa said.

The Regent smiled. "You didn't think I'd let you be the questing beast forever, did you? I couldn't risk your escape. Wisp is one line of defense against that, but I felt another was needed, so I laced the blood with poison and bound their substances together. When the poison activated, your body expelled it, along with all the questing beast's genetic material. You've lost the power to take that form."

"I've never vomited up an entire shape before," Howlaa said. "It was an unpleasant experience."

"The first of many, for a traitor like you."

"Regent," I said. "As Howlaa's witness, I must inform you that you are incorrect. Howlaa did not mean to harm the orphan. The fat man appeared and disappeared, and Howlaa and I were simply carried along with him. Surely there are others who can attest to that, testify that we appeared all over the city, fighting? Howlaa held on, hoping the fat man would fade and we would be taken to the world of the dreamer, but before that could happen… well. The dream engine was damaged."

"The *orphan* was *killed*," the Regent said. "You expect me to believe that, by coincidence, the last place Howlaa and the killer appeared was in that room?"

"We could hardly appear anywhere after that, Regent, since the dream engine was destroyed, dissolving the fat man in the process." I spoke respectfully. "Had that not happened, I cannot tell you where the fat man might have traveled next."

"He was a lucid dreamer," Howlaa said. "He'd learned to move around at will. He was trying to shake me off, bouncing all over the city."

The Regent stared at Howlaa. "That orphan was the result of decades of research, cloning, cross-breeding—the pinnacle of the bloodline. With a bit of practice, it would have been the most powerful of the orphans, and this city would have flourished as never before. We would have entered an age of dreams."

"It is a great loss, Regent," Howlaa said. "And we certainly deserve no honor or glory for our work—I failed to kill the dreamer. He killed himself. But I did not kill the orphan, either. The fat man tread upon it."

"Wisp," the Regent said. "You affirm, on your honor as a witness, that this is true?"

My honor as a witness. My honor demanded that I respect Howlaa's elegant solution, which had saved the city further murder and also destroyed the Regent's wicked dream engine. I think the Regent misunderstood the oath he requested. "Yes," I said.

"Get out of here, both of you," he said. "There will be no bonus pay for this farce. No pay at all, in fact, until I decide to reinstate you to active duty."

"As you say, Regent," Howlaa and I said together, and took our leave.

"You lied for me, Wisp," Howlaa said that night, reclining on a heap of soft furs and coarse fabrics.

"I provided an interpretation that fit the objectively available facts," I said.

"You knew I was the one dragging the killer around the city, not vice-versa."

"So it seemed to me subjectively," I said. "But if the Regent chose to access my memory and see things as I had seen them, there would be no such subjectivity, so it hardly seemed relevant to the discussion."

"I owe you one, Wisp," Howlaa said.

"I did what I thought best. We are partners."

"No, you misunderstand. I owe you one, and I want you to take it, right now." Howlaa held out zir hand.

After a moment, I understood. I drifted down to Howlaa's body, and into it, taking over zir body. Howlaa did not resist, and the sensation was utterly different from the other times I had taken possession, when most of my attention went to fighting for control. I sank back in the furs and fabrics, shivering in ecstasy at the sensations on zir—on *my*—skin.

"The body is yours for the night," Howlaa said in my—our—mind. "Do with it what you will."

"Thank you."

"You had the right of it," Howlaa said. "We are partners. Finally, and for the first time, partners."

I buried myself in furs, and reveled in the tactile experience until the exquisite, never-before-experienced sensation of drowsiness overtook me. I fell asleep in that body, and in sleep I dreamed my own dreams, the first dreams of my life. They were beautiful, and lush, and could not be stolen.

The End

We Go Back

We Go Back

My best friend Jenny Kay climbed in through my window and nearly stepped on my head. If I'd been sleeping a foot closer to the wall, I would've gotten a face full of her boot, but instead I just snapped awake and said "What who what now?" and blinked a lot.

"Oh damn," Jenny said in a loudish whisper. "When did you move your bed under the window?"

"Last week," I said, sitting up in bed. "I wanted a change." If you can't rearrange your life, you can at least rearrange yourself, and if your mom won't let you dye your hair blue, you can make do with rearranging your rooms.

Jenny Kay dropped from standing to sitting in one motion, making my mattress bounce, and landed cross-legged and totally comfortable. "Hey," she said. "So I need to borrow your ring." I couldn't read her expression in the dim moonlight from the window.

I looked at my right hand, where a thin silver ring looped my index finger, catching what light there was in the room and giving back twinkles. The metal grew cold against my skin and tightened a fraction, almost a friendly little squeeze. The ring—which wasn't really a ring—could tell when I was thinking about it. "Uh," I said.

Jenny nodded vigorously, a motion I felt in the jostling of the mattress more than I saw. "I know! I know. But I wouldn't ask if it wasn't important. I mean, you've had the thing for more than a year, and I've never asked once if I could use it, right?"

I glanced at my closed door—no glow under the crack at the bottom, which meant my parents had gone to their separate beds and turned out the hall light—and switched on my bedside lamp. Jenny was dressed in jeans and a sweater, all in dark grays and blacks, not her usual aggres-

187

sively flamboyant colorful mishmash style at all. Good for sneaking into people's windows, I guessed.

I sat up against the headboard, because when you're about to annoy your best friend, it's better not to be flat on your back at the time. "I wish I could," I said—not one hundred percent true, but Jenny was a fourteen-year-old genius, not a human lie detector. "But it's, like… part of me. You know? I'm part of the mechanism. I can't just take it off. It's linked into my, what's it called, socratic nervous system?"

"Somatic," Jenny said gloomily. She was almost as good at biology as she was at math. "The part of your nervous system that controls movement, which sort of halfway makes sense, I guess."

I shrugged. "So, there you go. The ring's not something I wear. It's something that wears me. Or we wear each other. What did you want it for?"

She looked away. "Nothing. An errand."

I sighed. "Tell me, Jay Kay. Maybe I can help. Is it about a boy?"

Jenny just bit her lip. Good enough. The past few months it's pretty much always been about a boy.

I took her hand. Me and Jenny go way back, and whenever I say that, older people laugh, because I'm fifteen and she's fourteen, and they're like, you're too young to even have a "way back." But I've known Jenny since she skipped first grade and ended up in my second-grade class, which means I've been her best friend for about half my life, and how many of you old people have a friendship with that kind of percentage? She used to hide me in her basement when things got too bad and I ran away from home, and she's the reason I've never failed a math or science class. I owe her. I'm not saying I'd kill for her or anything, but I mean, I like to think I'd help her bury the bodies.

"Okay," I said. "I'll help. Where are we going?"

"I don't want to get you into any trouble," she said. "It's my problem, I should really deal with it myself."

I shrugged. "Mom stopped doing the middle-of-the-night spot checks months ago. She even took the nails out of my window so I could open it when it started getting hot. I wouldn't say she trusts me, but I get by. I don't think she'll miss me as long as we're back by morning." I checked the clock. Four a.m. "We've got maybe an hour, hour and a half? If that's enough time, let's do it. Where are we going?"

She took a breath. "Seattle. Or, just outside it."

We were in Pomegranate Grove, Georgia. So she wanted to go pretty much right across the whole entire continent. "Okay. What's in Seattle?"

"That's where Craig moved," she said.

"Ohhh. So, uh, what did you have in mind?"

A meditative little smile touched her lips. Jenny was even better at revenge scenarios than she was at math, though she usually just made elaborate plans she didn't bother to carry out: she called it "gedankenvengeance." But Craig had hurt her in some very emotional and non-theoretical ways, so it didn't surprise me that she wanted to get back at him for real. "Nothing that will do any permanent damage. I just want to make him think he's haunted, possibly going crazy, and maybe leave a warning for the next girl he tries to screw over. Will you take me?"

"Of course."

She squealed happily and half-climbed out the window, returning with a dark gray duffel bag that clanked when it moved. "Revenge supplies," she said. "Don't worry, no explosives. Mostly just spray paint."

"Ha. Okay. You got coordinates?"

She slipped her phone out of her pocket. "Right here. Gotta love google maps. These numbers should take us right to the backyard. If you can get me into the house, too…"

"Not a problem. Just let me get dressed." Once I was ready—mimicking Jenny's dark color scheme, because sneaking around on the other side of the country in your pajamas is probably a bad idea—I read the coordinates off her screen. The ring on my finger squeezed in acknowledgment. "Shall we?" I said.

"I never get tired of this," Jenny said, and took my hand.

We leapt. Or jumped. Or jaunted. Or disapparated and apparated. Or translocated, warped, shifted. Or even just good old teleported. I've read a lot of science fiction stories in the past couple years, and there are tons of different words for what I'm talking about.

Which is: we went from here, to there, in less time than it takes me to tell you about it.

So how can I do this thing I do?

You know the old story: an ordinary kid finds her way to a strange world full of weird creatures, becomes involved in local politics or revolution or rebellion by accident, makes unlikely friends, and through pluck and ingenuity and the help of some magical allies or objects ends up defeating an all-powerful tyrant and being crowned king or queen.

That's pretty much what happened to me about a year and a half ago. Except instead of a fantasy kingdom with elves and unicorns, I went to a city at the center of all possible universes called Nexington-on-Axis, a place populated by refugee aliens from planets and asteroids and constructed habitats and energy clouds all across the multiverse (or maybe polyverse or omniverse—I've never been clear on the difference.) I did make friends and allies—a bodiless creature named Wisp; a deadly shapeshifter named Howlaa; a cyborg named Templeton who was kind of a jerk, actually; and some others. Together, we did overthrow an evil tyrant, though I actually rescued an imprisoned queen instead of becoming queen myself, which is a better deal—less work. And afterward... I came home.

Compared to saving a world, home is rough stuff. Of course Mom doesn't know about the universe-hopping, and with my history of running away from home and shoplifting (two things I've totally given up, believe me), she doesn't tend to trust me. My dad's got his own problems trying to win back mom's heart, and my brother Cal is off at his first year in college, studying advanced drinking and weed smoking, so I don't have anybody I can really talk to, besides Jenny.

At least in the other world, I had a purpose: defeat the Regent, help my friends escape, keep from getting killed. Back home, my purpose seems to be figuring out what my purpose is, and that's a lot harder. You can't be saving the world all the time. Sometimes you just have to get your homework done.

Oh, and there's one other way my story's different from the usual fantasy coming-of-age stuff. Instead of a magic ring, I have a highly advanced piece of alien technology that just happens to look like a ring, for the moment, because most of its mechanism is shifted into hyper-dimensions that human senses can't detect. It's called a jump-engine, and there are only a few of them in existence, and since I have one, that makes me one of the most powerful people in the multiverse.

Fat lot of good that does me.

We landed in a dark back yard, behind a house so big it looked like it should be a museum or something. I'm talking like four stories of big windows and bricks all climbed-over with ivy. More chimneys than I have fingers on one hand. The backyard had a beautiful white gazebo and an ornamental pond with a little arched wooden bridge over it and a garden shed bigger than my family's garage. I whistled. "Craig lives here?"

"His dad got a big promotion," Jenny said. "That's why they moved to Seattle."

"Some guys have all the luck." In a house this big, I'd probably be able to avoid my mom and my dad and my mom's boyfriend. (Don't ask. My parents are basically separated, except for complicated reasons they still live in the same house. It's about as much fun as you'd expect.) "I bet they have a wicked security system."

"I would imagine," Jenny said. "But probably not inside. Who wants to set off a motion detector when you're getting up at night to go pee?"

"Right. Where to?"

"Third floor. That room right up there should do. I think it's a library."

A library. Not even the library. It's like that one book on my summer reading list says: the rich are different.

I took Jenny's hand again, looked up at the window, and jumped. Line-of-sight teleporting is easy in some ways, though there's a chance of collision. The ring has failsafes to make sure my passengers and I don't end up inside any solid objects, but sometimes you bump into stuff. Fortunately we landed on top of a long wooden table, so the worst that happened was me banging my head on a curved brass chandelier. "Ow," I said—quietly—and we climbed down off the table.

"I'm not a hundred percent sure about the layout," Jenny said. "You want to stay here out of sight, and I'll see if I can find Craig's room? Shouldn't take me long to write 'I'm a liar' on his forehead with a Sharpie and upload a virus onto his computer from my flash drive. Maybe spray paint a little message in the hallway so his parents can find out what a jerk their kid is."

I yawned. I could've used that last hour in my bed, but if this made Jenny happy, I'd sacrifice a little consciousness. "Okay. Try not to get caught."

"If I get caught, I'll kick a shin and run in here and you can disappear us to safety."

"You and your crazy elaborate plans."

Jenny grinned, eased open one of the giant doors, and slipped out of the room.

Maybe fifteen minutes passed. I did my best to stay entertained, peering up at the bookshelves with a little penlight from my keychain—lots of leather spines, nothing that looked like it had been read in a long time, if ever—but it's stressful being in somebody else's house when you're not meant to be there, especially when your friend is committing pranks that might, looked at a certain way, be considered misdemeanors and felonies.

Then Jenny slipped back in, gave me a thumbs-up, and took my hand. "Home, Jeeves," she said.

I obliged. I even dropped her safely in her own backyard a half-mile from my house before bouncing home to my house (where, fortunately, quiet still reigned). I'm a full-service best friend, what can I say?

Teleporting. It's something I used to do a lot, but that trip with Jenny was only my third jump in the past eighteen months or so.

I know. Why don't I teleport every single day? You would, right?

But look: let's say you have total mastery of space. (Not time, unfortunately, just space.) You can go anywhere in the world, or for that matter in the universe, or for that matter in pretty much any possible universe, just by thinking about it. If it's a place you've never been before, maybe you need to know some coordinates in any of a million competing positional systems, to make sure you land in the right spot. But basically there's no door closed to you, no country that has to go undiscovered, no place you can't get to from here. Pretty sweet, right?

But let's also say you're a fifteen-year-old with a deeply suspicious mother who has a hair-trigger grounding policy and a tendency to do random spot-checks to make sure you're where you're supposed to be. You're pretty sure she spies on you through the GPS on your phone, so you can't take that with you, which is sort of like leaving part of your brain at home. You've got no driver's license, and really no ID at all (unless you count a YMCA membership card), and the only money you've got is your allowance, which isn't exactly enough to rent a room at the Cairo Ritz Carlton or book passage on a touring skyliner in the Outer Meta-Clouds of Cor Caroli. So as an obvious minor with no ID or cash, it's not ideal to wander around a foreign place where at best you don't speak the language at worst you don't resemble the dominant sentient species—you risk police attention, or getting mugged, or conned, or hit on by skeezy old guys, or eaten by aliens, and even if you survive all that, you teleport home in a flash only to find your mother waiting up for you to sneak back in. And then, bam: grounded under heavy surveillance.

If you wait until the dead dark middle of the night, mom definitely asleep, to jaunt across the world or the universe and have adventures every night the way other people have anxiety dreams—well, then you're exhausted the next day, you zombie-walk through school, get bad grades, get yelled at, feel lousy all the time. Most of the year I've got school, glee club practice, chores, homework, mandatory family outings on weekends, and community service for the time I got caught shoplifting. I'm busy. Summers are even worse. Mom's a big believer in over-scheduling.

Besides, when you can go anywhere, it's hard to figure out where you should go. You think you feel stressed out standing in the toothpaste aisle at the drug store looking at eight shelves of rectangular boxes, trying to figure out which one's right for you? That's nothing to trying to decide where in the entire multiverse you should spend the one free hour you can chisel out of a week.

Overall, being able to go anywhere and do anything can be pretty stressful, and the time when you can go off to college or even get your own apartment and really take advantage of the power seems like an awfully long way away.

And that's my life. Miranda Candle, the only person on the whole planet with a jump-engine, and it does me less good than having my own car and a driver's license would.

But, hey. Jenny was my friend. And I'll do anything for a friend.

A few days later, I got off the bus with Jenny Kay after school. She was still way up, in a great mood about her prank. Maybe getting revenge on a boy who pretended to like you and then made fun of you with all his friends is a dumb use of near ultimate power, but whatever: it made her happy. I'd peeked in on Craig's twitter stream and facebook pages and hadn't seen any comments about what Jenny had done, but that made sense, right? Who'd want to advertise the fact that someone had screwed with them in their own house?

We walked along the sidewalk, chatting. We lived so close together that a lot of days I got off the bus with her, hung around her house for an hour or so working on homework, then headed to my place for the usual tension-fest that is a Candle family dinner. Today there was a strange car in her driveway, a long black sedan. "Who's that?" I asked, and Jenny didn't answer, just shook her head and looked worried, which should have worried me, probably.

Her mom met us at the front door and gave me a tight smile. Mrs. Kay is nice enough, but about as old as my grandma. Her and her husband adopted Jenny after years of trying to have kids of their own, and they never knew quite what to make of the daughter they'd gotten. They were pretty religious, and things had been strained in that house ever since Jenny read the Bible cover-to-cover when she was eight and started pointing out all the plot holes and continuity errors. "Hi, Randy," she said. "I'm afraid you can't come over today—we have some visitors."

"What's going on, mom?" Jenny asked, but it was funny—she didn't sound curious, or annoyed. She sounded maybe a little scared.

"Nothing to worry about." Mrs. Kay flashed me another smile—all teeth, no warmth—and tugged Jenny into the house. And shut the door. And snapped the deadbolt shut.

Well, screw that. I looked around, made sure nobody was looking, and jumped into Jenny's house. Specifically, into a closet in her family room where they kept the vacuum cleaner and more Christian-themed board games than you probably knew existed. One of our go-to hide-and-seek spots as kids—Jenny especially love dhiding in that closet. I could hear voices in the room beyond clearly, though I wished I could see. I didn't dare push the door open even a crack, though—I knew the couch and chairs were arranged so somebody sitting in the right spot might notice me, and even if I vanished before they got the door open, it would ruin my chance to eavesdrop.

I wasn't spying. I was worried about my friend. I was information-gathering. But not for the first time, I wished the creatures in the city at the center of all possible universes had invented a ring that made me invisible instead.

"But did you see her in bed?" a female voice I didn't recognize said.

"No, but I saw her before bed at ten, and at breakfast at 6:30," her father said, in a pretty pissed-off tone.

Someone else was murmuring, maybe talking on a phone, and then a male voice said: "School attendance records confirm she was in her homeroom that morning at eight."

"It's about a five-hour flight each way," the female voice said. "If her whereabouts are unaccounted for from ten p.m. until 8 a.m., that's ten hours…" She trailed off.

"You know she didn't fly!" Jenny's father exploded. "This is ridiculous, she doesn't even have a driver's license, do you think she hitchhiked to Atlanta and caught a flight to Seattle and –"

"Of course not," the male voice said, soothingly. "It's impossible, of course. Even airport-to-airport, with no time spent waiting for flights, the timeline barely fits. Even if we thought you were lying about her being here at bedtime, and we don't think that, we have witnesses who saw her at choir practice until eight. Practically speaking, it's impossible. But we still have to investigate. Your daughter's fingerprints were found at a –"

"I have a question." That was Jenny's voice. Cold and quiet and barely contained. "Why, exactly, are my fingerprints on file at the FBI?"

I nearly fell out of the closet. FBI?

"They're not," the woman's voice said, sounding annoyed at having to talk to a kid. "But you were fingerprinted before your adoption, and again as part of a program to help find missing children in the event you were ever lost or abducted. When we came across prints we couldn't identify, one of our analysts expanded the search to every database we could think of. The real question is how your fingerprints ended up in that house."

"It's possible to fake fingerprints," the man said. "But we can't imagine why anyone would try to plant the prints of a fourteen-year-old girl from Georgia at a crime scene in Seattle –"

Crime scene? Okay, technically breaking in and vandalizing a boy's house is a crime, I get that, but it hardly seemed like something the FBI would care about.

"Obviously to make you waste your time on nonsense," Jenny's father said firmly. "If you're done here, my daughter has homework."

The agents—agents!—spun it out a little longer, but then they left. I didn't want to eavesdrop on Jenny and her family, so I jumped to Jenny's room instead, knowing she'd seek out privacy as soon as she could.

I had a cold feeling in my gut that there were things my best friend hadn't told me.

Jenny came in a little while later and shut the door, sliding home the bolt she used to lock her parents out. Her dad used to come in during the day and take that lock off, until one day Jenny replaced all the doorknobs in the house and refused to hand over the new keys until they respected her privacy. She was eleven when she did that.

She didn't look surprised to see me, just sighed and sat in the swivel chair at her computer, spinning to face me. She was so short the bottoms of her feet didn't quite touch the floor. Jenny's always been a tiny thing, but only physically.

"We weren't playing a prank on Craig, were we?" I said.

"We were not."

"So what were we doing?"

Jenny slouched. "I didn't want to lie to you. That's why I asked to borrow the ring. We were... crap. I was doing a favor for somebody."

"Who? And what kind of favor makes the FBI come to your house?"

Jenny sat weirdly motionless in her chair, and she wasn't looking me in the eye, which meant either she was lying or she was embarrassed about the truth. "I spend a lot of time online, you know that, and I'm good with computers. One place I go is on the darknet—it's sort of a shadow internet, you have to know the right people to get in, and there are a lot of guys there who maybe aren't so honest, but there are also a lot of geniuses. Anyway, I was chatting with one of them, and he was talking about how this big rich computer guy stole some of his research, and how he'd do anything to get his hands on some files, but the rich guy is super-paranoid and keeps everything on a local drive that's not even hooked up to the internet, he doesn't store anything in the cloud, and if he's got off-site back-ups they're in safe deposit boxes or something. And the guy's house is like a fortress, major alarm system, really tough to get inside. And, I don't know... I said I'd get the files for him."

I closed my eyes. "We broke into some rich guy's house and stole his computer?"

"No! No, I just copied some of his files. They're encrypted, I don't know what they say, but my friend on the darknet can take as much time as he needs to unscramble them. The whole thing should have been un-traceable, but I guess the rich guy had some kind of key-logging software or something, a way to tell his computer had been tampered with. I'm really sorry I lied to you, but –"

"Jenny. You don't really think this rich guy stole your friend's files, do you? I mean, come on –"

"Of course not," she broke in, voice rough and cutting as a ragged toenail. "It's probably industrial espionage. But it was easier all around if I let myself be used. I told my friend—not my friend, better to call him my client—that I knew some people who were experts at infiltration, and offered to act as a middleman to set up a job. It's like that old joke, on the internet, nobody knows you're a dog. They don't know you're a teenage girl, either. Anyway, I sent him some screenshots to prove I'd gotten what he wanted, and this morning..." She turned to her computer, tapped at the keys for a while, and then beckoned me over.

I squinted at the screen. It took me a while to realize what I was looking at. Possibly because I'd never seen a number with that many zeroes on it, outside of billboards advertising the Georgia lottery. "This is a bank account?"

"Yes."

"Jenny... you're rich."

"I guess so. You're entitled to a cut. I was trying to figure out how to give you the money secretly. I thought I'd set up a fake foundation and give it to you as a scholarship in a few years... Not much point in that now."

I felt numb, like my blood had been replaced by novocaine. I sat down on her bed. "You lied to me. You used me. What kind of friend are you?" I was tempted to slap her with my ring hand—one hit and I could send her anywhere I wanted, and right now, I wanted her far away.

"What kind of friend are you?" Jenny said, and I realized her stillness had been hiding anger, not shame. "You have freaking super powers, and you don't even use them. You took me, once, to the place where you basically saved the world, and gave me the whirlwind tour, but mostly just so I wouldn't think you were crazy when you told me about it. As soon as I saw that place, the aliens, the technology, I realized everything I thought I'd be working for my whole life was dumb. What's the point in being great at math, becoming a scientist, when we're just savages poking at rocks with sticks compared to the people in Nexington-on-Axis? They can build a machine that allows you to exploit quantum effects at the macro-level, making it possible for you to be anywhere in the universe basically instantly, and they can make it look like a ring, and give it to a teenage girl as a thank-you gift!" She stood up from her chair. "And you don't do anything with it. If I had that ring, I could be a superhero—or at least a supervillain, or something. You could do anything. See the pyramids. Pop over to Paris for a cup of espresso. Tour the ruins of Petra in Jordan. Rob a bank three thousand miles away, and be on the school bus an hour later with the perfect alibi. And that's just on Earth, you have the key to the entire universe, you've been places that nobody else on the planet even knows exist, and you still bitch about your parents and your schoolwork and whether some boy likes you." Her face was getting red, and spit was flying as she stood up from her chair, but she wasn't exactly shouting; Jenny knew exactly how loud she could be before her parents came knocking to see if she was okay. "Why did it have to be you? Why did you stumble into the amazing story? Why wasn't it me?"

I stood up and started backing toward the window, because I didn't like the way her eyes looked. "I never knew you were jealous. It wasn't all fun, you know. People tried to kill me. Actually kill me. I was hungry and dirty and scared a lot of the time. I was –"

"So you didn't even appreciate it," she said, shaking her head. "Better and better."

I took a deep breath and let it out slow. "We've been friends forever, Jenny Kay. Which is the only reason I'll let you get away with this."

She snorted. "What could you do?"

I punched her pillow. It disappeared, and—I knew—reappeared on my own bed. "One tap, and I could send you to the middle of rich computer guy's office, right now. Could be tricky for you to explain. Or I could just smack your computer and your bike and all your favorite shoes into orbit. Or slap you to Paris, see how you like being in a foreign country with no cash where you don't speak the language. That's just off the top of my head."

She sneered at me. I'd seen Jenny Kay show contempt for a lot of people—teachers, parents, other students—but never for me. I didn't much like it. "If you even try to mess with me, Randy, I'll –"

"Don't." My voice was low, but hard enough that Jenny stopped talking. "Don't try to threaten me. I've been threatened by things a lot scarier than you. Enjoy your money, Jenny. I hope it helps you get everything you ever wanted, because it lost you your best friend."

I was about to jump home when Jenny sat back down in her office chair, slumping, and covered her face with her hands. "I'm sorry, Randy." Her voice was muffled. "I didn't... I just needed the money. I should have told you, but I was trying to keep you out of it, and yeah, I'm jealous, but mostly, I was just desperate."

Jenny had already lied to me once, and I was tempted to just bail, but, all those years of friendship had to count for something. So I sat on her bed, about as far away from her as I could manage. "What did you need money for? Did you get into playing online poker or something?"

She uncovered her face and shook her head. "No. But I need to be able to support myself when I leave home."

I frowned. "What are you talking about?"

Jenny wiped away a couple of tears with the back of her hand. Her voice was very calm now. "I can't stay here. With my parents. You know how religious they are. Mom's been even worse since Grandma died. She goes to church three times a week now. Makes me go with her a lot of the time. They still make me sing in the choir."

"Sure, that sucks, I know, I have a hard time with my mom too, but you can stand it for a few more years, right? You've put up with it your whole life, and once you go off to college –"

"They're going to figure out I like girls," Jenny said calmly, and I felt like I'd just fallen through a trapdoor: nothing solid under my feet anymore at all.

"Um," I said.

"I heard them talking a few weeks ago. They suspect it already, I don't know how. Maybe it's just their usual paranoia, only this time, their crazy idea happens to be true. I can't hide it forever."

"Jenny... you're the most boy-crazy girl I know."

"So I convinced you, at least." Her voice was mournful. "I figured if I acted really, really interested in boys, it might throw my parents off, but it just made my mom more suspicious. I mean, she'd probably rather I was a slut than a lesbian, but neither one thrills her."

"Whoa," I said. "I'm sorry, I'm just processing, this is—how long have you known?"

She shrugged. "I guess I've always known. Maybe before I even knew there was something to know."

A thought crossed my mind. "Um, do you, uh, like…"

She rolled her eyes. "You wish, Randy. You're like my sister or something. Ew." I felt a weird mixture of relief and embarrassment and disappointment—hey, a girl wants to be appreciated. Then she grinned at me, and for a second, it was like old times between us. "But you see what I mean. If I don't get free somehow, they're going to ship me off to one of those camps where they try to cure your gayness. And when it doesn't work… I don't know what they'll do. Probably not send me to some all-female boarding school. Damn it. But something awful. Send me to live with my cousins in the middle of nowhere in Idaho. Keep shipping me off to brainwashing camp until I go crazy. Just kick me out of the house and disown me, maybe, once I'm old enough so they won't get arrested—like my aunt did to my cousin who got pregnant. Life around here has never been fun, but it's going to get ugly."

"So you want to get, what, emancipated?"

"Not so easy in Georgia. Pretty much impossible, for my purposes, unless I wait a couple of years and then get married to some guy, which, you know. Doesn't quite fix my problem. But I know some guys on the darknet, like I said. People who can set me up with ID, if I need to leave. I won't let my parents send me to some reeducation camp, Randy. There are a lot of runaways in this country. I'll be one with a bank account, at least."

Jenny is fourteen, but she looks about twelve. The thought of her, on her own, of what might happen… sure, she was smart, but there are plenty of nasty people out there who don't care how smart you are. "You can't do it," I said firmly. "Just take off on your own? You'll get killed."

She laughed. "So what's the alternative?"

I'm not saying it was the right thing to do. I know it wasn't. But she was going to run anyway. That's what you have to understand—I could let her take off on her own, and hope for the best, or help her, and make it a little more likely she'd stay alive

So of course I helped her, even knowinh the pain it would cause her parents, who really did love her—they just love Jesus and everything more.

I hadn't been to Nexington-on-Axis in a long time. I took Jenny, once, to meet some of my friends. This time, I went to see somebody I didn't even like that much.

Templeton looked even less human than last time I'd seen him. He'd replaced his two more-or-less human legs with a whole bunch of multi-jointed, spindly appendages that made creepy little tapping sounds on the concrete floor as he approached. His lab was full of half-built robots, some of them poking disconsolately at the wires trailing from their own top halves, others singing tunelessly. Templeton scuttled over to me, eyes telescoping out to look me over. "What are you doing back here? Shouldn't you be at a Justin Beiber concert or something?"

"I need a favor," I said.

"I'm not majorly into favors," he said. "I'm more into transactions."

I sighed. "Okay. Then do what I want, or I'll punch you into the middle of the sun."

"Brats today don't have any manners," Templeton said.

"Here." I placed a thin silver ring down on Jenny's desk with a little click.

She stared at it, then looked up at me, then looked at my hand, which was ringless. "Is that…"

"Yep."

"Randy." Her voice was breathy. "What did you do?"

I shrugged. "Went back to Nexington-on-Axis and got the biggest jerk and greatest engineer in the place to disconnect me from the ring." I felt weird, honestly, like I'd lost an arm, or at least a toe or something. "Then I got one of the city's ring-bearers to send me home. I didn't tell them why I wanted to take the ring off. Turns out when you save a civilization, they cut you some slack when it comes to asking questions."

"But your ring, why would you give it up?"

"They don't exactly hand out jump-engines like party favors," I said. "There aren't that many, and they're tricky enough to make that your whole secret bank account wouldn't even be a down payment. I couldn't get another one. So I figured I'd just give you mine."

Jenny's eyes were so wide, it made her look even younger than usual. "I can't. I can't take it. I—"

"You were right, when you said you'd do more with the ring than I do. I don't know, maybe it's because I got pulled into this whole big world-saving thing, with people chasing me and monsters and all that, but... I kind of like being home, even with my crazy parents and everything. I've had enough adventure for a while. But you need a way to escape. With this ring on, you can always get away, if you get in trouble. Anybody shoves you, you can shove back and send them to the middle of a cow pasture a thousand miles away. You can go wherever you need to. You can see everything. You should."

She picked up the ring, holding it between her thumb and forefinger. The silver sparkled, like there were flecks of starlight in the metal. "Do I just... put it on?"

"Pretty much. It's in fully-automatic mode. Think about where you want to go, or tell it coordinates, and... poof. Just be careful and don't jump into the heart of a star or something, okay? And maybe don't rob any banks. I still have a lot of bad karma from all that shoplifting I used to do. Get a job as a courier for human kidneys or something if you get short on cash."

She grabbed me and hugged me to her, and I could feel her heart beating, thump-thump-thump against my chest. "I'll come back and visit you," she whispered in my ear.

"You'd better. It's not like you'll have to buy a plane ticket first."

When I left her, she was still staring at the ring, not yet wearing it. But she'd put it on soon, I knew. And then it would be Jenny with the world at her feet. I won't say it was easy, giving up that kind of power, even to my best friend. But it was the right thing to do

Because we go back.

I honestly didn't think I'd ever see Jenny again after she disappeared. Her parents were devastated, and ended up moving away. I had to act pretty upset, too, and it wasn't hard. I was upset. I lost my best friend. At least it made my mom act a lot nicer to me, for a while, anyway, until she decided I'd had enough time to get over it. The FBI got suspicious and sniffed around a little more, but I doubt they found out much. Eventually, everything settled down, as much as it every does around my house.

About two years after Jenny disappeared, I was in my room, painting my toenails, waiting for Josh to call. (I was never as boy crazy as Jenny pretended to be, but boys? They're okay.)

My closet door swung open.

"Your room is messy," a grating, quasi-mechanical voice said. "Sign of a disorderly mind." Templeton strode in, with two legs again, though his knees bent the wrong way, and he had an extra joint or two above his ankles.

Behind him came Jenny, dressed in black, her hair chopped short and spiky, her grin as wide and wild as ever. I squealed and hugged her before I demanded to know what she was doing here, with him.

"He's even worse than you said," Jenny told me. "How can somebody who's barely biological at all anymore make so many dick and fart jokes? But he knows things about science nobody here has ever even stared to imagine. I mean, for a while I just jumped around on Earth, checking places out, seeing the sights, but I felt like I was wasting this amazing gift you'd given me, you know? I was just being a tourist. So... I made my way to Nexington-on-Axis, and talked my way in to see Templeton, and..."

"Made me take her on as a lab assistant." Templeton was looking at the posters on my wall like they were some especially disgusting species of slime mold. "More of an apprentice, really. She's not too stupid, your Jenny Kay. Anyway, she wanted to show you her journeyman work. She's spent the best part of the past eight months working on it. I made her bring me along because I like it when you get that dumb stunned look on your face."

Jenny reached into her pocket and pulled out a broad copper bracelet, with a sinuous wavy design worked into the metal.

"I'm guessing you didn't go all the way to the Nex to take a jewelry-making class," I said.

"At first I was just going to make you a new jump-engine," Jenny said. "The technology was already established, it wasn't even a science problem, just a practical engineering one. That seemed like the least I could do. But then I thought, well... maybe I can do better."

I took the bracelet. It wasn't as heavy as it looked. Barely felt like anything at all. But it made my fingertips tingle. "Jenny," I said. "What did you do?"

"It's obvious, in a way," Templeton said, looking at me with his complicated mechanical eyes, and if he hadn't had a metal grate for a mouth, I think he might have even smiled. "Talking about space in isolation is ridiculous, even Earth scientists know that, because –"

"Space and time are inextricably linked," Jenny Kay said, with a grin that could have lit up the dark side of the moon. "You know—the space/time continuum? You can't have one without the other. And if you can manipulate one..."

"Wait," I said slowly. "Are you saying... if I put this thing on..."

Jenny Kay put her arm around my shoulders. "Tell me something, Randy," she said. "Or actually, two things. First, are you still sick of having adventures, or are you ready to have some fun? And second—have you ever wanted to see what a real live dinosaur looks like?"

So that's it. Now we have all the time in the world. We can leave at midnight, take two weeks off, and have me back home a minute later by the clock. And what do you think Jenny and I do with all that time?

Yeah. We go back.

The End

Acknowledgments

I'd like to thank the following people, who have provided feedback, or advice, or donated to support the project:

Heather Shaw; Ginger Clark; Jenn Reese; Greg van Eekhout; Melissa Marr; Sarah Prineas; Michelle Ossiander; Ian Mond; Michael Jasper; Jennifer Theis; Edwina Thompson; Gary Singer; Jonathan McNeill; Elías Fernández-Combarro Álvarez; Patrick Waickman; Karen Graham; Bruce Copeland, Sarah Livingston.

www.ingramcontent.com/pod-product-compliance
Lightning Source LLC
Chambersburg PA
CBHW072056170626
46813CB00004B/1378